Death on the Pier

JAMIE WEST

First Published 2022

Printed and bound in Great Britain by Clays Ltd, Elcograf S.p.A.

ISBN 9781739762216 (paperback)
ISBN 9781739762223 (eBook)

Published by Brabinger Publishing, London
brabinger.co.uk

For Huckleberry, who snoozed nearby while every word was written,
and for Stuart, who read them all when I was done.

Prologue

I don't want to look, but I do. I can't help it. The all too familiar white paper sits neatly on my dressing room table. It's crisply folded in half and positioned with care. The text, which is now contained on the inside, can't be read without first opening it, but I don't need to do that. It's not the first time I've received a note like this and it's unlikely to be the last. Not unless I can think of a way to stop them.

I can imagine what the contents will be. No doubt it will be along the same lines as all the other notes. It comes accompanied by the same career-ending feeling of dread. It'll be written in the same chicken scrawl handwriting, the same blue-black ink. If the sender is right-handed they're almost certainly writing with their left, in some kind of attempt to hide their identity, but that's a futile effort. I know who wrote it. At least I think I do, but how can I know for sure?

I sigh as I open the note. As usual, there is just one simple sentence.

I will never allow you to succeed in this business.

There are no demands – there never have been any. No suggestion that whoever is sending them wants money in return for their continued silence. No suggestion of wanting anything at all. That's what makes them so terrifying; how can you reason with someone who wants nothing? This is about power.

I won't let them win. I can't. I will continue to be myself. In fact, I'll re-double my efforts in that regard. I refuse to show any hint that the notes have affected me. They don't bother me at all, I tell myself, although the feeling in the pit of my stomach seems to disagree.

Like all the previous notes I've received, I burn it. I watch as the fire licks around the edges of the paper, until the whole thing is consumed. Watching the curls of smoke rise is satisfying. A pile of ashes in an ash tray can't continue to have an effect over me. Keeping the note, re-reading it – that would be like having a constant reminder, a continual weight to carry. No. It's better that the notes are destroyed. That way I can pretend they don't exist. I can quite happily forget about the blackmail.

Until, of course, the next note.

Chapter One

Bertie was running as if his life depended on it, though of course it didn't. As he ran, he could hear his shoes splashing in the pools of water that had begun to form, scattered randomly across the pavement. He weaved and bobbed around the wet obstacles, doing his best to avoid the worst. It was when he darted across the road that the inevitable came. A loud splash was accompanied by a new sensation, the coldness of liquid seeping into his left shoe. The water had been gathering in the gutter – the drains unable to cope with the sudden downpour – and he had misjudged his jump. One foot had landed firmly on the pavement, but he had to step back to regain his balance; the only place to put his foot had been in the puddle.

This was the reality of the off-season in a seaside town. The seafront in Brighton, which had once been a tranquil, sunny retreat, was now cold and depressing. What had once been a gentle sea, scattered with dots of bobbing heads in brightly coloured swimming caps and waves that lapped softly onto the cobbled beach, now seemed less friendly. Strong winds whipped the waves into higher, more menacing peaks. Water pounded against the well-worn, smooth stones that were glittering in the wet.

Persistent droplets tamped down on the pavement, covering it in a thin film of water which shimmered in the bright diffused sunlight that fought to break through the grey cloud cover.

Bertie found solace under the wooden canopy of a refreshments kiosk that had been closed down and shuttered up; the summer of 1933 had well and truly passed. He pulled his long camel coat a little tighter around his body in a futile attempt to ward off the chill. Unfortunately, his umbrella was still sitting in the hotel room where he'd left it. He tried to console himself with the thought that an umbrella would have provided little protection, even if he had brought it with him. The thought didn't make him feel any drier.

He tried to remember when this had all seemed like a good idea. Hugh's phone call had come completely out of the blue. Would it be possible for them to meet up? Well, it had to be Brighton; Bertie was already halfway out of the door when he rang. Some might have thought that it was a touch narcissistic for him to seek out productions of his own plays so he could watch them, which is why he would have never admitted it to anyone. The truth of the matter was that he was genuinely interested in how they performed, especially when it was an older one that was rarely seen, like the one due to open tonight. Originally, he had been planning to see the production that evening, but with this last-minute change – and as long as there were no other delays in his journey – he should be able to catch the majority of the afternoon dress rehearsal instead.

Bertie had been unable to read Hugh's tone down the telephone line, which had made him unexpectedly nervous. Why would he call now, when it had been so long since they'd last seen each other? As far as he could remember, that had been on their final day at school.

Under the protection of the canopy, Bertie could feel water gently dripping from his head. He wasn't a vain man, but he had wanted to make a good impression after all those years. The extra minutes spent tending to his hair in front of the mirror had been wasted. The rain had washed all his efforts away.

The tone of the rain lightened.

It's now or never, Bertie thought. He left the safe shelter of the wooden cabin and darted towards the pier.

He stopped briefly under the roof of the entrance building to explain to the attendant who he was and what he was doing there. Rather than come out of the building to meet Bertie by the turnstile, the attendant hovered in the doorway. At the mere mention of the theatre, the man's eyes began to glaze over and he lazily waved him through.

As he passed through the turnstile of the Palace Pier, he noticed the entrance sign that hung above. Once it had been warm and welcoming, now it looked battered and tired. Although the signs and the white woodwork around the entrance had probably been freshly painted at the start of summer, the corrosive effect of the sea salt air had aged them prematurely. Today they appeared quite ominous.

The ground under Bertie's feet transitioned from the hard surface of the stone pavement to the wooden decking, which felt softer underfoot. The sound of his footsteps lowered in tone from a high-pitched tapping to a low "thunk".

Deckchairs piled high in wooden racks had tarpaulins pulled tight to protect them from the worst of the weather. A loose corner of the fabric had broken free from its restraint and flapped noisily in the wind. It seemed to make a poor substitute for the brightly coloured flags that would usually be waving gently in the breeze. Today they'd been stripped from their flagpoles, which stood bare, like the winter branches of a tree.

Looking down towards the far end of the pier, Bertie could just about make out the outline of the building towards which he was headed: The Palace Pier Theatre. Through the grey mist of rain, the silhouettes of the onion-shaped domes that decorated the top of the building were just about visible. While they weren't as large or ornate as the domes that adorned the Brighton Pavilion, they still did a pretty good job, giving the theatre a somewhat impressive and glamorous appearance.

Eventually, the theatre came into sharper focus; the painted black outlines and white exterior became brighter and more well defined the further down the pier he got. He darted under the wooden, Moorish-style arcades that encircled the building. Between the entrance doors, some black-and-white posters had been pasted up at the front of the theatre. In simple block text, they advertised the current show:

Arthur Cochran Presents
Celia Hamilton in
'Murder by Association'
by
Robert Carol

He sighed as water dripped from his overcoat. His surname was Carroll – with two Rs and two Ls. Bertie wondered how people got it wrong in the first place? It was always printed quite clearly on the front page of every script he'd ever written. In this case, he decided it probably wasn't too much of a loss. A show at the end of a pier and at this time of the year? He would be surprised if it was going to play with more than a handful of people in the audience each night.

Reading the top of the poster and the words "Arthur Cochran Presents" reminded him of a story a producer friend had once told him. It was their first big show in London and they'd wanted to arrive on the West End scene with a bang. As an extravagance, they splashed out on very expensive neon signage that read "Edward Peters Presents" to be mounted on the front of the theatre. Unfortunately, the first letter of the word "presents" had a wiring fault and for most of the run it read: *Edward Peters resents.* That had pretty much set the tone for the production that was rather badly reviewed. It was another year before Edward Peters got an opportunity to present another show in the West

End. The second time around, the expensive lettering was nowhere to be seen.

Bertie let his eyes drift down towards the bottom of the poster. There it stated: *Four performances only – Thursday to Saturday*. It seemed like a very short run. However, there simply wasn't the appetite for a full schedule of eight shows a week in the off-season. Brighton had the largest concentration of theatres outside London and audiences would prefer to try their luck on a show further inland rather than trudge all the way to the end of a pier on a blustery and miserable day. As he stood there in his sodden clothes, in the cold and the wet, Bertie knew exactly how they felt.

Pulling open the door and making his way in through the front of the theatre, he walked past a ticket window with the shutters pulled across. If he had hoped to be welcomed by the warm heat of the foyer, he found himself disappointed. The temperature inside the building was roughly the same as the temperature outdoors.

Bertie walked across the crush hall and up five or six steps. To his right, a sign indicated the way up to the circle, but he continued dead ahead, through the double doors and a half-open curtain that led into the back of the auditorium.

The Palace Pier Theatre was a decent size. Other than the vast Hippodrome, it was probably the largest stage in Brighton. It had a capacity that was comparable to most regional theatres and could easily accommodate shows on the first-class touring circuit. A year or two earlier, another one of Bertie's productions had visited the theatre as part of its national tour. It wasn't a popular venue to play at. You couldn't drive vehicles onto the pier, so any scenery and costumes had to be carried the entire length of the wooden deck by hand.

The local crew were used to this awkward endeavour, although the touring stage manager had found the load-in rather stressful. He remained in constant fear that a strong gust of wind might catch one of the flats – the large canvases stretched over wooden frames to form the scenery – and, sail-like, it would be whipped over the railings and out to sea.

Inside the auditorium, the sounds of the outside world were dulled a little, but waves could still be heard underfoot. If you left aside the noise, there were no real clues that this was a theatre sitting a little way out into the English Channel. The cream and brown paint colours of the auditorium were the mainstay of theatre interior design up and down the country. Nicotine staining from the many years of cigarette smoke rising from the audience had tinged the walls from clean cream to a murkier shade of yellow. Bertie had learnt that using brown paint on the decorative plaster detail that stretched up the walls and around the circle front was a clever design trick. Picking out just the highlights in gold leaf fooled the eye and made all the detail appear golden when, in reality, the expensive gilding was relatively minimal.

Bertie manoeuvred his way around a white column – though it was more of a pole – which was supporting the underside of the circle above it and was rather awkwardly positioned in the centre of the aisle. As he emerged from under the cover of the circle, the full height of the auditorium was revealed. The side walls crept up to join a gently arcing ceiling, which followed the curved construction of the roof. It would have been a complete semi-circle if it wasn't interrupted by a flat section of ceiling which stretched the entire length of the room. He was surprised to see that the majority of the flat ceiling wasn't the usual painted plaster, but glass.

Above the seats in the circle there were several large panels, each filled with dozens of square panes of glass. These panels stretched down towards the stage until the circle gave way to the stalls below and it transitioned into a magnificent, multicoloured stained-glass dome. Even with the lights turned off, he could tell that when it was illuminated from behind it must have looked spectacular. He could just about make out the different shades – green, blue and yellow, with the central band of the dome formed by clear, frosted glass. As he moved, the pieces of coloured glass caught the light at different angles causing it to shimmer and sparkle. Circular ceiling lights with a milky opal finish were dotted in a ring around the outside of the dome.

Bertie took one last look behind him, noticing a metal box hanging on the front of the circle rail with round holes cut in it. From within, bright spotlights illuminated the scene in front of him. He finally allowed his eyes to be drawn towards the stage, where a rehearsal was currently in progress.

It was not going well.

Chapter Two

'No, no, no!' bellowed a low, powerful, female voice, although Bertie couldn't tell where it was coming from. 'That's not how we rehearsed it. You stand on my right-hand side. *My* right!'

An actor, who looked like he was in his late-fifties, was dressed as a butler and peered out into the gloom of the auditorium with a confused expression on his face. He held his hand up to shield his eyes from the powerful stage lighting and waited patiently for the wisdom that could only be provided by a director.

'Robert, that is correct, I'm afraid,' came an exasperated voice in the darkened auditorium.

Bertie instantly recognised the voice as that of Arthur Cochran, the director and producer behind this production. Arthur had previously mounted another of Bertie's plays, but that was several years ago and before his current level of fame. They would still bump into each other at theatrical events, like opening night galas or at Drury Lane for the cutting of the twelfth-night cake. On those occasions, Arthur would always joke about missing out on the "big one" – he had turned down the option of producing the play that had turned into Bertie's first box-office smash.

Of course, no one really knew what made a hit show. Bertie certainly had no idea what it was about that particular show that had shot him from writing plays for the smaller, regional theatres to the prestigious West End. Now his name had gone from being a tiny, illegible smudge on the bottom of a poster to being displayed proudly on the front of the theatre in lights. Perhaps it was his clever plot – where it appeared that everyone had been killed by the end of the play, before the big twist was revealed – that had gripped audiences. It could equally have been the impressive settings or the brilliant actors that had made all the difference. All he knew was that as long as people were coming to see his plays, he'd keep writing them.

'Yes, sorry, Arthur. Sorry, Celia.' The actor repositioned himself. While he may have been dressed as a butler, he certainly didn't carry the calm demeanour of one. Quite the opposite, in fact. He was nervous and looked rather stressed. Even on this cold day, a thin sheen of perspiration could be seen on his forehead; it caught the light as his head moved. He turned around to address someone who seemed to be lying out of sight on the floor, holding his hands up apologetically.

'I must have written "*stage* right" not "*your* right" in my script.' His attempt to lighten the mood was unsuccessful.

'That's the *same* right,' came the same forceful, disembodied voice. It sounded unimpressed.

'Yes, I know,' Robert stammered. 'That was the joke.'

A stern-looking female face appeared from behind a squishy sofa that had been positioned in the middle of the stage: Celia Hamilton. The reason she was hidden behind the sofa, Bertie recalled, was that her character had been shot a little earlier in the play. Hers was, quite literally, the face that had launched a thousand ships when she played Helen of Troy in the eponymous film. That was when she was much younger and had softer features. Now her face seemed somehow more hardened. This might have been due to age, though, perhaps it was just that she was no longer being viewed through a soft-focus lens.

'I wouldn't have thought that now was the best time for joking, actually.' She glared out in the auditorium, seeing if she, too, could locate Arthur beyond the brightness of the lights. Taking her best guess at his position, she called out, rather hopefully, into the darkness. She ended up directing her speech roughly twelve feet to his right. 'Arthur, darling, I could do with a cushion or two behind here. It's not very comfortable, lying on the floor for all this time, you know.'

'Yes, Celia, dear. I'll see what we can do.' He indicated, by way of a sharp nod, to another girl on the stage who was dressed in a maid's outfit. Bertie took his best guess and assumed that this must have been Celia's dresser. It was fairly common practice for dressers or a stage manager's assistant to double up with a small acting part, keeping the show's costs down. She hurriedly left the stage, without a word, in her search for the requested cushion. She had very few lines in the show and even less to do. He suspected she wouldn't be missed for a while.

'Thank you, Constance,' said Arthur, in the direction of the departing girl. 'Right, shall we continue?' He had long since passed the point where he was attempting to disguise the impatience in his voice.

The stern face disappeared back behind the sofa again and the scene continued. Bertie knew that the disappearing face of Celia Hamilton had, until only a few years ago, been rather famous. She had made several films in Hollywood, where she currently lived. While none of them had been huge hits, she remained a household name, nonetheless. It was quite a coup to persuade her to return from America to star in this play, which even he admitted wasn't one of his best. He recalled that she and Arthur had previously been married, so perhaps the only reason she'd agreed was to do her ex-husband a favour.

Bertie cast his eyes over the rest of the stage. The scenery was a simple box set that had quite probably been recycled from an older production. It was a pretty good representation of a modern drawing room. The sofa was placed centrally on the stage. Celia's feet were just visible, poking out from one end. Three walls, convincingly painted to look like wood panelling, formed the sides of the room. In the right-hand wall, a large set of double doors that were currently open served as the main entrance to the stage. Through them, he saw that the cloth painted to suggest a hallway was less convincing, but it still did the job. In the left-hand wall, a set of French windows looked out onto some potted shrubbery, attempting to represent the garden beyond.

Sensing another presence in the auditorium, Arthur turned to see Bertie standing a few rows behind him. He was positioned behind a small sheet of wood that had been laid across the tops of the seats to form a makeshift table. A small lamp, with a dim glow, lit the pages of the script that sat atop it. He worked his way, with an awkward sideways shuffle, along the row of seats and greeted Bertie with a firm handshake.

'Bertie, what a surprise to see you here. You should have told me you were coming down. We seem to be getting through things a little quicker,' he added, conspiratorially. 'Now she's dead.' Arthur's eyes flicked towards the stage, although Bertie didn't require the extra clarification as to who had been causing the delays. 'As you know, she's up and alive in the second act, when we go back to before the murder happened. I expect things will grind completely to a halt again.' He tried to laugh it off, although his eyes didn't seem to portray the same emotion.

'I hope it hasn't been completely torturous. I know how these technical rehearsals can drag on forever,' said Bertie.

'No. Not *completely* torturous…' he joked in return. 'Now then, I hope you don't mind. We've made a few changes to the end of the act.'

'Mind? No, I don't mind at all,' he said, although this wasn't completely true. That depended entirely on what the changes were. If they happened to be better than what he'd written on the page, then he would absolutely endorse them – after all, the writer still gets the credit for them. If they made the whole thing worse – well – he'd just have to bite his tongue and hope no one blamed him. It was experience that taught him that a playwright's opinion didn't always have that much sway over that of a director. However, if the changes ruined the play completely ... well then, he might have to think very seriously about plucking up the courage to say something.

'We didn't do anything different with the lines though,' said Arthur, in an attempt to reassure him. 'Just improved a bit of the staging. We wanted to make it a bit more interesting.'

Bertie nodded in reply.

'We're coming up to it now, actually. At one point, earlier today, I thought we'd never reach the end of the first act. But it looks like we're in touching distance – that's if we don't stop again. I hope you like it.'

Bertie very much hoped so, too.

'Jenny's very good,' said Arthur, his attention proudly returning towards the stage again.

Jenny, evidently, was the young actress on stage wearing a simple yet refined black dress. Bertie vaguely recollected the plot and remembered she'd shot Celia's character a little earlier in the act. He tried to recall how the first act ended – something to do with the butler coming in after the body had been discovered. Robert, as the butler, was perspiring a little heavier now. These rehearsals were clearly taking their toll on him and certainly on his stress levels.

'...and I came in and found her like this,' Jenny said,

acting. 'I didn't know what to do, so I called for you.' Bertie inwardly cringed at his own clunky dialogue. It was safe to say that the dialogue in his plays had become a lot more refined in the many years that had passed since he'd written this one.

'Oh no,' replied Robert. He knelt behind the sofa for a moment before solemnly standing up again. He turned to Jenny slowly and spoke dramatically. 'She's dead.'

With a flash of light and a crack of thunder, the French doors flew open, accompanied by a howling wind.

'I'd better telephone the police,' boomed Robert, over the noise, before turning to exit through the double doors to the hallway – presumably where he might find a telephone. In previous versions of the production, this had been the final, solemn line. Now, to be heard over the added sound effects, poor Robert was very nearly shouting it.

The lighting dimmed until there was just a single spotlight that picked out Jenny, alone on stage. She turned, giving a haunting look out towards the auditorium before everything faded, leaving the stage in darkness.

After a few seconds, the powerful stage illumination returned, this time joined by the house lights. Bertie squinted, his eyes taking a moment to adjust in the brightly lit auditorium.

'Well,' asked Arthur, 'what do you think?'

'Bit dramatic, old chap, isn't it?'

'Yes, drama. Isn't it brilliant? And we changed it, so we've just got Jenny by herself at the end, you know, with

Constance crying in the background – although, of course, she's not here at the moment. I wonder where she's got to. Really focus down on Jenny. Besides, as you know, the butler needs to leave so he can call the police, otherwise, how would they know to turn up at the start of the next act?' Arthur finished proudly.

'Yes, I suppose that's true,' Bertie replied. Although he wasn't completely convinced that pedantry and the pursuit of realism were the best way to go about creating drama. The added sound effects and lighting were certainly doing their very best to make up for it.

A young man in a very dapper looking suit appeared through the French doors.

'I got a good crack on it that time!' He looked very pleased with himself. 'Oh, hello, Bertie,' he called out, recognising the playwright as he wandered a little further on.

This was Teddy Howard, a young, up-and-coming actor who had been making quite a name for himself in London. He had recently appeared in one of Arthur's productions at the New Theatre in St Martin's Lane. The play had been a hit with both the critics and the audience, receiving rather good reviews. The majority of the praise had been focused on Teddy in the supporting role. His handsome looks had not gone unnoticed by certain members of the audience and it appeared he now had a strong following of female fans.

'Yes, very good,' Arthur called back. 'The louder, the better. That's what I think. And remember to get it right on that cue line; that's really important.' He turned to Bertie in clarification. 'He's doing the thunder sound effect for us. May as well make use of him while he's not onstage.'

'Very resourceful.' Bertie was impressed. It was generally quite hard getting actors to do anything other than the bare minimum most of the time, let alone operate something as demanding as a sound effect.

Constance, wearing her maid's outfit, finally returned to the stage, somewhat nervously. In her hands, she clasped the requested cushion.

'Well, I don't need that now, do I?' snapped Celia, as she attempted to haul herself up from behind the sofa.

'Sorry, Miss,' she apologised and stood there holding the cushion, helpless.

'No, that's fine, Constance,' Celia commented sarcastically. 'I can get up perfectly well without your help.'

'Oh! Sorry, Miss.' Constance dropped the cushion to the floor and went to assist Celia as she stumbled to her feet.

Celia was a dominating figure, not in her stature or physical presence, but by the overbearing force of her personality.

'Do not apologise,' said Celia, sternly. 'I'm not interested in apologies, only that you do things correctly the first time round.' She flashed a pained smile, as if she'd offered valuable advice. 'Now, fetch me a cup of tea.'

Constance nodded dutifully and dashed off stage again.

'We *are* stopping for tea, aren't we?' Celia called out to the auditorium, to no one in particular. Oddly, while what she'd said contained all the typical words and features you might expect from someone asking a question, it certainly hadn't sounded like one.

'Yes, just a short break,' Arthur replied. 'We really should push on with the next act, though. We are starting to run a little behind.'

Celia pulled her head back at what she perceived as a small affront, stiffening a little. 'I can assure you, Arthur, that's not because anyone has been waiting on me.' Celia strode from the stage, heading back to her dressing room. She departed through the drawing-room doors at such speed the canvas-covered scenery surrounding them rippled in the movement of air that was left in her wake.

Teddy, who had jumped down from the front of the stage, was making his way along the central aisle in the seats. He gave a theatrical roll of his eyes as he reached Bertie and Arthur. 'That's not exactly true, is it?' he joked with a grin. 'We've only been stopping half the time because she can't remember the lines.'

'Don't be too hard on her,' said Arthur. 'She's been making films all these years and the majority of those were silent. Even now, you only need to memorise a page or two at a time when you're filming. I'm sure she's doing her best.'

Bertie wasn't sure if Arthur was making excuses to the group or if he was trying to convince himself.

'It's nice to see you again, Teddy.' Bertie smiled in his direction.

'Likewise. Have you met everyone else?' Teddy gestured towards the remaining two cast members who were trudging towards them. They appeared to be rather less enthusiastic.

'Robert Loughton,' announced the exhausted-looking actor in a booming voice, as he reached them. He extended a hand to Bertie, who politely shook it. 'I don't think we've met before?'

'I'm not sure,' said Bertie. 'Perhaps I've seen you in something?'

'Hmm… Vicar, was it?' His response was rather brusque. 'Done a lot of vicars, that's my usual fare. Plenty of butlers too, so you can understand how this isn't too much of a stretch for me.'

'And this is Jenny Ashcroft,' Teddy said. 'She's very good.'

'Yes, Arthur was just saying—'

'You won't have seen me in anything, though,' she said. 'This is my first proper role. I'm really quite new to all this.'

'But you're enjoying it?' asked Bertie.

'Oh, yes. I think acting is just wonderful.'

'Yes, I remember that…' recalled Robert as he let his body sink into one of the auditorium seats, shaking his head gently. He'd seen the same innocence that came with youth and inexperience in plenty of other new actors during his long career. He turned towards Teddy and Jenny to offer some wise words. 'In my experience, being an actor comes down to luck. Bad luck, most of the time – ha! But, if you're in the right place and the right role presents itself … well, of course, you could become quite famous. You can be as talented as you want, but it's luck you need.'

Jenny blushed a little, embarrassed at her outward display of excitement. She tempered her emotion, composing herself, speaking plainly and deliberately. 'Well, I'm grateful to be in this place at this time. That's all I can say,' she finished, putting a full stop on the matter.

'That's exactly it, Jenny.' Teddy beamed. 'Exactly it!' In quite a contrast to Robert, he seemed much more enthusiastic about the emerging actress. He turned his attention back to Bertie. 'What brings you down here?'

'I'm meeting an old school friend this evening, so I thought why not pop in beforehand?'

'Well, why not indeed?'

'It's been quite a while since anyone performed this play. I thought I'd check up on it and see how well it holds up. I'm staying for a few days, so it's turned into a kind of holiday, I suppose,' said Bertie.

'Well, why don't you bring your friend back with you tonight? Beef up the numbers a bit. We could do with a few more in the audience,' said Teddy, in a conspiratorial stage whisper. 'There's nothing like seeing a play while you're on holiday, is there?'

Robert emitted a short, loud laugh. 'Not exactly holiday weather, is it?'

Arthur's eyes looked ominously up at the glass ceiling. It was protected by the building's metal outer roof, but it was so thin it sounded as if the raindrops were falling directly onto the delicate panes of glass. It somehow made the rain feel more threatening. 'Yes, I thought I could hear the rain. Still can, I think. It's not the best weather for ticket sales…'

Arthur let the last few words tail off, leaving the thought incomplete. It seemed clear from the way he spoke that audiences weren't exactly flooding to the box office. It was no surprise to Bertie. There was a reason this show hadn't been on stage recently, and as hard as it was to admit, the truth of the matter was that it wasn't very good. Perhaps he was being overly self-critical of his work. It wasn't awful, by any stretch of the imagination, but he certainly wouldn't consider it his best work. It looked like even the draw of a former Hollywood star wasn't going to be enough to pull in the crowds.

'Let's keep our fingers crossed that it brightens up before tonight,' Arthur said in a voice that sounded hopeful.

'Don't worry,' said Teddy. 'I'm sure we can all march up and down the promenade and drag some unsuspecting punters inside. Now that Bertie's here, maybe he'll be able to drum up a bit of interest, too.'

'I'm not a star like Celia is, you know.'

'Absolute rubbish.' Teddy threw himself down into one of the theatre's seats, putting his feet up on the back of the one in front. 'You're the playwright of the moment, aren't you?'

Bertie sat in one of the tip-up seats, joining the others who were glad to get some rest. Each of them was dotted around in different rows. The seat let out a loud squeak as he flipped down the base.

Jenny very generously offered to make them cups of tea and disappeared to the back of the auditorium where there was an urn steaming away and a large metal kettle alongside some mint green earthenware teacups – the sort you might find in a church hall.

‘The problem with being the man of the moment, is that a moment is often quite fleeting,’ said Bertie.

‘Hmph, that sounds about right,’ said Robert dryly. ‘I’m telling you, if you see an opportunity, you’ve got to take it. No matter what.’

Bertie felt a little sorry for Robert. It sounded very much like he was speaking from experience. Bertie had met countless actors like him before. There were those actors who constantly found themselves work playing the background roles, never the lead. He wondered idly, was there an opportunity Robert had lost out on all those years ago at the start of his career? And now, would he always be looking back with bitterness about what might have been?

Jenny returned with two cups of tea, one in each hand, which she offered to Bertie and Teddy. ‘Well, this is a good opportunity for me, and I’m taking it.’ Her attempt at putting a positive spin on the conversation didn’t seem to impress Robert, who stifled a noise that sounded a lot like a disapproving cough. He clearly didn’t think much of this particular opportunity.

‘Now, Robert, there’s no need to take that attitude,’ said Teddy. ‘We may be in Brighton and it may be a little outside the peak of the theatrical season. The weather might be absolutely ghastly and it looks like we’re going to be playing to the stalls half-full tonight – that’s if we’re lucky – but that doesn’t mean that we aren’t going to do a cracking job of it, does it, Jenny?’ He caught Jenny’s attention as she returned with the final two cups of tea, one for Arthur and one for Robert, and directed his encouraging comments at her. ‘It doesn’t mean it isn’t going to be a wonderful night, when we get to put the play in front of an audience for the first time. Besides, if you do well Arthur might put you in one of his next shows in London, and I'm sure Bertie will be able to put in a good word for you.'

'Would you really, Mr Carroll?' Jenny's voice was sweet and earnest. She took a seat in the row in front of him.

'I see no reason why not.' In truth, he really could see no reason why he shouldn't put in a good word for her. Equally, he could see no reason why he should … not yet. There were scores of young actresses in London looking for work. In many ways, Robert was right. Success in the theatre was more about luck and being in the right place at the right time.

You know what, Bertie thought, *I will put in a good word for her when I get back to London.* Of course, that would be entirely conditional on whether she actually was any good or if Teddy was just being his overenthusiastic self.

'You'd put her in one of your revues, wouldn't you?' said Teddy, spinning round in his seat to face Arthur.

Arthur didn't respond. He was still standing in the row of seats a little distance away from the group, lost in his own thoughts. It took a moment, but eventually he emitted a questioning "Hmm" when he noticed that all eyes were on him.

'You'd put Jenny in one of your revues?' He turned and whispered theatrically to Jenny so that everyone could hear. 'You *can* sing and dance, can't you?'

'Not really.' Her face fell into an apologetic smile.

'Oh, I wouldn't worry about that! He put Celia in those revues, back in the day, and she couldn't hit a note with a bowl of rice.'

'That was a long time ago, when we were still married,' said Arthur, staying noncommittal.

'Love. It makes you do the strangest things,' said Teddy.

Bertie chuckled to himself. He suspected that love had nothing to do with it. His instincts were telling him that perhaps life at home with Celia ran a lot smoother whenever she was getting her way.

A young man popped his head around the proscenium arch. 'That's fifteen minutes,' he called out.

'Oh well, back to the land of dreams,' said Teddy, with more than a hint of sarcasm.

'Thanks, Charlie,' Arthur called back. 'I'll let you fetch Celia, then.' Charlie's head disappeared into the wings again, but not before Bertie caught a look of significant apprehension appear across his face.

'You should be paying that poor boy danger money, Arthur,' said Teddy.

'Stage managers are built of tougher stuff than you or me, Teddy. At least I hope they are,' he added, this time his voice tinged with a note of concern. No one was quite sure if he was joking or if he was being genuine.

The actors sidled out of their rows and the seats clunked back to their upright positions as they rose one by one. The teacups were returned to the makeshift tea station at the back of the auditorium before the actors returned to the stage. Teddy commented, to no one in particular, that there was no reason to rush as they'd be waiting at least another ten minutes for Celia to emerge.

In actuality, it took twenty.

While they were waiting, the cast sat around, glad of the extra rest. Teddy and Jenny sat on the sofa, with a quiet conversation taking place between them. Now and then, Teddy would make a quiet joke and Jenny would laugh. This was followed by a panicked, giggled "shushing" between them, hoping that no one would notice they were having more fun than anyone else. Across the stage, Robert sat on an occasional chair to one side. The extra time seemed to be to his advantage – his previously perspiring forehead was now almost entirely sweat-free. So confident was he in Celia's delayed return, he had decided to return to the stage, cup of tea in hand; he relaxed in the chair, sipping from it occasionally.

The calm didn't last for long. The storm was on its way – you could hear it approaching, the loud footsteps echoing down the corridor and then descending the steps from the dressing rooms to the stage. While the short break had a recuperating effect on the cast and they seemed a little more at ease when the rehearsal eventually restarted, it seemed to have had the opposite effect on Celia. She had returned even more irritable than before.

'Stupid girl,' she exclaimed at one point to the poor, set upon Constance. 'Why didn't you bring my script to the stage? Fetch it at once.'

Constance dutifully departed.

A little later on, she referred to Teddy as a 'dirty little liar' when he insisted that he was waiting for her to finish her line before he started his.

Even in the scenes when she wasn't appearing on stage, occasional clattering and banging could be heard, along with her loud exclamations of dissatisfaction. Bertie mused that perhaps the reason her Hollywood career had come to an end was that she was unable to fully adapt to the "talkies", where absolute silence would be required during filming on the newly built sound stages.

Celia's voice, which was deep and rich, was perfect for filling a theatre, but perhaps didn't come across with the right subtlety once it had been recorded and amplified to ten times its normal volume in a cinema. The sad truth was that she'd now reached an age where the roles were starting to go to the newer, younger starlets. Perhaps this was another reason she was exploring a return to the theatre. Bertie was comforted that his career wasn't dependent on either his looks or how old he was. With any luck, he would be able to continue to write plays well into his old age.

He noticed that Celia appeared to clash with Teddy more than the others. It might have been his overly cheery disposition that irked her the most.

'Are you smiling?' she demanded at one point, before striding away from him to the other side of the stage. Changing her mind, she strode right back over to him furiously. 'Don't smile at me. It's unprofessional.' Teddy opened his mouth in protest, but before he could make a sound, Celia interrupted, 'And don't talk back to me, either. I thought you were supposed to be the next big thing in theatre, but you look like the next big nothing to me.'

'Really, Celia? I thought I was doing rather well,' said Teddy, trying to lighten the mood with his retort.

'Rather well? You'd never get a job again, not if I had anything to do with it.'

Jenny didn't escape the cutting comments that came disguised as professional advice. 'Speak up, girl. If I can't hear you on this side of the stage, they'll never hear you at the back of the circle.'

Bertie thought this was rather unfair, not least because there probably wouldn't be anybody sitting at the back of the circle – certainly not based on the current ticket sales. In any event, he thought Jenny had a crisp, clear voice that floated elegantly throughout the theatre.

'I wish the rest of you would start performing at my level,' said Celia, commenting loudly to the group.

In many ways, it was true, Bertie thought. Celia was in a class of her own. Her stage presence was so strong it was almost tangible, even if her sledgehammer delivery of each line was a touch old school.

After another torturous two hours for the cast, the rehearsal finally concluded. Everything appeared to have gone to plan. The murder had been solved and the butler didn't do it – a trope that Bertie was always keen to avoid. At the very least, the actors knew where they should be standing, as required by the director, and they'd been able to deliver the majority of the lines correctly.

Arthur congratulated the actors on a job well done, although Celia had retired to her dressing room the very moment the curtain had fallen. He suggested that they all take the opportunity to get out of the theatre, have something to eat, and return ready for the first performance that was only a few hours away. Most of the actors nodded in agreement although Jenny, looking nervous, asked if she could stay and continue to rehearse by herself for a while longer.

The actors, now dismissed, went their own ways. Arthur had disappeared backstage somewhere, presumably to attend to Celia.

Bertie approached the front of the stage. As he got closer, he saw that what had looked like black-and-white tiles on the floor was actually a painted cloth stretched tightly over the stage. It was well-trodden and worn. It was thin enough that, in some places, the wooden boards underneath could be seen through it. Small black burns, caused by several productions' worth of cigarettes being stubbed out underfoot, were dotted over the surface, leaving it pockmarked with holes.

Jenny hadn't started rehearsing by herself yet and Bertie reiterated that Arthur was right. She really should make sure to eat something.

'Oh, Teddy said he'd take me out somewhere later, his treat. But I think I'm too nervous to eat anything.'

'Now, now. No one wants to be distracted by a rumbling stomach on the stage.'

'And I want to make sure I know exactly what I'm supposed to be doing and know all my lines.'

'I promise you, you know exactly what you're supposed to be doing already,' Bertie said. 'I've certainly seen worse rehearsals in my time. Besides, if you spend too much time worrying about what you're supposed to do, that *will* make you forget everything.'

Jenny smiled at him, reassured by his wise words. 'Thank you, Bertie. I'll just stay a little while longer, but I will take a break.'

'Is that a promise?' he teased.

'Yes. Yes, it is.'

He left her, still practising the lines under her breath. He walked towards the back of the auditorium, towards the exit. As he reached the doors, he turned back for a moment. The stage was empty except for Charlie and Jenny. Charlie skirted around the edges of the set going about his stage manager duties, tidying props and resetting furniture back to their starting positions, ready for the performance that night.

Jenny stood in the centre of the stage, going through the motions of one of her scenes. Bertie recognised it at once as the shooting scene. With the bright stage lighting now turned off, the working light from the wings cast long, eerie shadows across the stage. The figure of Jenny stood silhouetted in the gloom.

Slowly, deliberately, and with the gun held in her hand, Jenny practised taking her shot.

Chapter Three

'It wouldn't hurt to be a little more friendly with the others, you know,' said Arthur, bravely offering his advice.

'Don't be ridiculous,' Celia replied as she clipped on a pair of pearl earrings. 'I'm being perfectly cordial.' Her back was turned to him while she inspected herself in the dressing room mirror.

Arthur breathed out heavily through his nose, not wanting to antagonise her any further. The unintentionally sharp sound was more than enough to be considered a comment on the matter by Celia. Her eyes snapped up to meet Arthur's reflection in the mirror.

'I see,' Celia said haughtily, before she allowed her gaze to return to her reflection in the mirror. A few more moments passed in silence, but not awkwardness. They seemed to be relaxed with each other and comfortable with the quiet, although the whole atmosphere appeared to balance on a knife-edge. It wasn't long before Celia was unable to resist adding a further comment.

'I don't know what you think I'm doing here, darling, but it's certainly not to make friends. I came here to work.' The word "darling" fell somewhere neatly in between pointed and genuine affection. 'Now, I know it's been a while since I was in one of these theatre productions, but I assume that you – and the others who continue to work in it – still try to hold on to a modicum of professionalism during the rehearsal process.' She turned in her chair to face Arthur, resting her hand on the back like it was an armrest. The gesture added the full stop to the end of her sentence.

'Look,' started Arthur, with an apologetic tone. 'The last few days have been a bit stressful for everyone. I think they're frustrated with the amount of time the technical rehearsals have taken—'

'And, as I told you earlier,' Celia interrupted, 'that's not because of anything to do with me. I know *my* lines and what *I'm* supposed to be doing.'

'Yes, of course you do.' Arthur's reply was quick, although he didn't sound entirely as if he meant it.

It was convincing enough for Celia, though, who continued talking. 'It certainly isn't my fault if I get thrown off by Robert's bumbling around the stage or when Teddy just stands there with that ridiculous smile on his face. He's like a glassy-eyed fool.'

Arthur opened his mouth to speak but closed it again, recognising, with experience, that Celia wasn't quite finished.

'And I'm sure that girl, what's her name? Jenny? I'm sure what she does on the stage is perfectly acceptable for the amateur theatricals, or whatever it was she did around here before this, but the poor thing looks completely terrified most of the time. I feel quite sorry for her.'

This time, Arthur wisely kept his mouth closed. He expected that anyone would be terrified if they'd had to share a stage with her. He was quite certain that "sorry" was something Celia had never felt for someone in her entire life.

'It's not so much that she looks like a rabbit caught in the headlights, but almost as if the entire vehicle is bearing down on her, if you know what I mean. I've tried, haven't I? I've tried?' she said in exasperation.

'Yes,' said Arthur, somewhat automatically, although he wasn't quite sure what he was agreeing to.

'I've tried to advise her, given her my suggestions about how she might improve her performance, how she might improve her character. It doesn't seem to have had much of an effect, I'm sorry to say. Honestly, she's just a child and I—'

Celia was interrupted by the sound of a clothes hanger falling to the floor. She and Arthur turned in the direction of the disturbance to see an apologetic Constance and a crumpled garment on the floor. Apparently they had both forgotten Celia's dresser was still in the room with them, going about her duties for the evening performance.

'No dear, that's fine,' Celia said sarcastically. 'It's only Chanel, just drop it on the floor.'

'Sorry, Miss,' replied the flustered Constance who did

her best to rescue the clothing and hang it back up on the rail.

'I *was* going to wear it after the show. I assume you've arranged some kind of dreadfully dull drinks reception, haven't you?'

'Well, nothing too fancy. Just a few glasses of something in the bar, perhaps. It seems right, don't you think, to thank everyone for all their hard work?' said Arthur.

'Well, there you are then,' said Celia. She gestured with her palms facing upwards as if to say, what more do you want from me? 'I'm doing that, aren't I? And you accuse me of not being a team player. Honestly.' Celia turned back to face the mirror and started touching up her make-up.

'I can assure you I was not accusing you of anything,' Arthur apologised. Moving behind Celia, he rested two comforting hands on her shoulders, although they were quickly shrugged off so that Celia could continue attending to herself.

'It takes more than one type of person to make a team, you know.' Celia paused a moment to reapply her lipstick. 'There are those of us who are leaders and there are those of us who are followers. I'm a leader,' she added, sounding very pleased at the fact.

'I never doubted that for a moment,' said Arthur, under his breath. As he turned back to the room, he saw that Constance seemed to have wrangled the dress back onto its hanger and he hoped there wasn't too much damage done. When it came to Celia's clothing, a speck of dust was just as objectionable as a grease stain. Arthur didn't want to think about her reaction to something as outrageous as a crease.

'I have to lead by example. As the head of a company of players, naturally, they look up to me. If I let my standards slip … well, I don't know where we'd all end up. Merry hell, I would have thought.' Celia used a piece of tissue paper to blot away any excess lipstick, then carefully inspected the finish. She turned her head from side to side, her eyes fixed on the same spot in the mirror. The barest glimpse of a smile, almost a smirk, indicated that she was happy with the result. Celia caught sight of Constance in the reflection, who – now she'd finished dealing with the clothing rail – was watching her with intensity. In a daze, she hadn't realised that Celia had noticed.

'Didn't your mother tell you it was rude to stare?' snapped Celia. 'If you've got everything set up, you can go. I've no need of you anymore.'

Without saying a word, Constance nodded and then dashed out of the room with a glance at Arthur as she left. She looked close to tears.

'Well, she's a funny one,' Celia said dryly in Arthur's direction.

'Be kind to her,' he replied. 'She's in a new country. Everything is different for her.'

'I think we should look at replacing her, you know, when the show goes to London. I'm sure she's doing her best, but she is extraordinarily clumsy for a dresser.'

'Well, I'll bear that in mind. *If* this show makes it to London.'

'Jenny too. We'll have to find someone else for her.'

'Really, Celia,' Arthur protested. 'I think we'll look at crossing that bridge when we get to it and not a moment before.'

'I'm serious. You'll have to recast for the West End. She's really not at the same level. It would be unfair to her. Besides, she's always watching me too, like Teddy does.'

'Everyone looks at you, my dear; you're Celia Hamilton.'

'Well, I don't appreciate being gawped at. I find it quite off-putting. I think we should keep the fans in the audience, where they belong, and not up on the stage.'

Arthur had to resist the urge he had to enlighten her that Jenny was hardly her biggest fan. The two weeks of rehearsals had seen to that.

'It's not that I don't want to help her; in fact I feel rather kindly towards her.'

'You do?' said Arthur. This time he failed to disguise the surprise in his voice.

'It's just that I find it unnerving sometimes,' she continued, ignoring Arthur's comment. 'The way she stares. I think she's picked up some bad habits hanging around with that boy.'

'Teddy?' Arthur asked.

'Yes, he smiles. And that's just as infuriating if you ask me.'

'Oh, come on, Celia,' said Arthur. 'You can't come down harshly on the boy because he's smiling.'

Celia spoke coolly. 'No one's ever really that happy.'

'We used to be. Once.' Arthur paused, wistfully. 'You used to be.'

Celia responded to the comment with a disapproving look. 'What makes you think I'm not happy now?'

'Well, are you?'

'Arthur, if I was any happier, I think I might explode,' she replied, deadpan.

Arthur chuckled lightly. 'So you do still have a sense of humour?'

'Yes.' Genuinely – perhaps for the first time in a while – a smile crept across her features. 'But don't you dare tell anyone.'

'I wondered if you'd care to join me for dinner tonight, before the show. We could catch up on old times.'

'Drag up all that ancient history, you mean? If I have to think back to that long ago, it makes me feel like an old fossil. No, I don't think so. It's very kind of you to offer though, but I have other plans.'

'Other plans?' said Arthur, surprised.

'Yes. As much as I'd love to sit with you reminiscing about our years in London, I'd prefer for everything to remain as distraction-free as possible. I think I'll just go back to the hotel and have something light to eat in my room. I might even risk a visit to a little café, or something, although I worry I might have to disguise myself.'

'I think you might get away with it; it's not like the place is buzzing with journalists like it is in the West End or Hollywood.'

'Hmm.' Celia cocked her head at the thought. 'We'll

see, I suppose. Either way, I'd prefer to be alone, just for a while.'

'That doesn't sound like most actresses I know,' replied Arthur. 'I thought you all loved surrounding yourselves with people, being the centre of attention.'

'Honestly, dear. You make me sound like some kind of egocentric. That couldn't be further from the truth. There are times of course, as a personality, where one needs to place oneself in the middle of things. I promise you, Arthur, that I only do those things out of professional courtesy for everyone involved. For the publicity. It's part of the job, that's all. I much prefer being by myself, you know.'

'You do? I suppose that explains why you never remarried.'

'That's certainly not the reason.'

'You haven't found anyone who can live up to your high standards?' said Arthur, venturing his own theory.

'You really can be terribly perceptive when you want to, can't you? By which I mean, you're terrible at it. I think it's clear that I've managed quite well by myself over the years. Why complicate things with a man? Men, once they reach a certain age, seem to have a crisis of confidence and start doing idiotic things like running off with their poor young secretaries. Women, I find, are much more graceful in their progression into old age. We do it with dignity. If a woman *has* to resort to a younger man, it's only because the men of her own age become so unbearable. Present company excluded,' she said, with another hint of a smile.

'An assignation with a new young lover tonight, is it? No wonder you don't want me around.'

'Honestly, you do let your imagination run wild sometimes. I'll be dining alone. It's been nearly two decades since I was last on a proper stage. I want to be in my own thoughts at the moment. I could do without the distraction, quite frankly. Besides, what's the point of us talking endlessly about the past? It's all done now. I certainly have no regrets.'

'You don't?' asked Arthur. He sounded surprised, even though he tried to hide it.

'Why should I?' said Celia. 'I'm perfectly content with every decision I've ever made. Aren't you, Arthur?'

'Well, yes, I suppose I am,' said Arthur, thinking about it. He became more serious now. 'You don't ever wonder what your life would have been like if you'd stayed in London?'

'You don't ever think about what your life might have been like if you had moved to America?' she countered.

'I see your point.'

'Well, there you are, then. You can't keep looking back over the might-have-beens. You only get one life and sometimes you just have to take your chances and roll with it. Of course, I care for you very dearly, Arthur, but neither of us would be where we are today without making the decisions we had to make. Our paths were always meant to be separate. There are always hard decisions, sacrifices you have to make, but you can't say it didn't work out well in the end.'

'No regrets?'

'Absolutely none,' said Celia, firmly as she rose from the dressing table after one last look in the mirror.

'Well, if you change your mind, you know where to find me.'

'Arthur, darling, you should know by now that once I make a decision, it's almost impossible to get me to change my mind.'

A brief smile flashed across her features before she swept out of the room.

Chapter Four

The Ship Hotel sat on the seafront in between Brighton's two piers. The original building had been sited on Ship Street, allegedly constructed from a ship's timbers that lent the hotel its name. Bertie had seen the eye-catching advert when he was looking up train times in the *ABC Railway Guide*. It had appeared on the same page as the London to Brighton timetable, and seeing as he wasn't particularly worried about where he stayed – though the location seemed convenient enough – he had booked it straight away. He wondered if Hugh had done the same thing as, by coincidence, he had also booked a room in the same hotel.

There's a bewitching feeling about hotels, Bertie thought. Large hotels, even more so. There was a strange magic to the anonymity they gift to their guests, as they drift past each other in the hallways. There would be the meeting of eyes, perhaps a friendly nod of the head, and then you would continue on your way; you could acknowledge each other without saying a word. There were other patrons of the hotel that might be a little more forthright, emboldened by the fraternal bond between visiting guests, and would attempt to strike up a conversation with a stranger in the bar or lounge.

Here you would be proffered the same, time-worn questions: what's your name, where are you from, what do you do? Bertie was always tempted to invent a new persona each time someone asked – there was no fact-checking in a hotel. Anyone could be anyone and they could assume any identity they chose. He often contemplated the idea of inventing different characters that he could introduce himself as, although he never did. He didn't think he had the necessary acting skills to pull it off. The game would be up if he started laughing halfway through a made-up story of intrigue and adventure. Perhaps tales of derring-do weren't the way to go. Instead, would it be better to pretend you were something completely pedestrian, like an accountant? Surely that wouldn't prompt too many follow-up questions. Although, of course, there was always the risk that someone might genuinely require financial advice.

Being a playwright almost always prompted a cascade of additional questions: Do you know anyone famous? Would I have seen any of your plays? I didn't even know that was a real job… The last one, he would usually be too polite to counter robustly.

Bertie, although proud of the plays he had written, preferred to stay quietly modest about his achievements. Right now, his talent for enthralling murder mysteries was entirely in vogue and audiences were flooding to his plays. While he might be considered rather famous by those who followed the theatre scene, being a celebrity was not something he sought to be or aspired to. He was quite content with his entry in *Who's Who in the Theatre* and didn't feel he needed any more press coverage than that. Luckily, even the most ardent fans of the theatre would rarely know what the playwright looked like, something that established actors were unable to escape. It was rarely the case that he would be recognised by a theatregoer as he left through the stage door. That suited him perfectly.

Bertie sat in the lounge of the hotel. At this time of the year, it was almost empty. Now and then, a member of staff would pop a head in to see if any assistance was needed before dashing off again to attend to their other duties, covering the work of what would be two or more people in summer. The dark wood and stained-glass windows gave the room the feeling of a public house. A bottle of beer that was perched on the edge of the table in front of him and the cigarette smoke coming from the direction of his table partner only enhanced that effect.

'What do you reckon it's been?' asked Hugh. 'Fourteen years? Fifteen?'

'Something like that,' Bertie replied.

'Time flies, eh?'

Bertie nodded in agreement.

Hugh brought a match up, lighting his third (or maybe it was his fourth) Woodbine cigarette of their session. He picked the packet up, offering one to Bertie. 'Not taken it up yet?' asked Hugh through a haze of smoke.

'No, those things never really agreed with me.'

'Still collecting the cards, though?'

Bertie chuckled and shook his head. 'I've got no one to give them to me.'

The smell of the cigarette smoke took him right back to their school days when the pair of them would sneak off to smoke, or rather so that Hugh could smoke, out of sight from the other boys and the teachers. The cigarette cards would always be kept by Bertie if they were of interest.

'The Army Boxer series?' said Hugh with a chuckle. 'That was a favourite of yours, wasn't it?'

Bertie squirmed with embarrassment. His interest in that particular collection of cards was because the boxers would generally be posing with their tops off, something an adolescent Bertie found himself intriguingly drawn to, although he would have never admitted as much to Hugh.

'Association football too,' added Bertie. 'Although I'm not exactly an ardent follower of sports these days.'

'No, I didn't ever think you were.' Hugh shifted in his seat, taking another long draw on the cigarette. He leant back lazily in his chair. Behind the apparently relaxed exterior, Bertie could see an analytical mind that was continuously at work – was he analysing Bertie as they spoke? He suspected that Hugh was one of those people who could never really kick back and take it easy. It was his cold and shrewd mind that meant he had become the leading force behind the arrests of some of the country's most dangerous criminals and killers. A mind like that never stopped. It would always be mulling something over, an old case or the current one. He wondered, now, whether it was their school day memories that had the attention of Hugh's analytical mind.

'And are you?' Bertie asked. 'Still into your sports?'

'The boxing?' Hugh questioned in reply. 'I dabble in the Police League now and then. I'm afraid to say I'm not as sharp as I used to be, although I do pretty well. There's still the swimming, of course...'

Swimming in the river that crossed the bottom of the school grounds had been a common activity for the schoolboys during the warmer months of the year. Bertie, although dragged in against his will occasionally, generally didn't participate; he was more than happy to watch the others paddle up and down. Those that were more daring would climb the large tree on the riverbank, whose branches overhung the water, and dive in.

Bertie's preference for the water he swam in was that it was contained in a neatly tiled swimming bath. The clean white tiles of a swimming pool were far more preferable underfoot to the dank mud that squeezed between your toes in a river – the thought made him shudder. The most adventurous outdoor swimming Bertie did these days was confined to the Parliament Hill Lido.

'It's nice to see you again,' said Bertie, honestly. 'I know that we've kept in touch. But in person ... it's nice to see you again.'

'It is,' said Hugh, stating it as a matter of fact, 'although there's plenty in those letters I probably shouldn't have said. Things I really shouldn't have told you.' He leant forward, stubbing the cigarette out in the ashtray.

'There is?' questioned Bertie.

'I mean, things about the cases. I shouldn't really share them,' he quickly clarified. He looked at Bertie with his greyish blue eyes. They were captivating. When he spoke next, his voice was casual. 'Did you keep any of them?'

'The letters?' questioned Bertie. 'Some. But not all of them.' He lifted his cut-glass tumbler from the table. The weight of the heavy bottom was deceptive; the glass was empty. He placed it down again.

'I thought they might serve as an inspiration for your plays,' said Hugh.

'They have,' Bertie responded. 'They do. Although I don't think many of them could have been translated exactly to the stage. If I put some of those stories directly in a play, no one would believe them.'

'Ah, the old "the truth is stranger than fiction" routine.'

'But they were nice to get. Aside from hearing about your police cases,' Bertie said, before adding hesitantly, 'I'm glad we stayed in touch.'

'So am I.' Hugh lifted his beer bottle as a toast before draining the remnants.

'Do you even remember much from our school days?' asked Bertie.

'Remember much?' Hugh laughed. 'Only that the majority of it was cold and damp, and the food was terrible.'

'I don't remember anything. I don't know if it's because I've blocked it out or because there wasn't really anything to remember at all.'

Bertie's overriding memory of his school days was that there wasn't really a lot to do. Of course, there was schoolwork to be done and lessons to be taken. Except for that, the place was pretty unremarkable. There was never anywhere to settle. It almost felt like a large railway station, with plenty of space for people to aimlessly meander about in, but where the main function of the place was to sit around waiting for something to happen. Waiting for the next lesson, waiting for something to do, or waiting for the holidays when you could be free of the place for a few blissful weeks. Imagine what it would be like to spend all your time in a railway station that was large, cold, and echoey, but without the promise or the excitement of seeing any trains.

'You never told me why you wanted to meet up?' asked Bertie. He posed the question delicately; Hugh had somehow avoided the topic so far.

'I needed a break, I suppose. A holiday really,' Hugh replied. 'From work, from London. Brighton? Well, why not? It seemed like as good a place as any. Work is quiet at the moment.'

A holiday? It wasn't exactly sunbathing on the beach weather, although Bertie couldn't quite imagine Hugh partaking in such slothful activities. He wasn't the type.

'I didn't know murder was seasonal?' said Bertie, honestly.

'I wouldn't say it's seasonal, although maybe it's the heat in the summer? Perhaps it makes people do crazy things they wouldn't usually do.'

'I would have thought cases would rise in the winter

when it's colder and you're shut inside with a lot of people that you don't like very much.'

'True. But it does seem to come in waves, for whatever reason. For me, it's been relatively quiet for a month or so. That means one of two things… Perhaps it's going to stay quiet for a while.'

'And what's the other thing?'

Hugh laughed. 'That I'm due a murder any day now.'

'There's only one thing around here that's dying anytime soon,' Bertie replied with a smile.

'What's that?' Hugh sounded genuinely concerned.

'My play. Onstage. Tonight.'

At long last, one of the staff from the hotel shuffled into the lounge. Bertie was able to catch their attention and order another gin. He offered Hugh another beer as well, to which he agreed.

It was true. Bertie admitted he was worried there would only be a smattering of people in the audience tonight, even with a star draw like Celia Hamilton in the production. Hugh smiled, lighting another cigarette, the last in the packet. Poking around in the slightly crumpled packaging, he fished out the cigarette card for old times' sake. Looking back at him was a familiar face.

'How's that for luck? Celia Hamilton.' He tossed the card towards Bertie. 'The Stars of the Cinema series.'

The picture on the card was striking. It showed a much younger woman with softer features than the Celia he had seen at the rehearsal. It was one of those delicately lit, over-the-shoulder portraits where she looked every bit the Hollywood star. He turned the card over to read as their drinks arrived.

No. 68
Celia Hamilton
A former star of the London stage who now resides in America. Miss Hamilton won great acclaim for her breakout performance as Joan of Arc (1911). Perhaps her most famous part was playing the titular role in Helen of Troy (1919).

'Well. That is a coincidence. Look, I don't suppose you'd be interested in coming to see the play with me tonight? I have to tell you it's not one of my best. The construction of the thing is probably more interesting than what actually happens. You see the murder in Act One, then in Act Two you go back to before everything happened, which turns everything on its head. I suppose I was younger back then and far too clever for my own good. How about it?'

'Me? See a play? It's not really my thing,' he admitted, sheepishly. 'I'm more of a music hall man myself.'

'The place will be pretty empty. We can sit in the circle – I imagine we'll probably have it entirely to ourselves. Why not?'

'Well, why not, indeed?' said Hugh, with a twinkle in his eye. He raised his bottle of beer to Bertie, who responded with his newly freshened gin.

'So much for taking a break from work.'

Chapter Five

Bertie closed the door that led into the circle behind him and sighed, glad to be returning to his seat. Looking down from his vantage point above the stalls, he was pleasantly surprised. The circle, where he was standing as he watched the audience file into their seats, remained closed, as he had suspected. There were perhaps five or six rows' worth of people spread out over an area at the front of the stalls. The way in which they'd dotted themselves around the auditorium gave the appearance that the performance was much better attended than it actually was.

Plaster mouldings that looked like garlands of flowers adorned the front of the circle and the boxes. Set in the centre of each of the boxes were blue oval plaques containing cheeky cherubs in white relief. Their attention was turned towards the stage and seemed to bolster the audience numbers. The undulating curves of the circle front created the classic horseshoe shape of a traditional auditorium, which successfully managed to disguise the rather plain, rectangular shape of the exterior walls.

The warmth of pre-show chatter radiated from the awaiting audience members in their seats; it mixed with the sounds of the sea emanating from beneath their feet. Together, the resulting effect gave the auditorium an excitable buzz, something he hoped would be an encouragement to the nervous performers waiting behind the curtain.

Bertie skirted his way along the row at the front of the circle. In the centre of the row, Hugh was already seated, waiting for him to return.

Hugh peered down at the audience below. 'Not too bad, is it?' He spoke with the enthusiasm of a supportive parent.

'I've certainly seen worse in my time,' Bertie replied.

'Good seats too,' said Hugh, commenting on the view. 'I'm looking forward to this now.' He held the programme up so that Bertie could see it. 'Glad to see they spelt your name right,' he joked.

They hadn't.

'Well, this should be interesting,' said Bertie.

It would be. While the audience was sitting calmly in their seats, waiting patiently for the proceedings to begin, there had been a minor crisis unfolding backstage. Bertie, unwittingly, had been swept up in it. The Palace Pier Theatre was unusual, in that the dressing rooms flanked the sides of the auditorium at the circle level. As there were still a few minutes before the show started, He thought it would be a good idea to poke his head through the pass door that joined the auditorium and the dressing room corridor; he would give everyone a bit of last-minute encouragement.

It was something that, moments after he had opened the door, he instantly regretted.

'How about Bertie?' a voice exclaimed, as Bertie entered through the pass door. There was a small and energetic conversation occurring between the cast members who were gathered around. Teddy's voice rang out over the top in its cheerful and optimistic way.

'You could do it, couldn't you?' came Teddy's voice again.

Bertie wondered what "it" was, although he barely had a moment in which he could have attempted to make a guess. Nevertheless, he was pretty confident that he would be unlikely to want to do whatever "it" was. The entire cast, except for Celia and Robert, was gathered together, crammed into the small hallway with barely any room to move. Jenny Ashcroft stood the closest to him. She hopped from one foot to the other, looking nervous. Eventually, she noticed Bertie's confusion.

'Robert's gone off ill,' she said.

'Oh,' came his response, automatically. He didn't quite know how to respond or what he could do.

'Fancy being our butler, then?' Teddy's enthusiastic voice rang out – it was accompanied by an even more enthusiastic grin.

'Sorry, I write plays precisely because I have no interest in taking a single step anywhere near the stage.'

Bertie gave a sort of shrug to Teddy, whose expression changed from excitement to one of mock sadness.

He glanced around the faces of the small group, holding his hands up by way of apology.

'Spoilsport!' joked Teddy.

Arthur stood in the centre of the small group looking rather stressed, but still managing to keep control of the situation. The news had clearly arrived while the actors were getting ready. Jenny's hair was neatly pinned up in tight curls – ready for the wig she'd be wearing for her role – while her modesty was protected only by a dressing gown. Teddy – modesty be damned – was half-dressed without any shoes on. His shirt was unbuttoned and his braces were hanging down from his waist, dangling above the floor.

'No, it's all settled. Here's the plan, I will go on for Robert. I know the play well enough and if it turns out I need to carry the script around with me, then that's just what I'll do. Now, will all of you please go back to your dressing rooms and carry on getting ready,' he pleaded. The group nodded in agreement. 'Constance, would you tell Celia I'll be along to her room in a moment to explain what's happening?' Constance gave a slight tilt of her head in response to Arthur and disappeared obediently down the corridor.

'Five minutes,' called Charlie, who at that moment only just had the presence of mind to look at his pocket watch. 'Four really,' he admitted, a little more quietly to anyone that still happened to be paying attention to him.

'Fun, isn't it?' said Teddy brightly, to no one in particular. He gave Bertie a wide smile before turning down the corridor to put on the remainder of his clothes. Jenny turned to Bertie, looking a little paler than she did earlier in the day. Before he could give her an encouraging look or a supportive word, Arthur had started to speak to him. Jenny hurried off, like a startled rabbit, along the corridor in pursuit of Teddy.

'Sorry about all this, old boy,' Arthur said, putting a friendly arm around Bertie. He wondered whether the comforting gesture was an attempt at steadying Arthur's nerves or his own. 'Bloody Robert's gone and picked himself up a bug or something. He did look pretty terrible earlier, but that's Robert, isn't it? It's not like he's ever looked the absolute peak of health.' Arthur relinquished his hold around Bertie. 'I suppose I'd better … well, you know…' He trailed off and took a breath in an attempt to strengthen his resolve. He turned to face Bertie, with an expression that was hard to decipher. His mouth remained open as if no words would come. 'I'd better see if I can fit into Robert's costume,' said Arthur eventually. He started down the corridor towards one of the dressing rooms. 'I don't know what it says about the state of my health that we're roughly the same size.'

'If there's anything I can do?' Bertie let the question hang there, knowing full well there was nothing he could.

Arthur turned back to face him without breaking his stride down the corridor. 'Shout out the lines whenever I forget what they are.' He laughed. 'No, no, I think everything's under control now. At least I hope it is…'

Arthur certainly looked nervous about the whole thing, but then he would. Bertie would have been.

'Look, must go and see Celia. I'm not sure she'll be exactly pleased, but what can you do...' With that, Arthur turned, disappearing around a kink in the corridor and out of sight.

Bertie gave a final glance over at Charlie, who was the last remaining person in the corridor. Like any good stage manager at a moment of crisis, he was standing by, in a state of readiness, nervously consulting his watch.

Hugh laughed as Bertie, now back in his seat, relayed the events to him. 'They're not going to cancel, then? Put it off for the night?'

'Have you never heard of the phrase "The show must go on"?' said Bertie. 'It's something that we theatre folk slavishly adhere to, even if it's despite our better judgement.'

There's something admirable about the mentality of performers, Bertie thought. Even on a night like this one, when the theatre was largely devoid of an audience. The fact they would plough on and do the best they could, regardless of circumstance. The oft-used phrase, he had once learnt, was coined in circuses. If a performer was injured or an animal escaped, the show would always continue in an attempt to spare the audiences of the panic and horror, by way of distraction: "The show must go on."

He wondered if this oft told backstory – always making sure the show continued, regardless – was instead a myth perpetuated by unscrupulous producers. He suspected, then as now, that they would be unwilling to cancel a show and then have to return the box office takings to the audience.

Bertie had heard stories of "doctor theatre" where actors' illnesses would mysteriously vanish the moment the curtain went up, although, more often than not, those illnesses were inflicted on themselves by an overindulgence of alcohol the night before a matinee performance, without leaving enough time to recover.

He had listened to tales that were relayed to him about actors who had sustained injuries on stage, including broken bones, and wouldn't miss a beat for the rest of the performance only to double over in pain the moment the house lights were brought up at the end of the show. Actors were strange and wonderful people. *There's being a hero,* he thought, *but there's also taking things a bit too far.*

The curtain, neatly framed by the proscenium arch, glowed a rich red. This was another nifty trick, in Bertie's opinion. It was quite likely that the house tabs were rather faded and dusty. A couple of bright lights with a coloured gel filter – these had the nickname "curtain warmers" – lit the curtain, making it appear a rich colour and much more luxurious-looking than it really was.

Bertie had discovered, over the years, that the many tricks of set design weren't reserved solely for once the curtain had risen. Often, expensive-looking marble columns in theatre auditoriums were nothing more than skilfully painted plaster or even papier mâché. The artifice of the theatre was just as present in the buildings themselves as it was on the stage.

As the house lights began to dim, jaunty music

started to play. After a moment, the curtain rose, revealing Celia Hamilton in a striking dark red dress. She was preparing drinks, as dictated by the play. Gentle applause met her appearance, causing an almost imperceptible twitch of the corner of her mouth in polite acknowledgement. Bertie supposed it was a far cry from the reception she would have once garnered at a movie premiere. It caused him to wonder what it was that had brought her here. Had she really reached the sunset of her career in Hollywood? Although to give her credit, perhaps she had missed working in the theatre. Many actors do.

The long tedious days on a film set, with only a director, a camera operator and an uninterested crew as your audience, were nothing compared to the instant gratification that you would get from an auditorium filled with people. If she'd wanted to get back into the theatre, why hadn't she found a role in London? He pondered still. Surely, a role for someone like her wouldn't have been too hard to come by. While the movie industry might have turned their back on her, he was certain she'd enough of a following for people to queue around the block for returns in the West End. Why come to this dead spot in Brighton?

Maybe it had been too long since she'd been on the stage? This little jaunt down to the south coast was, perhaps, a confidence-boosting exercise, something where she could test and refine her skills as a stage actress once more. This seemed more likely. Even the best knife dulls and needs sharpening occasionally. From the little Bertie knew about Celia, he was sure she'd never put herself in a situation where she wasn't one hundred per cent confident in her abilities. She would never risk looking the fool.

Bertie had worked in the theatre long enough to realise how fragile an actor's confidence could be. Critics could be harsh. One amusing adjective, to produce a more entertaining write-up, could blight an actor's career for years. The echo of a comment from a review of a long-forgotten show could creep into the audition room and make it easier to choose a different actor for the role. The adage goes: you're only as good as your last show. And while that's generally true, it's always the bad ones that seem to cast the longest shadows.

The play progressed through the first few scenes without incident. When Arthur finally appeared as the butler, Bertie was surprised to see him without a script in his hand. While his acting wasn't exactly what you'd call stellar, he knew all the right words, he said them in the right place and stood in roughly the right position. There were people that were happy to call themselves professional actors who didn't always have the requisite skill to do all three at once.

Watching the production turned out to be more enjoyable than he had expected. He hadn't thought about this play for a great many years, let alone remembered the majority of its contents. Some of the lines sounded reassuringly familiar, while there were others he barely recognised. There were even a few funny lines he'd forgotten about, which caused him to laugh out loud.

Teddy had been right; Jenny was an excellent actor. None of the nerves Bertie had witnessed before the show or in the rehearsal were showing. *Even Celia must be impressed*, he thought. Unfortunately, she had much more difficulty hiding her attitude towards Arthur's butler. He recalled how she'd admonished the rest of the cast for not performing at her level earlier in the day; Arthur's butler seemed to be well below her par.

The audience, for the majority of the act, played their part well. They laughed in the right places and they gasped when the action demanded it. Teddy, much to Celia's disapproval, would occasionally play a line directly at the audience in an attempt to wring the largest possible response out of them. He threw a few raised eyebrows and facial expressions in their direction – breaking the fourth wall – to get some additional, and unscripted, laughs. You couldn't stop Teddy from being Teddy. He clearly wasn't taking the production quite as seriously as he could have done. Bertie couldn't blame him, this was end of the pier entertainment after all and some of the dialogue left a bit to be desired.

The scene of the murder was dramatic indeed. In a moment of anger, Jenny's character removes a gun from her purse and shoots Celia, apparently due to the hideous way she's been treated her whole life, something which, based on her experience during the rehearsals, wouldn't have been exactly a stretch of the imagination for her.

It was an intense scene between the two of them. Arthur had staged it so that the full company was on stage when the gun went off, even though the other characters weren't actually in the room with them; it was quite modern and effective. You could see the characters react to the sound of the gun going off, each from a different point of view: Teddy's character in the garden, Constance's maid in her quarters and the butler in the kitchen. In the second act, each character describes what they were doing when they heard the gunshot – or the noise that they'd mistaken for something else – like a champagne cork popping or a car backfiring. Bertie thought it added a bit more interest to the staging and still avoided ruining the twist ending. It was something that he certainly thought was an improvement over the original production.

When Jenny fired the gun, the loud report made the audience jump. Celia then performed such a dramatic and realistic death that it garnered an appreciative round of applause. She quickly fell to her knees behind the sofa, using the back of it to prop herself up, before finally disappearing from view. Bertie found her acting enthralling. Even from their vantage point, which was a fair distance from the performers, every subtle movement could be clearly read. She really managed to make it look as if the life was fading from her eyes.

Stuffing the gun back into her purse, Jenny dashed off the stage, leaving the body hidden behind the sofa to be discovered in a few minutes, at the end of the act.

Bertie glanced over at Hugh and was surprised to find him engrossed in the action. When they'd met earlier, Hugh's features had looked more rugged and stern in the light of the hotel lounge; it had made him look every bit the tough guy that he was. But here, in the reflected glow of the light that was being bounced back from the stage, his features were softened. He looked much more like his younger self, the one Bertie had remembered.

Sensing Bertie's gaze upon him, Hugh turned to look at him. 'Show's great. I think she probably did it,' he joked in a whisper, pointing in the direction that Jenny had departed and returned his focus back to the action.

The act was now nearing its end. Arthur entered, as the butler. Constance, performing as the maid, was acting distraught after the body had been discovered and was crying in the corner of the room. And now it was time for Arthur's masterpiece of sound effects and drama – the one that Bertie had witnessed earlier in the day.

Arthur crouched down a little behind the sofa to inspect the body.

'Oh no,' he announced dramatically. 'She's dead!' With a crash of thunder, the windows flew open. The sound of howling wind and yet more thunder filled the room. Arthur's butler stood up and dashed out to the hallway to call the police, leaving Jenny and Constance lit only by a single spotlight.

The exciting staging had its effect and the audience responded as loudly as they could with their applause, impressed by the final moments.

Arthur had filled in valiantly for the butler, which hadn't seemed to dilute the response of the audience. If Bertie hadn't known any better, he would have hardly thought a last-minute substitution of an actor had taken place. There were undoubtedly plenty of far worse performances he had seen in his time.

The applause continued as the curtain fell.

The play had gone well, under the circumstances. The

murder victim had been shot, the body had been discovered, and we knew who did it because we saw them fire the gun.

It was only when a loud scream rang out from behind the curtain that Bertie and Hugh realised something had gone horribly wrong.

Chapter Six

Bertie and Hugh rushed backstage as quickly as they could. As they made their way onto the set, they saw the actors gathered around the sofa. Jenny was sitting on it, sobbing uncontrollably. Teddy sat next to her, doing his utmost to console her, but it seemed to be having little effect. Arthur, Constance and Charlie stood around Celia in silence. She was still lying, unmoving, on the floor.

'What's happened?' asked Bertie.

The instant he asked, he knew he wouldn't need an answer. A small pool of dark red liquid surrounded Celia, slowly staining the canvas floor cloth that had been stretched over the wooden boards. The viscous liquid glistened in the intense light coming from the lighting battens, hung overhead.

'She really is dead,' said Arthur plainly, in shock. 'I should...' He stammered over his words. 'I should call the police.'

'No need,' replied Bertie. 'They're already here.' He

indicated to Hugh, who stepped a little further into the stage light.

'Nobody touch anything,' Hugh stated. 'Nobody leave the stage.'

'Is that really required?' asked Arthur.

'Yes, I'm afraid so,' Hugh replied. 'Where is the gun?'

'It's back on the props table, stage left,' said Charlie. 'It's been there since Jenny brought it offstage.'

'I must ask you to stay here until further notice. I'll ask you to empty your pockets of anything you might have, one by one, as a matter of routine. So let me know if you currently have anything on yourself, any props or belongings.'

'Should I go and tell the audience to leave?' said Arthur.

'I can do that,' Charlie offered.

'No, ask them to hold tight for a few more minutes. We should make sure we have all their names and addresses before they leave. I'll call the local station to notify them of the events and make the necessary arrangements. Everyone should remain here for the time being.'

'Is that really necessary?' Arthur questioned. With a lack of anything else to do with his hands, he was anxiously fiddling with the silk flowers that sat on one of the tables.

'I'm afraid so. It shouldn't take long.'

'Oh, what's the point!' Jenny exclaimed from the sofa. 'It was me, wasn't it? I was the one who shot her.' She suddenly fell silent, shocked at her own words. The remaining thoughts spilled out in a confused jumble, becoming more hysterical. 'I didn't think … the whole time I thought it was acting. I thought she was acting … she was lying there, dying, the whole time. I did that, didn't I?' She collapsed back into Teddy's arms while the group stood there in silence, dumbfounded.

All the while the sound of the disconcerted audience murmuring and chatting could still be heard through the curtain.

Using the phone on the stage manager's desk, Hugh took a moment to call the local police station, arranging for several members of the Brighton Police Force to be swiftly dispatched to the theatre. Hugh went through the actors one by one, asking them if they had anything on them and getting them to empty their pockets of any belongings. There wasn't much to be found. Anything of personal value to the actors would have been locked away in their dressing rooms.

Only Charlie had anything of use on him. He carried the usual accoutrements of a stage manager: a penknife, a stopwatch, several pencils and a set of keys.

After being dutifully checked by Hugh, Charlie stepped out in front of the curtain to explain to the audience that the performance would be cancelled due to the "indisposition" of Miss Hamilton. He announced that everyone should remain in their seats for the time being and that there was nothing to worry about as a policeman was already in attendance, something he instantly regretted. At the mention of the police, the murmuring and chattering among the audience members increased in intensity.

'Look here,' Teddy protested as he tried to comfort

an inconsolable Jenny in his arms. 'Do we have to stay here on stage with a dead body? Can't you see how upsetting it is for her? For all of us. Can't we go somewhere else?'

'Is there somewhere else?' Hugh asked Charlie, as he returned through the curtain. 'Even if we can just leave this room.' He indicated the set surrounding them.

Bertie tried his best not to find Hugh's reference to the set as a room funny. It didn't seem particularly appropriate to find anything amusing at this moment in time. Charlie explained that there was plenty of room upstage of the set for them to gather, if they would like.

Hugh was considerate, but firm in the handling of the situation. He guided Teddy and Jenny towards the area Charlie had suggested, Arthur and Constance followed. Arthur was consoling Constance and gently comforted her, explaining that everything would be all right. She had a cushion that she was clutching against her tightly, apparently for comfort.

Bertie marvelled at Hugh's efficiency. Once the cast members had left the set and it was just the two of them remaining, he watched Hugh immediately set about the place, taking in everything about the scene.

'Stand over there,' Hugh said to Bertie. He spoke quietly, almost conspiratorially.

'What?'

'Stand over there,' Hugh repeated in the same hushed tone. This time, it was more impatient. 'I want to you be that girl. The one who was holding the gun.' With a flick of his wrist, he pointed vaguely in the area Jenny would have been standing, while keeping an eye on the door through which everyone had just left. It felt like they were doing something secret, something forbidden. It was almost as if Hugh had forgotten he worked at Scotland Yard. Surely he was free to investigate whatever he wanted?

Bertie moved over to the position he thought Jenny had been in when she fired the gun. As he did so, he caught a glimpse of Celia's body, which made him turn away impulsively. The blood had soaked into the canvas covering the stage.

'What is it?' asked Hugh, nonplussed.

'Sorry,' replied Bertie. 'I just can't stand the sight of blood.'

'You're joking?' Hugh exclaimed, before realising that maybe he had exclaimed a little too loudly. 'You're famous for writing murder mystery plays, and you can't stand a little blood?' he added in a quieter voice. 'That's brilliantly ironic.'

A little blood? It was hardly a little, Bertie thought.

'Fine,' Bertie said. 'I'll do my best not to look at it.' Keeping his eyes focused on Hugh, he managed to avoid looking down at the floor and repositioned himself. 'I think she was standing about here.'

'Okay. Shoot me,' Hugh said.

Bertie held out his hand and pointed at Hugh with two fingers: the obligatory gun mime.

'So, she was standing there, and the victim—'

'Celia,' Bertie interrupted.

'Yes, of course,' Hugh said. 'Celia was standing here.' Using his arms, both of them outstretched, he traced a line between Bertie's "gun", through himself, and out to the wall of the set behind where Celia had been standing. He inspected the painted canvas. 'No sign of a bullet,' He turned back to Bertie. 'Although a little pea-shooter like that, the bullet probably never made it through.'

'Right,' replied Bertie, who was starting to feel a little queasy at the way Hugh was delivering his frank analysis. 'Everyone was onstage at the time. We saw what happened.'

Hugh nodded in agreement, then suddenly stopped. 'No, not everyone. That chap who hangs out backstage?'

'You mean Charlie, the stage manager?'

'Exactly. Charlie, the stage manager. While everyone was on stage, he could be roaming around back here doing whatever he wanted.'

'I can't see it myself, but I suppose it's possible,' Bertie pondered.

'Now then, Bertie, we have to keep an open mind. All possibilities, however unlikely, are still very much possibilities until they can be definitely eliminated.' Hugh took one last look around the place. There didn't seem to be much more that could be gleaned from the murder scene at this time. 'Well, come on then. Time to go and interview our suspects. We'll have to get as much out of them as possible before the local police arrive and take over.'

'We?'

'What?' Hugh said, with a noticeable twinkle in his eyes. 'Don't you want to help me solve this mystery? I know for sure that you didn't do it. You were sitting right next to me. That's the only thing I do know about this case.'

'I don't know if I could solve a murder,' said Bertie. 'I don't know if I'd be any good at it.'

'Rubbish. You've written some of the best murder mystery plays in living memory. This time, you just need to unravel the mystery, instead of having to make it up.'

Bertie wasn't convinced. He didn't think it was as easy as Hugh thought it was, to swap from being a creator of fictional crimes to a solver of real-life ones. It wasn't as simple as rearranging a mathematical equation – another thing he thought he probably wouldn't be very good at.

'Besides,' Hugh continued, 'you know the theatre, you know the type of people who work in it, you know all the lingo. Think of it as being an interpreter. I think you're going to be very useful to me.'

'Well, I can give it a go, I suppose.' Bertie gave a kind of hopeless smile; he was already getting the feeling he might be in over his head.

The pair of them exited through the doors and headed to the rear of the stage where the cast had gathered. Unlike on the set, here there were no lighting bars or pieces of scenery suspended above them. The roof space appeared to go up forever, the theatre's features fading away into the darkness. The back wall of the stage was painted a dirty white with several large heating pipes running across. Bold black letters declared firmly: *No Smoking*. The wall only rose up by twelve feet or so before it levelled out and became a kind of storage platform. On it, a jumble of old bits of scenery and folded backcloths were stored haphazardly – there was a bit of what looked like a sash window poking out propped up next to a shabby door frame. Much of it was battered and looked like it had seen better days. The dusty pile loomed ominously over them.

Jenny seemed much quieter now. She had found a wooden chair to sit on and was holding a glass of brandy. Teddy was crouching nearby and was consoling her.

'For the nerves,' Teddy said, indicating the brandy. 'I hope you don't mind? Charlie had a bottle in his desk.'

'No, that's fine,' Hugh said. 'Normally, I would take this time to establish everybody's whereabouts, but I already know that. You were all on stage, in full view of myself, Bertie, and all the other audience members. While we haven't found the bullet, we have established, from our brief examination of the crime scene and what we witnessed, that it's quite likely the fatal shot was fired from somewhere in the backstage area.'

Bertie noted that Hugh's voice had become noticeably more well-spoken and formal while he was making the announcement to the group.

'Well, clearly,' said Arthur. 'We all saw what happened.'

'Please, Mr…?'

'Cochran, Arthur Cochran.'

'Mr Cochran,' Hugh continued. 'Without the bullet, we cannot yet establish the full facts and whether the bullet that killed Celia Hamilton came from the gun that Jenny fired. Until we do, we're making sure we explore all the possibilities.'

'There are other possibilities?' questioned Teddy, sounding hopeful. He gave Jenny an encouraging look, although she was too preoccupied with her own thoughts to notice him.

'I would be unwilling to rule anything out at this stage,' replied Hugh.

'But I did it,' came a small voice. 'I shot her.' The voice was much stronger this time. Jenny stood up. 'It was me.'

Hugh turned to face Jenny. Teddy stood up beside her in defence, resting a comforting hand on her shoulder. 'What's your name?'

'It's Jenny Ashcroft, Inspector.' Jenny's voice had lost its confidence again and emerged with a slight waver.

'Then, Miss Ashcroft, can you explain to me the reason you wished harm to Miss Hamilton?'

'I…' Jenny faltered, lost for words.

'Any reason you might want to wish her ill?'

'I don't know,' said Jenny, eventually finding the words.

'You don't know?' Hugh repeated.

'I suppose … I didn't think she was very nice. She was very mean to Teddy, too.'

'What I mean, Miss Ashcroft – Jenny,' Hugh lowered his voice to a soothing tone, 'is did you plan to kill Celia Hamilton?'

'Plan?' Jenny repeated back to him.

'Did you plan, in advance, to commit murder this evening?' Hugh asked.

'No,' said Jenny. 'But that doesn't matter, does it? I still did it. I still killed her. I still murdered Celia.'

'Miss Ashcroft,' Hugh said, with the slightest hint of a smile. 'It makes all the difference in the world.' He turned his attention now to Charlie. 'Did you see anyone in the backstage area during the performance?'

'No. There was no one else back here. Just me.'

'You're absolutely sure of that fact?'

'As sure as I can be. I suppose it's possible…' he said slowly, without completing the full thought.

'Absolutely sure that no one else could have been backstage, specifically during the period when the shooting scene is happening onstage?' asked Hugh. 'Where were you at that point during the show?'

Charlie pointed towards the desk that was positioned at the front and to the left-hand side of the proscenium opening. 'I was downstage, there, at the stage manager's desk.' Bertie knew that Hugh wouldn't know his upstage from his downstage.

'And from that position,' Hugh continued, 'would you be able to see the other side of the stage?' He looked at Bertie for assistance with the correct terminology.

'The stage right wing,' he added helpfully.

'Yes, the stage right wing,' Hugh confirmed, with a smile of thanks flashed in Bertie's direction. 'Would you be able to see it from your position?'

Charlie, realising – along with the others – that perhaps there really were other possibilities, let out a low, reluctant sigh. 'No, I wouldn't.'

'You're not suggesting that someone else could have crept in and shot Celia?' asked Teddy in astonishment.

'Oh, come on, we're not expected to believe that are we?' said Arthur.

'Right now, I'm entertaining all and any possibilities, and I'll continue to do so until the facts of the matter eliminate them,' Hugh explained to all of them. He turned back to Charlie. 'And can anyone vouch for you? Your whereabouts?'

Charlie seemed taken aback that suspicion might be falling on him. 'No,' he replied in a quiet voice. 'There's no one back here but me. I do everything, change the lights, set the props and bring the curtain in and out. It's just me…' His voice trailed away. His face fell with the realisation he was the only one on the stage without a concrete alibi. Normally, he'd be thankful for his position, hidden out of view from the audience. Tonight, it seemed to be a liability. He was the only person who no one knew where he was.

Hugh cast his eye over the group of people assembled. Jenny stood with Teddy by her side. With a shaky hand, she took another sip from the glass of brandy. Arthur leant against the wall with an expression of disbelief at the events occurring around him. Next to him stood Constance, who seemed shocked into silence. Charlie sunk to the floor, sitting on it cross-legged. Using his hand, he grumpily propped his head up. He clearly wasn't thrilled at the thought of becoming a key suspect in the investigation.

'Well, I think we've got a clear picture of where everyone was at the time of the murder. Everyone was on stage, with the exception of Charlie here. We know the shot, because of the angle that Celia was standing at, almost certainly came from the backstage area. But if we assume that no one else was back here…' Hugh trailed off.

'What does that mean?' questioned Bertie.

‘It means that our murderer must be here right now,’ Hugh said. His tone was grim. ‘Unless there’s someone we haven’t thought of? Anyone else who’s unaccounted for?’

At that very moment, the door to the stage swung open, banging loudly against the wall. A portly figure stumbled in, panting in exhaustion with laboured, heavy breaths. He tottered a little further towards them. As he stepped into the light, it glinted off his profusely sweating forehead.

‘Sorry I’m late!’ boomed Robert Laughton. ‘Bit of a dicky tummy, I think. I’m feeling much better now, though.’ He smiled, looking around at the surprised faces. He brought his hands together in a loud, contented clap and beamed. ‘I could probably go on for Act Two if you think that’s a good idea?’

Chapter Seven

After the shock appearance of Robert Laughton, it took a few moments for the others to regain their composure. It was, Bertie suspected, the most dramatic entrance Laughton had ever made in his career. Distracted by the goings-on of the evening, Bertie – and the others too – had entirely forgotten that there was another actor in their midst.

'What's going on?' the red-faced actor asked, in response to the strange expressions that appeared on the faces watching him.

The poor man looks like he's close to collapse, Bertie thought. He must have run down here, full tilt. Something that would have been rather punishing for a man who hadn't likely moved at that speed for a great many years.

'Who's this?' Hugh asked.

'I'm the butler,' Robert joked. He still hadn't quite grasped the gravity of the situation that was laid out in front of him. 'Robert Laughton,' he added, reading the look on Hugh's face, who was trying to work out who this mysterious intruder was, and offered his hand in introduction.

'The actor Arthur was filling in for?' asked Hugh with realisation.

Robert confirmed with a nod. 'That's the one.' He realised that Hugh was unlikely to accept his handshake and let his arm drop back by his side. 'Don't know what happened really.' He talked at a volume that was entirely inappropriate to his distance from Hugh. He was one of those actors whose voice appeared to stay at the same level, whether they were performing on the stage or talking to someone standing next to him. 'Felt absolutely awful earlier on. Bloody terrible, actually. But now it seems to have passed. Still not feeling top-notch again, mind you, but certainly, I'm well enough to show up and give it a go.'

'That is apparent,' said Hugh.

'What's happened? Everyone looks so serious,' said Robert, looking around the room. 'And who are you?'

'I'm afraid it is serious,' came Hugh's reply. 'I'm Detective Chief Inspector Hugh Chapman. I'm afraid to inform you that Miss Celia Hamilton has been shot.'

'Good Lord! You mean just like in the play?'

Everybody had been relocated to the studio at the front of the building on the top floor. A number of local policemen, accompanied by a police doctor, had arrived to help manage the crime scene. Several constables were left guarding the stage as the audience were shepherded out of the auditorium. Another joined them in the studio to take the fingerprints of the cast members while they were waiting to hear what would happen next.

Hugh had suggested that they may be more comfortable up there. Bertie wasn't so sure. On a sunny day, the large windows that dominated one wall of the room would have flooded the studio with light. You would have had a clear view back along the pier and of Brighton itself. In the distance, you would be able to see the yellow and mahogany cars of the Volk's Electric Railway, happily trundling back and forth.

On a cold, dark evening like this one, the view was not quite as hospitable. An inky blackness was the only sight through the large windows tonight.

The darkness of the night sky had the effect of transforming the windows into large mirrors. Slightly wavy imperfections in the glass distorted the image a little. It wasn't as extreme as a funfair mirror, but it created an unflattering look, nevertheless. They reflected back the gloomy expressions of the figures waiting in the room.

Teddy, Arthur, Constance and Robert sat on some dusty wooden chairs with nothing to do but wait until they were told what would happen next. Wait and wonder how the battered upright piano, that sat on its worn castors, had ever got into the studio. It certainly wouldn't have fit up the tiny staircase they'd just climbed themselves. A constable, who had finished the process of taking their fingerprints, was quietly keeping watch over them all.

Bertie and Charlie had remained on stage while Hugh went to negotiate with the sergeant in charge.

Bertie strained to hear the conversation, although couldn't make out much of it. They remained in awkward silence while they waited for it to conclude. Hugh still had some questions to ask about the events of the evening and asked if anyone would have a thorough overview of what had happened during the show that night. Bertie told him that it would be the stage manager.

Eventually, the sergeant left to give instructions to the other nearby policemen and Hugh approached Bertie, giving him a surreptitious thumbs up. 'They've agreed to let me handle the case,' he announced, 'because of my reputation for working on high-profile cases and being here, on the scene, when it happened. It took a bit of buttering up, but I think I convinced them. We have to keep the local police fully informed of our progress, but for now, they're letting me lead the investigation.' Hugh allowed himself a smile in Bertie's direction. 'As I'm in charge, that means me and you.'

Turning his attention back to Charlie, Hugh took his place at the stage manager's desk on the tall stool sat in front of it. On the sloped surface was a copy of the script, lit by the faint glow of a bulb. In pencil, neatly written, were all the cues for the play. Cues to raise and lower the curtain, lighting changes and sound effects were all clearly marked. In a second column next to them were all the moves the actors made during the show. Sometimes they were accompanied by a small diagram of the stage with arrows and initials illustrating the movements. At the top of the desk, where the slope became flat again, a telephone for calling the various parts of the theatre sat on its surface.

The desk was placed against the back of the proscenium. If there hadn't been a wall there, Charlie would have been looking directly out towards the auditorium. Using his feet, Hugh swivelled on the stool to face to his right, where there was a tall gap between the proscenium arch and the wall of the set. Through it, he could see a thin slice of the stage and a decent portion of the drawing-room set. The view was mainly the area downstage of the sofa; the rest remained obscured. Turning further around on the stool, until he was facing away from the desk, he could see a trestle table. It was positioned next to the doorway that led into the set through the supposed "hallway". On it were placed all the different props used in the show. Underneath each prop was a label, in the same neat handwriting he recognised from the script.

Sitting guiltily above its own label was the gun. It was currently being attended to by a policeman who was using a small kit from a tin to dust for fingerprints.

'And you can keep an eye on everything from here?' Hugh asked, turning on the stool to face Charlie.

'Yes, pretty much. All the comings and goings,' he replied.

'Even though, to follow the script, you have your back to the props table and that entrance?'

'I'm not sitting there for the entire show,' explained Charlie. 'I'm the only person working backstage on this show, so I have to run around doing all the different jobs. I might have to go here to operate the curtain,' he said, indicating a loop of rope that descended from the ceiling to the right-hand side of the desk. The rope went around a pulley bolted to the stage floor and then disappeared back up into the void above them. 'It's counterweighted, so it's not a lot of effort. And then I might have to go over there to change the lights at different points during the play. This one is relatively simple, though. Lights up and lights down at the start and end of each act.'

The "there" that Charlie indicated was a panel with switches and levers that poked out the front of it. The panel stretched a short distance along the wall. Each lever, Charlie explained, was attached to a "dimmer" which controlled the voltage and subsequently the output of each light.

Next to the desk, there was something that Charlie called a panatrope. It looked like a large record player, but with two turntables. He explained how this was used to play music and sound effects during the show. A white button, with an etched label marked "Go", was riveted on the front by each turntable. When the button was pressed, the needle would drop onto the record from its pre-set position and play the required sound effect.

'But you have practical sound effects on this show as well, don't you?' commented Bertie. 'You and Teddy were operating them in the dress rehearsal.'

'Yes, that's right,' said Charlie. 'I think Arthur prefers the traditional way sometimes. Besides, it can be a lot easier to time things correctly when you're doing it manually, like a crash of lightning. Those panatropes can be fiddly things to work. If you're just a touch out when you pre-set the needle, you might end up accidentally playing, say, a car backfiring instead of the gentle birdsong that you actually want. You can see how that doesn't always go down well with the actors and the director, even if the audience finds it hilarious.'

'Where are these practical sound effects?' Hugh asked, looking around.

'On the other side of the stage,' Charlie said. 'Would you like me to show you?'

Hugh nodded.

Charlie led them round to the opposite side of the stage. 'There's a wind machine and a thunder sheet. They've got to be on that side, so it sounds like the noise of the wind comes through the French doors. I've also got to be on that side to push the doors open with a broom handle as well,' added Charlie, as they arrived. He nodded in the direction of a broom handle that was propped up next to the French doors on the back of the scenery.

'A broom handle?' said Hugh, surprised.

'Sometimes the old ways are the best,' Charlie replied with a smile. 'I just knock them open with it.'

Hugh chuckled. He had no idea that such a dramatic effect would have been created by such simple means.

Next to the French doors, there was another props table. It was much smaller than the one on the other side and contained far fewer props. A small garden trowel and a potted plant sat waiting for their entrance, things that Hugh assumed must have been used in the second act, as he didn't recognise them from the first half of the performance.

The wind machine was a sheet of canvas stretched

over a wooden drum that had thin wooden ribs attached to the outside. A large handle on the side allowed the operator to turn the drum, which simulated a wind noise as the ribs rubbed against the canvas. It was positioned behind a cloth that was painted to look like a garden, hung just beyond the French doors. Some fake shrubbery in pots sat in front of the canvas – an attempt to disguise where the cloth met the floor and make it look more convincing. Next to the wind machine hung a large, thin metal sheet. This produced the sound of thunder by giving it a sharp shake, as Charlie skilfully demonstrated.

Hugh looked over the two pieces of equipment. 'So, who did what?'

'I did the wind machine. Teddy did the thunder.'

'After you pushed open the doors,' Hugh clarified as he stepped through the doors onto the stage. He swung one of the French doors on its hinges. It moved effortlessly, without a sound.

'Yes, that's right. Then I'd run back round to the other side – we swapped and Teddy kept the wind machine going. I needed to do the lighting change and bring in the curtain. That's the end of the act.'

'That seems like a lot of work,' Bertie commented with amusement. He wandered over to Hugh, who was still inspecting the other side of the French doors.

'You get used to it. It was complicated and it took a lot of rehearsing, I can tell you that,' said Charlie. 'But we got it right in the end.'

'And there was no one else around here,' asked Bertie, 'while you were doing the sound effects? Other than Teddy, I mean.'

'No, everyone else is on stage.'

Hugh put his arm through one of the empty window frames on the door and punched Bertie on the arm, lightly.

'Where's the glass?' Hugh asked.

'There is no glass,' said Bertie. 'You can get unwanted reflections from the lights. Cheaper too. The bonus is that you never have to clean them and there's no risk of them ever getting broken.'

'What about the shooting scene?' said Hugh. 'Would anyone be around here?'

'No,' replied Charlie. 'As you know, everyone else is on stage at that point during the show. You saw it for yourselves.'

'But you wouldn't know for sure, would you?' said Bertie. 'You said yourself, you only come over this side of the stage for the end of the act.'

'Yes, that's right,' confirmed Charlie.

'So, someone else could have arrived, without your knowledge, during that scene?' Bertie continued.

'Yes,' Charlie said. 'At least I suppose that's possible. But who would—' Charlie broke off, without being able to finish the thought.

'Robert?'

'That's a bit of a stretch isn't it, Bertie?' Charlie said in disbelief.

'Perhaps, but perhaps not,' Bertie pondered. 'It's the easiest thing in the world to fake an illness. He is an actor, after all.' He turned to the inspector. 'What do you think, Hugh?'

Hugh was still mulling his own thoughts over. 'So far,

we have a few possibilities. Someone else could have shot through the French windows, making it look like Jenny did it. There's no glass to be broken by a bullet and the angle would work. That actress could have done it in plain sight of the audience—'

'Jenny?' Bertie clarified. 'Seems like a pretty bold move to me!'

'Quite. There's also the possibility someone in the theatre swapped the bullets in the gun without her knowledge.'

'If someone else shot from here, that means we could be looking for a second gun, doesn't it?' asked Bertie.

'That's exactly right,' said Hugh. 'See, I told you that you'd be good at this.'

Bertie felt flattered – slightly – and rather proud of himself. Then he remembered that an actual murder had been committed, and his excitement faded a little.

'But wouldn't we have heard two shots?'

'That wouldn't necessarily be the case,' said Hugh.

'You mean if there was a silencer?' said Bertie enthusiastically. 'On the gun?'

Hugh smiled. 'A silencer, in the way that you refer to it, doesn't really exist,' he explained. 'That's just something you read about in thrillers and fiction. What a silencer really is, is a suppressor. The reason it's not called a silencer is that you can never silence a gun completely, only make it a lot quieter. There'll always be some sort of noise produced by a firing gun; it can't be eliminated altogether.'

'But if two people fired a gun, with the sound of one of the gunshots suppressed, at the exact same time, you're saying that it would be hard to distinguish one shot from the other?' Bertie asked.

'It would take unbelievably precise timing, of course, but something that's not impossible,' Hugh nodded. 'Once we've had the police surgeon retrieve the bullet, we'll know more about the type of gun we're looking for.'

'So, Robert might have been able to do it?' said Bertie, feeling queasy.

'He is one potential suspect,' he replied. 'But there are others I can think of right now. Like you,' he said, looking at Charlie.

'Me?'

'Yes,' continued Hugh. 'There's no one who can vouch for your movements during the show. Like you said earlier, you're the only person back here. There's no reason why you couldn't have come round here during that scene and fired through the window with a second gun. There's also no reason why you couldn't have swapped the bullets in the original gun.'

'But I've got no cause to kill Celia,' Charlie protested.

'But, of course, you would say that,' said Hugh with the hint of a smile.

'I would have thought,' said Charlie, in an attempt to prove his innocence, 'if Robert came back here to shoot Celia, it would be the easiest thing for him to drop the gun off the side of the pier. It was, what, fifteen or twenty minutes after we finished before Robert showed up? He could have done anything in that time.'

'He's right, Hugh,' said Bertie. 'If Robert did come here with a second gun, it's probably lying somewhere at the bottom of the English Channel right now.'

'Well,' said Hugh, 'in that case, maybe we should look at the one gun we do have.'

As they headed back to the props table in the other wing, Bertie observed the rear of the set. It was formed by frames of wood with diagonal bracing, covered in canvas. The back of each flat was stamped with the name *Brunskill.* He recognised the name of the scenic workshop that had built the set. More faded black text read *Dinner at Eight – Tour*, confirming his suspicion that this was indeed a recycled set.

As they walked around it, he noticed that, because of the way the box set was designed, there really was no other entry point into the room or any way that you could see inside it. The view from Charlie's desk provided the best view and, even then, it only permitted you to see a thin slice of the action.

When they reached the props table, the constable was packing up his fingerprinting kit.

'Any luck?' asked Hugh.

'We've got a couple of clear prints and a few other smudges,' the constable replied.

'Great, well, let's see if we can match them up to anyone upstairs or to Charlie here.'

'Yes, Sir.' With a sharp nod of the head, the constable set off up the dressing room steps at the side of the stage.

Hugh picked up the gun from the props table. It was a small, semi-automatic pistol – small enough to fit in the palm of his hand.

'An interesting choice,' he commented.

'Is it?' asked Charlie. 'Not really my thing, I'm afraid.' He gave an apologetic shrug. 'I suspect Arthur chose it more for the look than anything else. A practical decision, too. It needed to be small enough to fit into Jenny's purse. That's important for the way it gets used in the show.'

'There were others to choose from?'

'Yes, not a huge collection,' Charlie recalled. 'There was a revolver, an old starting pistol, I think, and this one.'

'Well, a starting pistol would have certainly made things easier,' said Hugh.

'It would?' asked Bertie.

'For a start, it's impossible to fire real bullets from a starting pistol,' said Hugh.

'So, this is a real gun?' Bertie sounded surprised.

'Oh yes,' Hugh replied, 'this is definitely a real gun and very much capable of firing very real bullets.'

'But we've only got blanks,' said Charlie in defence. 'We wouldn't have a real bullet anywhere near the building.'

'I'm sure you wouldn't,' said Hugh, slipping out the gun's magazine. From it, he ejected three shiny, brass-coloured cartridges on the table one by one. He clicked open the top of the gun and dropped a fourth out of the firing chamber. 'Four cartridges remaining' He turned to face Charlie. 'How many does it hold?'

'Six,' he replied.

'So, two were fired.'

'That would be one from the dress rehearsal, one from tonight.'

'You didn't reload it or check it again before the performance?' Hugh asked.

'Didn't seem much point in re-loading it, like I said, it holds six.'

'Right,' said Hugh, turning the gun over in his hands.

'What's that engraving on the side?' asked Bertie, who had been watching over his shoulder. The initials *BBL* were neatly stamped on it. 'The manufacturer?'

Hugh thought about it for a moment. 'I'd put my money on Barclays Bank Limited, myself.'

'A bank?' said Bertie, with mild surprise.

'Yes,' replied Hugh, 'lots of banks used to supply these to members of staff for self-defence when transporting money or valuables, things like that.' He turned the gun back over to the other side, showing it to Bertie. 'Webley and Scott – that's the manufacturer. Small, easy to use, and fairly reliable.' He placed it back in its spot on the props table.

'Between the show and the dress rehearsal,' asked Bertie, 'it was left here?'

'No,' Charlie answered. 'It's kept locked in a safe. I've worked on enough shows to know that even with blanks, guns can be dangerous things.'

'So, no one could have got to it before the show?' said Bertie. 'None of the actors?'

'I don't see how. I'm the only one with a key. I get it out of the safe, right before the show begins, and I put it on the props table.'

'But it's possible that someone could have got to the gun during the first act and switched out the blank for a real bullet?' said Bertie.

'It's unlikely,' said Charlie. 'I keep a pretty close eye

on the props table for most of the show.'

'Any of the actors,' asked Hugh, 'or Jenny herself. Could they have put a real bullet in?'

'Do you think that's what happened?' said Bertie.

'I'm not sure yet. It seems the simplest and most obvious solution. In my experience, it's often the simplest solution that eventually reveals itself as the correct one. But we've got a few more things to find out first. For example, what was the motive? Did she have the opportunity, before the show or during it, to make the switch?'

'After the rehearsal,' said Bertie, remembering, 'she was here by herself. She stayed afterwards to continue rehearsing by herself.'

'Is that right?' Hugh asked Charlie.

'Yes, that's right. I also stayed behind to reset everything on the stage back to the start of the show, so she wasn't alone with the gun. After about twenty minutes – perhaps half an hour – we left.'

'All of you?' confirmed Hugh. 'Jenny?'

'Yes that's right, when she was done rehearsing, I locked the gun away.'

'Where did you go?'

'Just home. It's not far from here.'

'You live by yourself?' said Hugh.

Charlie looked a little sheepish for a moment, then replied, 'With my mother.'

'I see,' said Hugh, 'so she'll be able to confirm all of this?'

'Yes, that's right.'

'Did you go straight home?' Hugh asked.

'Pretty much. Me, Teddy and Jenny, we all ended up

leaving together. He was outside having a breather, waiting for Jenny to change. Smoking is banned in here, you see.'

'I'm surprised you could light anything in this weather,' commented Bertie.

'It's not too bad, depending on the direction of the wind,' said Charlie. 'You get pretty good at knowing where the sheltered areas are after you've been working here for a while.' Charlie put his hands in his pockets, shifting the weight from one side of his body to another.

'Did you two stay outside long?' said Hugh. 'Did you talk about much?'

'Not really, just about the show. This one and the last one. We'd done one together up in London. I think the pair of them were going out for dinner together, but you'd have to ask them.'

'And then you all left?'

'Yes. We all walked back along the pier together. When we got back to the shore, they headed off their way and I headed off in mine.'

'And all this time, you had the safe key on your person?'

'Yes. The key went in my pocket at the theatre and that's where it stayed until I got it back out again before the show, to unlock the safe,' said Charlie.

'But to be clear about it,' Hugh said. 'You didn't get the key out at any other time?'

'To check I had it, you mean?' asked Charlie. 'No, I can't say I did.' He looked between Hugh and Bertie, looking for some assurance he'd done the right thing.

'And between here and your house, you didn't meet

anyone?'

'In that weather? It was very quiet. There was no one at all.'

'Well, I think that's all for now,' finished Hugh. 'Unless you've got anything else you want to ask, Bertie?'

'Me?' he said, caught unawares by the question, forgetting he was supposedly an equal partner in the investigation. 'No, I don't think I've got anything else to ask.'

'Great. Well, in that case, Charlie, perhaps you should go and join the others upstairs.'

Charlie nodded and headed up the dressing room stairs, making his way towards the front of the theatre where the others were waiting in the studio.

'What do you think of this key, then?' said Bertie as soon as Charlie was out of earshot. 'I got the impression you were trying to get at something?'

'I don't know,' replied Hugh. 'I thought there might be something there. Could someone have lifted it from him at some point? He said he didn't check if he had it until he was back at the theatre again.'

'You mean someone picked his pocket?'

'Yes, you lot are all very touchy-feely in the theatre, aren't you? "Darling" this and "darling" that.'

Bertie threw a disapproving look at Hugh as he played the stereotype. As far as he knew, since he had arrived in Brighton, no one had called anyone else "darling", although he knew what his friend was getting at.

'We're not *all* like that,' he protested. 'Although you try remembering a whole theatre full of names on your first day. Sometimes – and yes, I admit it – we all have to resort to using the word "darling" from time to time, but only when our memories betray us.'

'So, you don't think there was anyone he might have come into contact with? Anyone who might have had the opportunity to relieve him of that key?'

Bertie ran through the possibilities in his head. 'He was outside with Teddy, if that's what you mean?'

'You think he could have pulled it off?'

'Lifting – to use your terminology – the key?' Bertie paused to think. 'It doesn't seem likely, to be honest. I don't know if he quite has the subtlety to pull it off.'

'But we did learn one more thing…' Hugh left the sentence unfinished, encouraging Bertie to complete it.

'You're looking at me very expectantly, right now,' he said. 'I'm not sure if I *did* learn anything.'

Hugh smiled, giving one more hint. 'While Charlie was tidying up?'

It took Bertie a few more moments, but eventually, he got there. 'Jenny was onstage, with the gun. Charlie said she was never alone with the gun, but if he was distracted at any point, there might have been an opportunity when she could have interfered with the gun. It wouldn't take more than a moment or two to slip a bullet in surreptitiously.'

'Quite right,' congratulated Hugh. 'She could have done anything with it and we know that Charlie didn't check the gun before the show. He put it directly on the props table.'

'So that means…'

'Yes,' said Hugh. 'The next person we speak to should be Jenny. Let's see if that brandy has worked.'

Chapter Eight

Hugh used the telephone on the Stage Manager's desk to call up to the studio. Talking to the constable who was keeping an eye on them, he arranged for Jenny Ashcroft to be escorted down to the stage. While they waited for her to appear, Hugh spoke to Dr Grant, the police doctor, who had finished his inspection of Celia Hamilton's body. Her body had now been removed, leaving the stage empty. Behind the sofa, a large brownish stain on the tattered floor canvas was the only remaining sign that a dead body had been lying there a few moments earlier.

'Anything of note, Doctor?'

'Nothing too out of the ordinary, I'd say. She died of a gunshot wound to the heart. After being shot, I expect she would have lost consciousness almost instantly. Death would have followed a few moments, perhaps a few minutes, later.'

'Will we have to wait before we can retrieve the bullet?' Hugh asked.

'The bullet? There is no bullet. There's an entry

wound, just slightly to the left of the breastbone' – he indicated the location on his own chest – 'and there's an exit wound on her back. You seem surprised,' said the doctor, seeing the look on Hugh's face.

'I would have thought a small gun like that and from that distance—'

'Well, yes, it is unlikely,' said the doctor, 'but not impossible. Of course, it depends on the exact path of the bullet through the body. If it missed the right organs, there's no reason a bullet might not make it all the way through. Have you not found one yet? Well, I suppose it must be around here somewhere.'

Bertie thought it strange that the police doctor didn't seem very concerned about the missing bullet. However, this was only his first murder investigation, so he assumed that the doctor knew what he was doing.

'We'll have a hunt around, then. See if we can find it,' Hugh said.

'There's not much more I can tell you, I'm afraid,' said the doctor.

'Will you know any more after the autopsy?' asked Bertie.

'There won't be an autopsy.' The doctor's response was blunt, a comment on Bertie's inexperience. 'What killed her isn't exactly a mystery.'

'Are you able to take a guess at whether the gun we have here is the murder weapon?' asked Hugh, hopefully.

'Not categorically, no, and without the bullet...' He offered a shrug by way of apology. 'That said, based on the size of the wound, it was almost certainly a gun of around that calibre.'

'Well, thank you, Dr Grant. You've been most helpful.'

With a sharp nod, Dr Grant turned on his heels and set off with purposeful strides.

After he'd gone, Bertie asked, 'Have you ever shot a gun, Hugh. On a shooting range, say?'

'Of course,' he replied. 'I'm a Chief Inspector. We all know how to handle guns.'

'The first time you fired a gun, how accurate were you?'

'Not very,' Hugh recalled. 'Although, with quite a bit of practice, I'm pretty good now. I wouldn't exactly say I'm a sharp-shooter or anything like that though. Why do you ask?'

'Do you think Jenny's fired many guns?' said Bertie.

'I don't know that she would have had much reason to.'

'Well, that's what I think too…'

At that moment, the door from the front of house area clicked open. Through it returned the constable accompanied by Jenny Ashcroft. She was still wearing the outfit from the play, a sleek black dress, except now she had Teddy's jacket draped over her shoulders. Hugh gestured to her, encouraging her to continue down the aisle and join them on the stage. She hesitated.

'Is she…' She stumbled over her words a little. 'Is she still there?'

'No, Miss Ashcroft,' Hugh said in a comforting voice. 'The body has been removed.'

That seemed to be enough to satisfy the young actress who proceeded onto the set. The constable who'd escorted her in remained at the back of the auditorium on guard. Jenny sat in a large armchair, positioned downstage from the sofa, far enough that the stained canvas floor remained out of sight. Hugh and Bertie sat down, taking their places on the sofa together.

'You seem to have calmed down a little,' said Hugh.

Jenny nodded, gently. 'Yes, I was in shock before. Teddy wanted to accompany me down, but I said I'd be all right. I suppose I'm still in shock now, just a different kind of shock. You see, I was horrified at what I'd done. I don't imagine you'll be surprised to hear, Inspector, that I've never actually killed anyone before.'

She spoke lightly, the words floating out of her, as if she wasn't quite present in the moment.

'I've come to terms with it now,' she said. 'At least I think that's what it is. Or perhaps, I realise that it's something I'll have to come to terms with – in time.' The phrases came in a flat monotone. Emotionless. 'What's going to happen to me now?'

'Right now, Miss Hamilton? Nothing,' replied Hugh.

'Nothing?' she questioned, shocked. His response had a slightly restorative effect, the glazed-over expression faded a little. 'But I did it. You should be arresting me for murder, surely?'

'And is that what you did?' asked Hugh. 'Did you murder Celia Hamilton?'

'Yes,' she replied with conviction.

Hugh shifted in his seat a little before leaning forward. 'Now, we've been over this. Can you tell me why?'

'Why?'

'Yes. Why? Why did you want to kill Miss Hamilton?'

'I suppose I didn't like her very much,' she replied. 'She wasn't very nice to me and she certainly wasn't very nice to Teddy. Is that not a good enough reason?'

'I shouldn't say so, Miss Ashcroft. Not enough by half,' Hugh replied. 'You seem to be confessing to a crime that you had no reason to commit.'

'But I did commit it. Isn't that enough?' she questioned, looking confused.

Bertie leant forward, rising from the sofa. He knelt next to Jenny in an attempt to comfort her. 'What we're asking, Jenny,' Bertie said, 'is, did you plan in advance to kill Celia tonight? Did you put a real bullet in that gun?'

'Oh no,' replied Jenny, her face even more relieved now. 'I didn't do any of that.'

'Then how can you be a murderer?' Bertie said. 'How can you be a murderer if you never had any intention of committing murder? That's right, isn't it, Hugh?' Bertie glanced over at his friend to provide further encouragement, or at the very least, confirmation. He offered neither, an unreadable expression on his face.

'I suppose you're right,' she replied. Bertie nodded in encouragement. 'I didn't have a reason to kill her. Why would I?'

'Exactly, Jenny,' said Bertie, still in soothing tones. He stood up, moving over to her, resting a hand on her shoulder for support. 'I think you've been involved in some kind of tragic accident and we just want to get to the bottom of it, to understand what has really gone on here.' He looked at Hugh again. This time, he snapped out of his thoughts.

'A tragic accident it may be, but someone still planned a murder tonight, and it worked,' said Hugh with a grave note in his voice.

'Does that mean I'm going to go to prison?' said Jenny, emotion now creeping back into her voice.

'I couldn't say, I'm afraid,' Hugh replied. 'What's important is that we find out who did plan this murder, who switched the bullet in that gun and which one of you really wanted Celia Hamilton dead.'

'I don't know who would want to kill anyone,' Jenny said. 'I know Celia isn't exactly the easiest person to work with and she can be very nasty when she wants to be. But if someone thought that was enough to kill her…' Jenny had started to speak more lucidly now. She'd somehow convinced herself she was a murderer, but it seemed like her conscience was clearing and logic was returning to her assessment of the situation.

'You said she wasn't getting along with Teddy,' said Bertie. He relinquished his supportive hold on her shoulder and joined Hugh on the sofa.

'Oh Teddy,' said Jenny, in a tone that was approaching motherly. 'He's been wonderful to me, very supportive.' Bertie nodded in response, encouraging her to continue. 'Yes, he's been very good to me, so I don't want to say a bad word about him.'

'But if you had to?' said Bertie, with the hint of a smile.

'Well, he's becoming very popular, isn't he?' she replied. 'I don't know too much about these things, but it very much seems to me he's on the verge of becoming quite a famous actor. Sometimes – and only sometimes, mind you – he can be a little bit… How would you put it, cocky? Now, it's all in a very harmless, charming way, if you ask me,' she hurried to add. 'But, of course, it would rub Celia up the wrong way. She could be quite harsh with him at times. It was her way of knocking him down a few pegs, I suppose. Telling him to stay in his place, stick to what he knows, that sort of thing.'

'I understand,' said Bertie. 'And how did you get on with Celia?'

'I think she could be impatient with me. She would try to offer me advice, in her own back-handed manner. I tried to ignore it most of the time. I think she really did believe she was helping me, but instead it just seemed to shatter my confidence. Everything is still very new to me, you know. I don't suppose I got it any worse than the others, mind you.'

'And how was the show? How did it feel?' he continued.

'Oh, I thought it was just wonderful!' She beamed. For the first time, Bertie noticed, her face really lit up. 'Finally getting the opportunity to perform in front of an audience for the first time was such a thrill. Now, I know that there weren't very many of them, but that didn't bother me. It was still an exciting experience.' Her face fell. 'I expect that's the last time it will ever happen.'

'How do you mean?' said Bertie.

'Well, even if I don't end up in prison, I'm hardly going to be top of the list for any acting work again. I started out wanting to be a famous actress – don't we all? I don't want to become famous for something like this…'

'I…' stuttered Bertie, a little lost for words. 'We're getting a little ahead of ourselves, aren't we?' He looked at Hugh, who simply shrugged. 'And what else do you remember from the play?'

'Well,' Jenny paused. 'Everything felt a little different.'

'Different, how?' Bertie said.

'Well, we had Arthur filling in, and he did everything a little differently to Robert. I thought he was very good, mind you, especially at the start. But as the night went on, I think he couldn't quite remember where to stand or what to do.'

'It's not surprising, is it? I would have expected him to at least carry the script with him?' said Bertie.

'Oh no, he knew all the lines.' Jenny said, impressed with the director's talents. 'He was very good like that. And, of course, nothing was different enough that the audience would notice. It's only if you'd seen the rehearsals and known exactly what it was supposed to be like that you'd be able to see any difference. He'd just stand up a bit later than Robert or come on too early for an entrance. Little things like that, nothing of any real consequence.'

Bertie looked over at Hugh, who spoke. 'The shooting scene. How did that feel?'

'It was the same as it always was,' said Jenny. 'Although…'

'Yes,' said Hugh encouragingly.

'Everything felt a little different with an audience

there. The way we performed the scene, it felt different from rehearsals. Celia's performance was so believable, she looked shocked. But of course, that must have been because she was…' Jenny trailed off, unable to complete the sentence. 'Oh, isn't it awful!' she exclaimed, dropping her head in her hands. 'The whole time, we all thought she was acting, but she wasn't. It was for real. She was there, dying, in front of us all.'

'Now, now, Jenny,' said Bertie, comforting her, in an attempt to stop her from becoming overwhelmed again. 'It's all right. You're doing a great job by telling us all this. Isn't that right, Hugh?'

'Yes, that's right, Miss Ashcroft. You've been incredibly helpful. I just have a few more questions for you. It won't take long.'

Bertie thought Hugh sounded more officious than comforting, but the words seemed to do their job.

'Very well,' said Jenny, who repositioned herself in the seat, sitting a little more upright. Her resolve stiffened, knowing she was almost done.

'Can you tell me your movements from after the rehearsal this afternoon?' Hugh asked.

'I was with Teddy the whole time,' she said. 'He waited for me after rehearsal.'

'You stayed behind and rehearsed a little by yourself, didn't you?' Hugh said.

'Yes, that's right. It was just that some of the blocking – our positions, where we stand – it had changed earlier in the day.'

'What specifically had changed?' asked Bertie, curiously.

'Oh, nothing much, really. Just a few tweaks here and there. My entrance had changed from how we rehearsed it and Arthur was very particular about how we all stood for the end of the act.'

'You were rehearsing the shooting scene when I left,' Bertie added.

Jenny thought about this for a moment. 'Yes,' she said after a short while. 'Yes, I probably was.'

'Had that changed?' asked Hugh.

Jenny's face lit up with realisation. 'Yes,' she recalled. 'Yes, it had, now you mention it. It was a lighting thing. The lights are something we don't have in the rehearsal room, of course. It was the way the light was coming in the window. I was casting a shadow over Celia. Now, she didn't like that at all...

'It was Robert's suggestion, I think... I moved downstage, so I wasn't directly in front of the window. That way, I wasn't blocking the light coming in through it anymore, and she could be lit nicely. I could still do what I needed to do, with the moves and the acting and everything, so that hadn't changed. Robert's very experienced at all this. He's been doing it for so long. He knows all the tricks of the trade. He'd be the one who would often give me suggestions of how I might say a line or where I might stand.'

'And when you were rehearsing by yourself, did you have the gun?' Hugh asked.

'Yes, I had it the whole time, then I put it back on the props table,' Jenny replied. 'That's where it ends up in the show. When I was finished, I let Charlie know I was done. I expect he made sure it was locked away, like he always does. Then all three of us walked down the pier together before we went our separate ways.'

'So, I want to be clear about the movement of the gun during the show,' said Hugh. 'When do you collect it from the props table?'

'It stays there for the whole act,' Jenny explained. 'I only collect it right before the scene when I need it. I put it in my purse and go on for the scene. I thought I was going to have to carry it around with me for the whole show, but I didn't in the end.'

'Why?' asked Hugh.

'Well, I didn't mind the weight actually, but it was quite heavy. We were worried that every time I went to put it down on a table or on the side it would make a clunking noise – so that wouldn't do. That's why we changed it, so now I collect it right before I come on for the scene.'

'And where does it go after the scene?' Hugh said.

'I drop it off – my purse and the gun – back on the props table.'

'You leave the gun in the purse?' Hugh said.

'Yes.'

'And it would stay like that until the end of the act?' asked Bertie.

'That's right, it doesn't get used by anyone else until the second act.'

Hugh, who seemed to be following Bertie's line of thought asked the next question. 'I don't know if you were aware, Miss Ashford, that when we found the gun, it was sitting on the props table, not in the purse, but in its labelled spot. Would that surprise you?'

Jenny thought about it for a moment, then spoke. 'Yes, that would surprise me. I definitely left it there, as usual, in the purse. But perhaps Charlie took it back out and reset everything on the props table. He's very efficient like that.'

Hugh made a note and underlined it in a small black notebook, where he was keeping a record of their conversations. He would make sure to ask Charlie this at some point.

Hugh continued the questioning. 'Between the end of the rehearsal and the show, what were your exact movements?'

'Well, the three of us – that's me, Teddy and Charlie – all walked to the end of the pier together. Charlie went off his way, Teddy and I went off ours. We went for some afternoon tea. I don't know the name of the café, but it won't be hard to find. I suspect it's the only place that's open at this time of the year. He very kindly took me there and said it would be his treat because it was a special night for me, my first ever professional performance. We stayed there until we had to come back here for the show.'

'Can you remember any of your conversation?' asked Hugh.

'None of the specifics. He was just saying how exciting it must be for me, it being my first proper play. But he was mainly talking about himself, which I was quite relieved about, to be honest. It took my mind off the show and my nerves.'

'Then afterwards, you came directly back to the theatre. You didn't stop on the way?'

'Yes, that's right. We both came back and went straight to our dressing rooms to get ready. It was a little later on when all the kerfuffle started about Robert.'

'And how did that go?'

'Well, I don't think Arthur was very keen on doing it at the start, but he seemed to come round to it in the end. It was the only option. We couldn't afford to lose Charlie if he had to fill in. He had far too much to do backstage. From what Constance told us, it sounded like Robert would have been rather upset if we'd had to have cancelled on his account. So, Arthur it was.'

'Well, that seems to be all, Miss Ashford,' said Hugh.

'I'm free to go?' she asked.

'Free to go back upstairs, for now,' replied Hugh.

'But you don't want to arrest me, or anything,' she said, sounding almost disappointed.

'Not just yet, I'm afraid, Miss Ashcroft.' Hugh raised a hand, indicating that they were done to the constable who was waiting at the back of the auditorium. He escorted Jenny back to the bar.

As the auditorium door click shut behind them, Bertie paced backwards and forwards a little. 'I'm not sure what to think anymore,' he exclaimed, sounding a little more dramatic than he had intended.

'No, neither do I,' Hugh replied. 'Unless we find further evidence of a second gun, I think we have to assume that the gun that killed Celia is the gun we have here. The one that Jenny was holding.'

Bertie looked at Hugh. 'The only person who could have killed her is Jenny. No one else went near.' The whole thing seemed impossible. 'But to shoot someone in the middle of the stage like that. It seems very bullish, doesn't it? Having the nerve to do something like that, in full view of everyone?'

'It does seem rather fantastical, doesn't it?' Hugh said. 'But you tell me, you know actors, you know what they're like.'

'What do you mean by that?' questioned Bertie.

'Well, they don't live in the real world like us, do they? This all feels like something incredible, from a movie or – perhaps – from one of your plays?'

Hugh rose from the sofa, taking a step into the open space of the stage in front of them. 'This is a place of performance, after all.' He smiled, opening his arms out wide, rotating gently on the spot. Bertie wasn't sure if Hugh was just stretching, after a long period sitting down or making a grand theatrical gesture to emphasise his point. Hugh let his arms fall back down by his side. 'Are we seeing things as they were meant to be? Or how we, the willing, watching audience, were meant to see them?'

'What I want to know is, did Jenny know there was a real bullet in the gun? Did she put it there?' Bertie wondered aloud.

'It didn't appear as if she did…' Hugh trailed off.

'What is it?' said Bertie.

'Well, how good an actress do you think she is?' asked Hugh. 'You said she was very good, didn't you?'

'She is,' confirmed Bertie. 'She is very good.'

'Then who's to say that what we've just seen, everything she said, this interview,' Hugh said. 'Who's to say, that all this wasn't just one great performance?'

Chapter Nine

With Hugh's opinion being that there was nothing more to glean from the crime scene, he and Bertie headed up to the studio where the cast were patiently waiting.

Teddy and Charlie sat at a small trestle table with Jenny. She was nursing what was probably by now her second or third glass of brandy. Arthur and Constance sat side by side, their chairs angled in towards each other, while Robert was slouched grumpily by himself in the corner.

'Look,' said Arthur, standing as he saw Hugh and Bertie enter. 'Are we going to be kept here all night? It's been a long day for all of us.'

'No, you're quite right,' agreed Hugh. 'I suggest that you all go home for the evening. It is getting rather late, after all.'

Hugh explained that he had already obtained the details of where they were currently staying, thanks to Charlie who had kept that information in his stage manager's notebook. The theatre would now be sealed until further notice. There would be policemen stationed around the theatre, at all times, to make sure that nothing would be disturbed at the crime scene. In the morning, they would continue their investigations into what had happened and until that was concluded everybody present should not think about making any plans to leave Brighton.

'Can we go to the dressing rooms to collect our things?' asked Constance politely.

'Regrettably, no,' said Hugh to the disgruntled sounds of protest by the others. 'I'm sorry, everything must stay undisturbed at this time.'

'Come on,' protested Arthur. 'On a cold night like this?'

'We will find you blankets to keep you warm,' said Hugh decisively.

This seemed satisfactory enough, or at least Arthur couldn't find any further words of complaint. His mouth opened and closed noiselessly.

'Then it's all settled,' Hugh said, before promptly turning on his heels and leaving the room. He would go and settle the finer details of the plan with the other police officers. It left Bertie stranded, awkwardly, in front of everyone. They all looked in his direction with expectant faces.

'What's this, then, Bertie,' said Teddy, still enthusiastic, despite the late hour. 'Are you going to help solve the murder?'

'Um, I'm not sure,' replied Bertie, honestly. 'I suppose I am, although I'm not sure how much use I'll actually be.'

'Rubbish,' replied Teddy. 'I think you'll be great at this. All those plays you've written over the years. You've got a great mind for murder.'

'I suppose we'll see, won't we? I want to reassure you that Hugh's very competent, you know. He's one of Scotland Yard's finest detectives. I don't know how much help he'll need, quite frankly.'

'Well, if Jenny didn't do it,' said Teddy, giving her a friendly squeeze of the hand, 'I'm sure we'll find out in no time who it actually was.'

'That's what she's saying, is it?' said a grumpy voice from the corner. 'That she didn't do it?'

'Yes, Robert, that's correct.' The reply came from a calm female voice that Bertie was surprised to find was Jenny's. He was a little taken aback by Jenny's coolness. Perhaps now she'd been able to take a little more time and absorb the details of the situation. Perhaps it was down to the third glass of brandy. 'Someone else must have switched the bullets in the gun because it certainly wasn't me. I don't know the front end of a gun from the back.'

'Hmph!' Robert scoffed loudly. 'Well, that's exactly the sort of thing that a murderer would say.'

Teddy, leapt to Jenny's defence. 'Now, look here, Laughton. If that's what she says, then I believe her. Besides, if anyone should be worried about it, it's me. I'm letting her stay with me tonight, so I can make sure she's okay. I'm not having her take the bus all the way back to Saltdean by herself. And I'm not a bit worried I'm going to be murdered in my sleep. Not worried in the least.'

An awkward silence fell over the room once Teddy had finished his speech; there was nothing left to say.

A few minutes later, Hugh returned to the studio with the promised blankets and ensured that everyone was safely dispatched back to their digs. Together, leaving the darkened theatre behind them, Bertie and Hugh walked the short distance from the pier, back to The Old Ship Hotel.

'How do you do it?' Bertie asked.

'Do what?'

'I have about five hundred different possibilities swimming round in my head right now. Who could have done it? Who was where when?'

'My advice,' said Hugh, 'is to try to not think about it. Otherwise, you'll never get to sleep.'

'Yes. Well, that might be easier said than done,' Bertie smiled.

'There're plenty of ideas swimming around in my head too,' said Hugh, returning Bertie's smile. 'You should just let them. What I've found – in my experience – is that as more facts come to light, they will start to favour one idea more than the others. Those facts start to clump together. Eventually, the solution will present itself. But you shouldn't try to discount any of them right now, not right away. You need to trust yourself, trust the process. That's what works for me. At this moment, every thought that you have is still entirely possible, no matter how impossible it might seem.'

'Every thought?' said Bertie, knowing that Hugh couldn't possibly know some of the wild theories that were swirling around in his head. Now that he had spent much of the afternoon and an entire evening with Hugh, he was embarrassed to admit that not all his thoughts were completely focused on the murder.

'Of course!' said Hugh.

'Well, I'll do my best, but I imagine it will be a somewhat restless night,' said Bertie sadly. 'Maybe this will all look different in the morning.'

'Well, I'm only down the corridor if you really can't get any sleep. I can't imagine I'll be getting much either' Hugh smiled. 'Unfortunately, that's just the way it is when you're trying to solve a murder.'

'Are you joking!' Bertie exploded.

Hugh stood there with a beaming smile on his face. 'Not really.'

The pair of them had arranged to meet outside the front of the hotel first thing. Bertie was surprised to find Hugh wearing loose-fitting trousers and a polo shirt under his jacket, instead of the smarter clothing he had been wearing the day before.

'Swimming? In this weather?' Bertie exclaimed, after Hugh had explained the reason for his casual attire. He thought that the idea was absurd to the point of it being a practical joke. 'Don't you think that's a little bit ridiculous?'

'No,' defended Hugh, still smiling. 'It's good for the soul, good for the mind. It helps you to get things clear in your head.'

Bertie responded with a sarcastic look, feigning concern. 'I'd much rather take a long walk to get things clear in my mind instead, wrapped up nice and warm in my coat and scarf. It also comes with the distinct advantage that I won't end up feeling like an ice cube when I'm done.'

'Suit yourself,' said Hugh. 'I'll meet you at the theatre in – say – twenty minutes, half an hour?'

Bertie nodded in agreement. Hugh set off down one of the long ramps that descended from the esplanade, down towards the beach. The sun was still low in the sky and Hugh's figure cast a long shadow across the shingle as he headed towards the shoreline.

A little further along the beach, a few fishermen had unlocked some of the brick arches that extended underneath the road, readying their boats and equipment for the day. During the summer months, it wasn't uncommon for the fishermen to supplement their income by providing pleasure cruises to willing tourists. Bertie thought that the lingering smell of mackerel from the morning's catch would do nothing for his unfortunate susceptibility to seasickness.

Hugh stripped off his clothing to reveal a pair of dark coloured swimming trunks underneath – anyone watching must have thought he was quite mad, Bertie thought. He turned back, spotting Bertie at his vantage point high above the beach, and waved. He turned to face the sea, and with a few bold strides, bounded into the water. When the water was deep enough, he dived beneath the waves without a flinch. He didn't seem to notice that the temperature of the water must have been positively arctic!

Bertie went and sat in a nearby shelter that had a

bench facing the sea. The sun shone crisply over Brighton this morning. It if wasn't for his breath, rising in clouds of condensation in front of him, it could have easily been a bright summer's day. The sunlight glinted off the water and the West Pier – on Bertie's right – reflected back its warm glow.

He turned his head back to the left, surveying the theatre on the Palace Pier. This seemed to be the exception to the rule. Whether it was just the position of the sun – coming from behind the pier, causing everything to appear in silhouette – or Bertie's knowledge of the events that had happened there last night, it somehow left a dark, ominous void on the horizon.

He watched Hugh take several long, powerful strokes that carried him swiftly along in the water, parallel to the shore. After a little while – he was beginning to feel quite inadequate after watching Hugh's display of athleticism – Bertie decided to leave the shelter and head along the esplanade in the direction of the theatre. Hugh had his method for clearing his mind and mulling over the problems of the case; Bertie would try his own. His was a lot less wet.

He let his feet carry him, automatically, one foot after the other, along the pavement. The very scientific technique, known as wandering, was one he had used many times before. If he was stuck on a particular plot point or trying to come up with a line of dialogue, he'd set off around the block of his apartment building in Belsize Park. If it was a problem that arose at the theatre, he would weave his way around the roads in the West End.

Whenever he was stuck with a problem, thinking on his feet always seemed to help.

The difference was, when it was his plot, Bertie was able to do whatever he wanted. He was the one in charge. Usually, he would be able to think up solution after solution, alibi after alibi, and then he would choose the one that would serve the production best. Maybe that would be the most unexpected idea, or perhaps it would be the most dramatic. However, the current situation was completely different. It was someone else's job to be in charge of the plot and characters this time.

As he passed by the Palace Pier, he noticed a small crowd had gathered. The turnstiles were locked and a policeman was in conversation with someone who was being turned away from the entrance. He had expected the crime scene at the theatre to be sealed off, but it looked like the entire pier had been closed too, at least for the time being. A few other figures loitered nearby. It seemed likely that these were not members of the public, waiting for the pier to re-open again, but members of the local press. It was obvious now. He hadn't really considered that Celia Hamilton's death would be news, but of course it was. It wouldn't be too long before the number of reporters grew as they were joined by others from the national press, travelling down from London. He continued to walk by without stopping. No one noticed him. Why would they? Now he was involved in the case, he expected that this may well change by the end of the day and didn't relish the thought.

Leaving the pier behind, Bertie didn't know where to begin. He – and a hundred other people in the audience, including Hugh – had seen the murder take place. He shuddered inwardly at the thought: Celia Hamilton dying in front of a room full of people without a single one of them realising that anything was wrong.

He tried to think of it through the eyes of one of his fictional detectives; often the simplest explanation was the right one. Well, the simplest explanation was that Celia Hamilton was shot by Jenny in full view of the audience. In fact, that was the one thing they could be sure of: the time of the murder. Everything else was much harder to explain.

Why would Jenny, someone who had never met Celia Hamilton before starting on this production, and someone who wouldn't benefit in any way from her death, shoot her? He thought about his plays. In them, he would disguise people's histories from the audience, so they could be revealed in a dramatic fashion at the right point. But, in real life, could you hide your past so easily? He didn't think so. If there was some connection between the two that they weren't seeing yet, it would eventually be uncovered.

In his head, he went through all the different plots he had written over the years. Did any of them compare to this one? He wasn't sure he would have been able to think up such a horrific scenario in the first place. It was gruesome.

He thought about *Murder by Association*. In the play they'd performed last night, everything appeared one way but, in the second act, things were turned on their head. Not murder, but suicide made to look like murder. The trick of the play was, what the audience sees in Act One turns out to be a misinterpretation of what happened, based solely on what was heard. In Act Two, the real events were revealed with the same dialogue taking on an entirely different meaning. Jenny's character condemns herself to the gallows to save Celia's from the indignity of suicide. The failing of the play, and why it wasn't one of his best, is that it was never convincingly explained why she decides to take the blame. Still, it made a very dramatic twist that almost no one in the audience saw coming.

Was there an impossible twist hiding in plain sight in the case of this very real murder? Something that, when looked at another way, made everything appear completely different? Could Charlie or Robert have taken the opportunity, during the shooting scene, to fire a second shot through the window while everyone else was on stage? None of it made any sense to him whatsoever. He was keeping his fingers firmly crossed, hoping that when he and Hugh started to interview the others, things might start to fall into place. Right now, he hadn't a clue.

Bertie stopped walking, realising his feet had carried him well beyond the pier. He turned back, surprised to find he had walked a lot further than he had been expecting. He glanced down at his wristwatch – a lot more time had passed, too. He hurriedly set off back to the pier. At this rate, Hugh might even beat him there!

Chapter Ten

In the end, Bertie and Hugh arrived in front of the pier entrance at almost the same time. Hugh had dried off and changed back into his smarter clothes, looking much more like a police detective again. His hair betrayed him though – it now had the giveaway thickness and texture of someone who had been swimming in saltwater. Bertie thought it only enhanced his rugged good looks. As Hugh saw Bertie arriving, a huge grin appeared across his face.

With a wave of acknowledgement at the policeman on duty, Hugh escorted Bertie through the turnstile. He ignored the calls from the group of reporters that had grown in size since Bertie has passed by earlier.

'I see the swimming worked then,' Bertie said, regarding Hugh's expression.

'Not only that,' Hugh replied, 'I've had a message!'

'Divine inspiration?'

'No.' Hugh rolled his eyes in a playful manner. 'From the police. They called the hotel. It's the fingerprints.

They've confirmed that there were only two sets of fingerprints on the gun.'

'And whose are they?' questioned Bertie.

'Charlie's and Jenny's.'

'That's it?' said Bertie. 'So, it has to be one of them, right? Charlie or Jenny must have switched the bullets.'

'Perhaps…' Hugh replied. 'Perhaps not.'

Bertie sighed, trying to see how this new information helped them. It didn't seem to make anything clearer to him. 'I don't see how this gets us any further.'

'Every new fact gets us further towards something. I don't know what that something is, but closer towards it we are,' Hugh said, his wise words sounding more cod-philosophical than he had perhaps intended. 'Real life isn't like a play; every clue isn't always going to reveal something to us immediately.'

'I wish it would,' said Bertie.

'What matters in real police work is information. As much information as possible. It might not mean much when you find it and it might not mean anything for a long time after that. But the more information we have, the more dots we can connect. Eventually, a pattern will reveal itself. It always does.'

'I'll take your word for it,' Bertie replied. 'At least you seem to have some sort of faith in the process. To me, it just seems like yet more noise to be added to the jumble of thoughts that I already can't make any sense of.'

'Don't worry, Bertie,' said Hugh in an encouraging tone. 'You'll see it all works out in the end.' He smiled again and the pair of them set off towards the theatre at the end of the pier.

As they walked, Bertie let this new information swirl around in his head. He let it mix around with everything he already knew, trying to see if anything would emerge from the haze. Hugh certainly seemed positive that it would, but nothing came.

'But knowing whose fingerprints appear on the gun must tell us who fired it? Who must have killed Celia?' asked Bertie.

'No,' corrected Hugh. 'Knowing whose fingerprints were on the gun tells us only one thing, who held the gun.'

'Then, if that's the case, either Jenny or Charlie must have been involved. Even if they didn't fire the gun themselves, it must have been one of them who swapped the bullets.'

'Or…?' pushed Hugh, encouraging Bertie to look beyond the obvious.

'Or,' said Bertie, thinking about it carefully, 'if someone else did change the bullets, they were wearing gloves.' He turned to Hugh with an annoyed expression. 'Well, that's irritating. Add that to the list of things we need to find out about – see if we can find any gloves lying about the place.'

'Seems pretty sensible to me,' replied Hugh. 'Although we still don't know how they got hold of the damn thing in the first place; it was apparently in sight or locked in the safe at all times.'

They continued towards the theatre. Hugh explained that he had asked Robert Laughton to meet them there. There was a restaurant at the back of the theatre building which they could use to interview him; his movements from the previous night were still unaccounted for.

When they reached the theatre, they didn't go through the front door as these were securely locked with padlocks and chains wrapped around the handles inside. Instead, they walked past the entrance and along the side of the building. As they ducked under the cover of the arcade, Bertie recognised the distinctive frame of Robert Laughton in the distance. He was already waiting underneath, by the side door. He appeared a little out of breath and was looking impatiently at his watch. Robert didn't seem particularly happy about being summoned at this time of the day, but Bertie didn't think he ever seemed particularly happy about anything. A policeman stood nearby, keeping a watchful eye on him while he waited.

Robert caught sight of Bertie and Hugh approaching. 'Oh, there you are.'

'Apologies for being a little late, Mr Laughton,' said Hugh. 'I was a little delayed because of my swimming.'

Hugh retrieved a key from his jacket pocket and went to unlock the door to the restaurant. Robert looked at Bertie, seeking a further explanation for Hugh's comment. All he could offer was, 'I know, it's ridiculous, isn't it?'

The door swung open, allowing them in. Bertie led the way up a few steps until they entered the empty restaurant. Opposite, large windows offered an impressive view over the top of the boating pond at the pier head and out to sea. The blunt arrow-shaped pier jutted out like the bow of a ship. With nothing in the distance but water, you could be almost forgiven for thinking you were standing on the bridge of an ocean-going liner. The view was framed by the arcade that wrapped around the outside of the building; its repeating horseshoe arches mirrored the profile of the onion domes on the roof. From their vantage point inside, the curved outlines seemed to suggest portholes, which only added to the effect.

With a nodded indication from Hugh, Robert pulled out a chair and seated himself at one of the round tables which, like the others, was without its tablecloth and dining paraphernalia.

Hugh remained standing and was walking slowly around the edges of the room. Various posters were hung up on the walls advertising events and productions from this year's summer season – no one had got round to taking them down yet. He looked at each of them in turn as he spoke. 'Have you performed in Brighton before?'

'Yes, at least two or three tours of mine have come through here,' Robert recalled. 'Could be more… You see it all blends together these days. The Theatre Royal, definitely. The Grand, possibly… No, definitely The Grand, now I think about it. Of course, it's a cinema these days, but it was a good little theatre back then. *Marie Rose*? I think that was the play, but it was a good few years ago now.'

'Never here, at the Pier though?' said Hugh, turning to face Robert.

'No, I think I'd remember trotting out into the middle of the ocean every day,' he replied with a chuckle. 'Thought I was going to be blown out to sea on more than one occasion! Seems like a bloody silly place to put a theatre, if you ask me, but I suppose they thought it was a good idea at the time.' Robert turned sideways on the chair to follow Hugh's progress around the room.

'And this play?' asked Bertie. 'How's this one been?'

Robert turned to him with a knowing smile. 'Is the author looking for a compliment?' he announced in mock grandeur, raising an arm to Bertie in reverence before he slumped back into the chair.

Bertie smiled back with a chuckle. 'Not at all. I'm sure you're just as aware as me that this isn't a timeless classic by any stretch. Although I have to say that, in its defence, it's not quite as bad as I remember it being.'

'Didn't pull in an audience, I'm sorry to say, did it? I don't think Teddy has ever had the experience of playing to a house that wasn't packed to the rafters. I expect this whole experience has been quite a disappointment to him.' In contrast, Robert's tone suggested that this wasn't his first experience playing to a less than enthusiastic auditorium.

'You're in digs with Constance, is that right?' said Hugh.

'Yes, that's right. Not last night, though.'

'Oh?' questioned Hugh.

'That's right. Old Cocky put her up in his place for the night.' Hugh looked at Bertie for clarification on the term "Cocky".

'Arthur,' Bertie explained.

'Yes, that's right. Arthur,' Robert repeated. 'Put her up where he's staying for the night. Regency Square, very fancy. I think she's rather delicate. Very sensitive. Young people often are these days, don't you find? He's rather fond of her, you know. She only got a couple of lines in this one. Lucky for her. She's not exactly the best, is she? But her real job was to be Celia's dresser.'

'Celia's dresser?' Hugh asked.

'Yes, I imagine it was probably included as a condition of Celia doing the job, or something like that, her own personal dresser. The rest of us have to make do all by ourselves, of course. God knows what else Arthur had to do to persuade her to come back for this little play in the first place. Lots of money I would imagine – ha! Makes sense. That's probably why there wasn't much to go around, in terms of wages, for the rest of us in the supporting roles. Still, it's work, isn't it?' Robert shrugged. 'Arthur had some idea that, being an American, Constance might be a reassuring presence for Celia; she'd been out there a long time and had got used to the American lifestyle, their way of things.'

'Constance is American?' said Bertie, surprised.

'Oh yes, didn't you spot the accent? She tries to cover it up in the play when she talks, although not very successfully, I have to say. I suppose she's trying her best – no real training as an actress, as far as I can tell. She only came over a few weeks before we started rehearsing. I don't know if she paid her own way or if Arthur helped her with the travel arrangements. I suspect he did. As I said, he's very fond of her, is old Cocky.'

'You mean fond, in a romantic sense?' asked Hugh.

'Ha!' exclaimed Robert. 'I wouldn't put it past him, you know, it could be. Could be. Although, he's old enough to be her father, isn't he – sly dog? Of course, if that was the case, they'd have to have kept it pretty quiet in front of Celia, wouldn't they?'

'She'd get jealous, you mean?' said Hugh.

Robert scoffed again. 'I don't know if Celia was the jealous type, to be honest with you. Vindictive, yes. But jealous? No, she was too proud for that. I don't think Celia had any romantic feelings towards Arthur after they split up, none at all. But if she couldn't have him, she'd make damn sure it would be difficult for anyone else to. Not because she wanted him back, just because she could.'

'You seem to know her quite well. Have you worked with her before?' asked Bertie.

'Know her quite well? I don't have to. She's notorious!' replied Robert. 'There *was* a play we did together. She would have been very young. So would I, for that matter. But it was just a small part, nothing to write home about.'

'Do you remember the play?' said Bertie.

'Not even a little bit,' said Robert. He closed his eyes in an attempt to aid his memory, but after a moment or two, he shook his head. 'No. Something to do with Ancient Greece, I think. Togas and sandals, that sort of thing. Other than that, I couldn't tell you a thing about it.'

'It can't have been that long afterwards that she left for America, now I think about it. Yes, she was always destined for greater things – she used to tell us that herself. Used to lord it over us once she'd decided to make the move out there. Well, it wasn't all plain sailing like she thought it would be. She would boast about the work she had lined up when she arrived, but none of it came to fruition in the end. I'm sure she fabricated the whole thing. It was probably the best part of a year before she landed her first job. Now, if you believe what she says in those magazine interviews, she was waiting for the right role to come along. Well, that's a bit of revisionist history for you. If that's what she wanted to tell herself... Like I said, she was too proud.'

Hugh looked at Bertie. They seemed to be getting somewhat off the subject.

'Your digs,' Bertie asked, 'nice landlady?'

'Oh yes, she was fine,' said Robert. 'I tell you, I've had a fair few battle-axes in my time, but this one was pretty good. You could buy in some food or leave some money with her and she'd be able to whip up something pretty respectable for your tea.'

'She was?' asked Hugh, wondering why Robert's answer had come in the past tense.

'She's not there anymore,' Robert said.

'Why not?' said Hugh.

'Gone off to visit her sister in Scotland. Apparently, she goes this time every year. Gave us a bit of a reduction on the rate and left us to fend for ourselves after a few days here. Pretty thankful, really. I'm not sure how many more greasy breakfasts I could take.'

Bertie looked at Robert and wondered much the same thing.

'I'm not the best cook,' Robert continued, 'but I can muddle through. Constance is pretty good about it, though. She's been sorting out that end of things for both of us. A bit fussy for her own good sometimes. She'll ask me how I want my sandwiches cut, triangles or squares. I don't know that I've ever even thought about it before, let alone have a preference. Sometimes we'll have both because she can't make up her mind.'

'Yesterday,' said Hugh, 'what were your movements after the rehearsal?'

'Constance and I went back to the digs for something to eat.'

'Did she cook?' asked Hugh.

'Yes, nothing too fancy, just some meat paste sandwiches and a pot of tea.'

'Is that all?'

'Yes.'

'And you ate the same thing?' said Hugh.

'Yes. At least, I think so,' replied Robert.

'And then a little later you felt unwell?' asked Hugh.

'Yes, well, I'd been feeling a little peaky all day. When you travel around as an actor and you're visiting new places, you're always picking up some sort of bug or another. Each provincial town has its own distinctive collection of its own provincial bugs.'

It was something that rung true to Bertie. It was not unusual for a cast to make it through rehearsals to opening night in fine fettle, but as soon as the first night was out of the way, that's when the colds and sniffles started. The stress of the intensive rehearsal period was rumoured to weaken your immune system, making you more susceptible to picking up new bugs. After the first performance is out of the way, and everyone relaxes, that's when the illnesses hit you. All at once.

If you were lucky, you might have an understudy in

place, although it was more likely that someone would have to fill in at the last minute. Usually, it would be one of the stage management assistants, script in hand. He wondered if Arthur hadn't been willing to go on last night, would Charlie have attempted to stumble through it instead. He got the impression that Charlie, like him, was much happier when he stayed well out of the limelight.

'Constance was very good about it all,' Robert continued. 'She was very kind to me. She made sure I had everything I needed, said she'd let everyone know what had happened, and said she was sure they'd be able to work something out to cover for me. I was pretty gutted to be honest. I've never missed an opening night in my entire career. Not one. I didn't want it cancelled on my account.'

'And that's why you showed up at the theatre later?' said Bertie. 'You didn't want to break that record?'

'Well, I started to feel better almost instantly. After about an hour, I reckoned I would be up and able enough to do the second act – so off I dashed.'

'The time between Constance leaving and you arriving at the theatre? Can anyone else confirm your whereabouts?' asked Hugh.

'Now look here,' Robert protested. 'I don't like what you're suggesting.'

'I'm not suggesting anything,' replied Hugh calmly.

'I'm sure you already know there's no one else who could possibly confirm my movements last night.'

'That's…' Hugh left the word hanging while he searched for the word. 'Convenient.'

Robert scoffed loudly. 'Ha! Convenient? I don't find it bloody convenient at all. I've got no way of proving anything. Under suspicion of being a murderer? It's ridiculous. I was ill, I was in bed. You were all there at the moment I arrived. I couldn't possibly have been involved in anything to do with it.'

'Yes, but you said you felt better. What was it? "Almost instantly"?' said Hugh.

'So, you're suggesting that I somehow hot-footed it over here and shot Celia?'

'I might be suggesting it,' said Hugh. 'Right now, it's merely one of the many possibilities that I'm entertaining.'

Robert switched his gaze to Bertie and then back to Hugh. 'And how am I supposed to have done it? Dressed up as Jenny and took her place centre stage? It's preposterous. From what I understand about it, you were all watching, weren't you? You all saw who shot Celia with your own eyes, for goodness' sake! I don't know how you think it could have been me?'

'But you could have swapped the bullets, couldn't you? Or you could have arrived just in time for the shooting scene and shot Celia with a second gun?' asked Bertie.

'A second gun? Swapped the bullets?' Robert spat out the words, each one in increasing disbelief.

'Yes,' continue Bertie, unperturbed. 'That gun is placed on the props table at the top of the show. You're a professional, you've been doing it for years! You know the show inside out. You would know the moments when it's left unattended. You could swap the bullets and leave no trace at all. No fingerprints.'

'No fingerprints? Tell me, how exactly am I supposed to have managed that?' said Robert with a resigned sigh.

'Your character, the butler,' said Bertie. 'Butlers wear gloves.'

Bertie turned to Hugh, who tilted his head and nodded, impressed. He turned back to Robert, who was suddenly very quiet. A thin sheen of perspiration was just starting to appear across his forehead.

Chapter Eleven

Hugh locked the side door of the restaurant while Bertie watched Robert totter, dejectedly, into the distance, escorted by the policeman who had been waiting outside. After he watched them disappear around the corner at the front of the theatre, he leant against the white weatherboard cladding and sighed.

'It's infuriating, isn't it? This bullet thing,' Hugh commented. 'I don't think I've ever had a job where the crime scene was preserved so perfectly. No one had a chance to move things around and no one else came through – so where is it? It was lucky that we were both there.'

'It was lucky that you were there,' corrected Bertie. 'I wouldn't know the first thing about sealing off a crime scene – preserving the evidence or whatever it is you need to do.'

Hugh had made sure that the stage area had been thoroughly locked down in the moments after the shooting and no one had been allowed to return to their dressing rooms. It was unlikely, then, that the bullet would be found anywhere other than the stage.

'Do we need to search our suspects then? Their digs?' Bertie asked, in an attempt at being helpful. 'In case one of them removed it without us seeing.'

'I don't know if there's any point,' he replied reluctantly. 'As our helpful stage manager pointed out, destroying or getting rid of evidence couldn't be easier in a place like this. Especially something as small as a bullet.' Hugh tapped the wooden decking with his foot. 'A quick nudge down a gap between the boards and it's gone forever.'

Bertie had to admit, he didn't know very much about firearms or ammunition. But the gap between the boards looked, to him, conveniently bullet sized.

That must be the reason Hugh was so keen to search everybody before they left the stage last night, he realised. He didn't want anyone taking or removing anything, as it could be, quite easily, made to disappear. Bertie laughed quietly to himself, as a memory occurred to him.

'Something funny?' questioned a puzzled Hugh.

'No, I was just remembering,' said Bertie. 'A friend of mine once told me that he was in a dreadfully dull play in Eastbourne; they also have a theatre on a pier. The crew had so much time in between their cues, they used to cut holes in the floor and see how many fish they could catch during the performance. I have to admit, I always thought he was pulling my leg. Now, I'm not so sure.'

'I wonder how many they caught,' said Hugh thoughtfully. Bertie smiled at this somewhat earnest comment. 'Still, it illustrates a point, I suppose,' he continued. 'Getting rid of evidence on this pier is something that can be done just as easily in there as it is out here.'

Bertie wondered to himself: there was all the chance in the world that their missing bullet could have been knocked down a stray hole in the stage and into the sea. It was also possible that it was done, not on purpose, but by complete accident.

They took a few steps along the side of the building where Hugh knocked on a door – it must have been an emergency exit, as there was no handle on the outside. After a few moments, there was a rattle of chains on the inside and the door swung open.

A constable appeared in the doorway and, recognising Hugh, he let them enter. Once they were inside, he set about wrapping the chain around the handles again and locking them with a padlock.

After climbing three or four steps, Bertie was surprised to find themselves standing on the stage. No wonder the noises of the outside world managed to creep into the theatre. It was so close.

'Do you want to go round the dressing room and search for clues?' asked Hugh.

'We sound like the Hardy Boys,' responded Bertie with a laugh.

Hugh shrugged in response. 'Sometimes the Hardy Boys knew what they were doing,' he said with a smile.

'There are dressing rooms on both sides of the stage, although they didn't use the ones on this side, only the ones on stage...' Hugh paused for a moment, turning to face the back wall, and pointed to the other side of the stage with his left hand. 'Stage left?' he ventured.

Bertie chuckled. 'You're very close. Stage right. It's done from your point of view when you're looking out towards the audience.'

'Dammit,' muttered Hugh under his breath. 'This way please!' he announced, as he set off across the back of the stage. Bertie followed him across and up the steep wooden stairs that led to the dressing rooms. Hugh followed the corridor as it zigzagged around the dressing rooms. It was wide enough for one person to walk comfortably and only just enough for two people to pass. It would have been quite an ordeal to navigate them on a big show with actors, dancers and dressers squeezing past each other, rushing to make their cue.

Bertie could never quite relax in the dressing rooms of actors, even when he was invited in. He always felt like he was intruding into an intensely personal space, which made him feel a little awkward and uncomfortable. Actors, as far as Bertie could tell, seemed to bring with them all kinds of charms and keepsakes. A collection of items would be built up over time and transported from theatre to theatre. Letters or notes from admirers would be displayed, presumably to build confidence in one's own talents. Small items collected on an actor's travels, to which they might ascribe a successful performance and hope that they might bring further luck in the future, would be held on to and guarded possessively.

They started their search at the far end of the corridor, working their way back towards the stage. In each of the dressing rooms, all the usual items could be found sitting on the long built-in dressing table that stretched the length of one wall. The table was divided into several positions that each had its own mirror attached to the wall and half a dozen light bulbs around them. Sticks of greasepaint, with the paper sheath unravelling around them, were dotted around. They lay, half used, on the table top or poking haphazardly out of make-up boxes. Each stick had a different number written on them. Presumably, the numbers made some sort of sense to the actor when they were applying them – creating highlights and contours that accentuated their features under the intense glare of the stage light, making their expressions more readable – but what each number actually referred to had always remained a complete mystery to Bertie.

He felt rather intrusive sifting through the various items, searching for clues that he had no idea what they looked like. 'I'm not entirely sure what I'm supposed to be looking for, to be honest,' he admitted to Hugh.

'You've spent more time in these kinds of places than I have,' said Hugh. 'Is there anything that looks out of place to you, anything that you wouldn't normally expect to see?'

Not wanting to disappoint Hugh, Bertie carried on poking around in the belongings. He inspected an old copy of *The Era* newspaper. It had started as a general newspaper, but as time had gone on, it became more and more focused on theatrical news. Now it was referred to as "The Actor's Bible" and no self-respecting actor would be seen without a copy tucked under their arm.

The paper lay in Teddy's spot and was dated some four months earlier. He expected that it contained a favourable notice from Teddy's excellent performance earlier in the year – with some quick maths, he judged that it would have been around that time. There were two kinds of people who worked in theatre, Bertie thought: those who admitted to reading their notices and those who pretended they didn't.

Bertie was one of the ones who pretended they didn't. While he didn't read every notice religiously, his faithful secretary, Gertrude Williams, would keep and file away anything that she felt was important. She also kept her own archive of *The Era* and *The Stage*, sending a stack of them off each year so they could be bound together into a thick volume. Programmes from each of his productions were stored tidily in cardboard archival boxes, along with the various drafts and revisions of each play. She held an almost encyclopaedic knowledge of this archive in her head and for the parts of it not committed to memory there were hundreds of notecards from which she could look up and cross-reference any kind of theatrical information you required.

She would often field calls from producers who were trying to track down a certain actor that had appeared in a production. On occasion, even journalists from newspapers would get in touch when they were looking for background information for some story or other.

It was all very impressive. Bertie supposed that the whole archive would have to be donated to a museum one day. Space in his flat was limited and there would come a point where it would no longer fit in the room that he had set aside to be her office. As long as she carried out the rest of her work with the same dedication and efficiency – which she did – Bertie felt that the sacrificed space was a price worth paying. Also, it couldn't be bad for business with all those directors, producers and journalists regularly calling. At the very least, it meant that his telephone number had remained a permanent fixture in all their address books.

As they finished their search, nothing seemed to be out of place in Teddy and Robert's dressing room – at least as far as Bertie could tell. Jenny and Constance's room was much the same, although it was a lot emptier. Presumably, Jenny – being new to the industry – had accumulated far fewer bits and pieces to be displayed in her place. There was a small note from an aunt, wishing her luck, that had been pinned up next to the mirror.

Constance had even fewer possessions displayed. Because of her double duty as Celia's dresser, alongside playing a small role, it would have left her with very little free time to spend in her dressing room. Presumably, she'd travelled light on her trip over from America, which Bertie also thought would have contributed to the lack of paraphernalia. Two small photos, one of which he assumed was of her family, were pinned up at the side of the mirror. It was an assumption, as there wasn't exactly a strong family resemblance between her and her parents, but they certainly looked like a happy family group.

Bertie directed Hugh's attention towards the photograph 'What do you think? Parents?'

'Could be. I don't look very much like my parents either.' Clearly he was thinking along the same lines.

At least they looked very happy, Bertie thought. In the photo, the family was sitting on the steps of a large, open porch, in front of a timber-framed building. Perhaps it was a farmhouse. It certainly looked pretty rural.

Above the family photo was a second one – a small portrait of Constance. She was a little younger, perhaps fourteen or fifteen, but still unmistakably the same person. Her expression was hard to interpret. She was neither smiling nor frowning, just neutral. The background was dark and inky; any details of her surroundings had been lost in the blackness.

He unpinned the photo from the wall, looking at the back of it for any further information. There was a smudged stamp for a newspaper he'd never heard of based in Arkansas. He pinned the photo back in its place.

Bertie thought about his own flat, back in London and the photographs he had displayed around it. Naturally, there were photos of events like first nights, shaking hands with a producer or two. There were holiday snaps with friends. Birthday parties. He couldn't think of any photographs that were only of himself. For that reason, the photo seemed a little strange. Perhaps there was some other implication to the photo, might it have been a reminder of a significant moment from the past? It must have been, if it was taken and printed by a newspaper.

With nothing else of interest being discovered, Bertie and Hugh moved along, past the kink in the corridor, to the star dressing room. This room was closest to the stage. Because of the zigzag in the corridor, the walkway was now between the dressing room and the outside wall. The room didn't have any windows that opened directly to the outside. Instead, daylight filtered through the exterior window, across the corridor, and through a second window in the dressing room wall. Through this window, you would have been able to see all the comings and goings of the actors as they moved from their dressing rooms to the stage. A bonus for Celia, who he was sure would have taken delight in keeping an eye on everyone.

A small hand-lettered card, neatly written, was slotted into a brass holder on the door. It read:

CELIA HAMILTON

Hugh nudged the door open, and they stepped inside. This room seemed a little larger than the others; even though it was physically the same size, it only had one dressing room table. The furniture in the room which, at one time, had been new and ornate, but after years of use by the many actors passing through, now had an air of faded grandeur about them.

The large dressing table – with an equally large mirror – sat against one wall. A four-panel screen had been placed next to it – blocking off a corner of the room for privacy while the occupant was changing. On the dressing table there was a large make-up box with the top unfolded open. Tubes of Max Factor were neatly displayed in rows alongside several brushes of various shapes and sizes. This was the Hollywood influence, Bertie mused. Robert's sticks of Leichner greasepaint, with their tattered paper casings that tore off as the stick wore down, looked positively medieval in comparison to this sleek-looking set.

Underneath, the make-up box contained three slim drawers. These looked like they were designed to hold larger items, like jewellery, and upon opening them he saw that they did. Working his way down through the drawers, one by one, he could see some very expensive-looking necklaces and earrings. He suspected that the jewellery was just expensive-looking, rather than the real McCoy. These were apparently for stage use only. The items weren't in complete disarray, but surely genuinely valuable jewels would have been treated with a touch more care. The valuable jewels, which Bertie was certain Celia would have brought with her, were probably locked securely away, back at her hotel.

When he reached the third drawer, he was surprised to see that it contained something altogether more interesting. Sitting neatly on top of a small stack of press cuttings and photographs was a crisp, flat piece of paper with a few scrawled words written on it.

'Hugh,' said Bertie, getting his attention and beckoning him over. 'What do you think about this?'

In messy, unidentifiable handwriting, a few simple, but effective, words were written:

Remember. I know your secrets.

'Blackmail?' asked Bertie.

'It certainly looks that way, doesn't it?' said Hugh, inspecting the paper closely without removing it from the drawer. 'It will be hard to tell much from the handwriting. I'd say they've deliberately gone out of their way to disguise it – perhaps they used their non-dominant hand to write with.'

'Fingerprints?' Bertie asked.

'Possibly. I think we should get it checked out.'

Every time Hugh made some kind of reference to Bertie and him being a crime-solving team, it took him by surprise, but each time there was a strange tingle of excitement. Not only had Hugh been listening to his thoughts on the crime, something that he was under no obligation to do, but he had also discovered a real life, genuine clue. He felt as if he was only a magnifying glass away from being a real detective. At the start, he had thought that Hugh was simply humouring him by asking him to be involved. The more time they spent together, the less it seemed that was the case. And, while at the beginning Bertie didn't know how useful he would be, he now found himself wanting to impress Hugh, like an obedient dog would his owner.

'Who would blackmail Celia?' asked Bertie.

'I imagine she's a very rich woman,' said Hugh, 'and everyone has some sort of scandal in their past – especially your sort of people.'

'My sort of people?' Bertie responded.

'You know, the film and theatre type,' said Hugh with a smile. 'Famous people.'

Bertie smiled back. 'I'm hardly famous, Hugh.'

'Of course you would say that. You're far too modest. But that doesn't mean it's not true. On the other hand, people like Celia Hamilton don't always appear to be at all modest. I'm sure she's built up many enemies over the years. Professional rivalries, if you will.'

Bertie thought that she probably had. People like Celia naturally dominated any room they entered and that wouldn't always sit well with everyone else. The rehearsal he had witnessed yesterday was only the start of it. When you're the most famous person in a room, you have a kind of power: people find it very hard to say no. It's also very easy to wield that power, without understanding the effect it can have on others, though, of course, Celia Hamilton knew exactly the power she could hold over someone else and would wield it with precision. If she was unhappy with how things were progressing in the rehearsal room, she'd make damn sure that everyone else would be unhappy as well.

'I'm sure she did have enemies,' said Bertie. 'Positive, in fact. But enemies to the point of blackmail? It seems a stretch. To the point of murder? Well, that seems even more unlikely.'

'You can forget about unlikely,' Hugh said. 'She *was* murdered. We know that it happened. That would very much indicate that it's not unlikely at all.'

Bertie couldn't fault his reasoning. Although he didn't think what you might call a "professional" disagreement or a rivalry in the rehearsal room could lead to murder. But who knew what secrets lurked in Celia's past? Certainly, something that she'd prefer to be kept out of the papers might just be well worth paying for.

'Maybe the price started to go up and she no longer wanted to pay?' Bertie thought aloud.

'Although, you've got to wonder, if the goal of blackmail is to extort as much money as possible, having your target be dead seems a little counterproductive,' Hugh stated. 'What it does tell us, though, is now we know she had enemies. And that those enemies were here in Brighton – if not right here in this theatre.'

Chapter Twelve

'Did you get on with Celia?' said Hugh, posing his first question.

'No one ever really "got on" with Celia Hamilton,' came the reply. 'We all just put up with her.'

A wry smile was visible through the cloud of cigarette smoke as Teddy exhaled. He leant casually against the white railings of the pier, one foot lifted, with the sole of his shoe pressed up against the painted cast iron. He wore a stylish camel-coloured coat with a long navy scarf that draped around his neck, protecting him from the chill. Bright, cool sunlight lit the scene. It looked like something right out of the pages of a Picturegoer magazine. Teddy let the ash from his cigarette fall towards the decking. It was carried away on the swift breeze before it could reach the wooden boards.

Bertie was watching, sitting on one of the benches that covered and sheltered from the wind. The benches stretched out in a long line in front of the theatre, splitting the pier in two along its length. Hugh stood nearby, putting his questions to Teddy. There was no doubt, in Bertie's eyes, that Teddy looked every bit the star performer. It was just that his real-life career hadn't quite caught up with the way he chose to carry himself or the style in which he dressed.

For some performers, their careers never really matched up to the impression they tried to cultivate. Bertie was sure that Teddy's career would catch up to his persona in a few short years. Throughout his own career, he had seen many actors come and go, but there were few with the kind of star quality that Teddy had. Celia Hamilton had it too. Of course, it's almost impossible to put your finger on what describes star quality. By its very nature, it's something that's indefinable, but the one thing he thought always linked together star performers was a sense of effortlessness.

You could always spot the people who were destined for this higher level of success – they would always stand out. All around them, everyone else, like dancers struggling to keep up in a chorus line, would look like they were having to put in more work to achieve the same ends. They would be surrounded by people doing the same steps, but it always seemed much harder for them to disguise the effort they were putting in. Instead, when you caught sight of someone who looked destined to become a star, it would come across as completely effortless to them. It would seem completely natural, like they didn't even need to try at all. Even if offstage they were a bundle of nerves, that would all fade away the moment they stepped on the stage. It was clear to see that this was the place where those performers felt the most comfortable. It was where they came alive. If he were a gambling man – and he wasn't – Teddy was an actor who Bertie would have happily put money on to become a star.

Teddy had it. Whatever "it" was.

'Did you "put up with her"?' Hugh responded.

'Oh, I'd say so,' came Teddy's cheerful reply. 'I certainly did my bit. I tried to be nice to her at the start of rehearsals. I even asked her for advice. I thought she might like that. I asked her, what if I wanted to get into films and things? But it was clear that she had no intention of helping me out. She said she didn't want to see any more people like me get into the movie business.'

'What did she mean by that?' said Bertie from the bench.

'What did she mean by it?' said Teddy quickly. 'Nothing, as far as I can tell. She just wanted to make sure to keep me in my place. She didn't want a young upstart like me getting ideas above my station. The movie business was for people like her, not for someone like me. I daresay if Celia's high standards were what you needed to meet in order to work in Hollywood, there wouldn't be anyone around to make the films. Nothing was ever good enough for her.'

'You think she was threatened by you?' said Hugh.

'Threatened? I don't think Celia Hamilton felt threatened by anyone. She just didn't want other people – younger people – to have success, as if there was only so much work to go around. The longer you keep everyone else down, the longer you stay up. I suppose that was how she saw it.

'The thing you have to understand about people like

Celia is they always have to be the most important person in the room. They have to get all the praise. They have to get all the attention.'

'And putting you in your place, that was how she made sure that she stayed the most important?'

'Of course,' replied Teddy. 'She's a very famous woman, you know. No one becomes that famous by pure talent alone. You have to fight for it, make sacrifices for it. Well, if that's what you have to do to get into films, quite frankly, I don't know if I want anything to do with them. I think I might just stick to being rather good in plays. It seems to be going quite well for me so far.'

'You *do* seem to be doing quite well at it,' Bertie said. 'So why on earth did you feel the need to come down and do a play in Brighton, especially at this time of the year?'

'Blackmail,' Teddy replied with a smile.

Hugh and Bertie stiffened a little and their eyes darted towards each other.

'Blackmail?' repeated Hugh.

Teddy took one last drag on the cigarette before flicking the stub, sending in a soaring arc, into the sea. 'I suppose you could call it that,' he said. 'You know Arthur produced the last show I was in, and a very good show it was, too. It was a good part, very good for me. I'm sure you saw the reviews. But a supporting part all the same.'

Bertie nodded in response. He had indeed seen the glowing notices that Teddy had received and the ones that he suspected were contained in the newspaper that sat on his dressing room table.

Teddy lit another cigarette before continuing his

story. 'Arthur said he had a lead role for me in his next big play, but only on the condition that I'd come down here and do this one first. He said the money wasn't going to be great, but it would be fun. Well, he certainly was right about one of those things; the money is terrible.'

'You were okay with that?' asked Hugh.

'I didn't mind, really. I've done well enough in my career so far that I don't have to worry about money all that much. I don't mind Brighton, it's a nice enough place, so I didn't see anything wrong with saying yes.'

'And what did you think about the choice of show?' asked Bertie.

'Well, very excited that it was going to be one of yours, of course,' Teddy said, with a twinkle that was directed in Bertie's direction. 'I've never done a Bertie Carroll before – even if it was one from a few years back. Still, a Bertie Carroll is a Bertie Carroll, isn't it? Quite frankly, I think he wanted a play with a small cast. I don't think he had a lot of money to put into this one. I imagine Celia Hamilton doesn't exactly come cheap. That's why we've got Jenny, poor girl. I'm sure he's paying her a pittance, but she doesn't know any better. She is very good though, you saw. Very good, but very green. I hope she hasn't been too damaged by the Celia Hamilton treatment. She didn't get it bad as me, thankfully, otherwise I think she'd have lost her confidence altogether.'

'Why Brighton, do you think?' Bertie said.

Teddy looked thoughtful. 'I expect that Arthur had some idea that he could have got it to transfer into town at some point. This was still Celia's first stage role in –

what – fifteen years? Even though she puts up a pretty good front, I think she was understandably nervous about it. That's probably why she turned out to be even more insufferable than we all expected, taking it out on everyone else. I suppose it was something in the way of a try-out. If it went well down here and she performed well – remembering all the lines would have been a good start – then perhaps Arthur would transfer it into town. It would have made a killing. Celia would have been a big box office draw.'

'Have you seen this before?' said Hugh, reaching into his inside coat pocket.

Hugh took out the note they'd found in Celia's make-up box and held it up for Teddy to see. As Bertie watched, he saw that there was a brief moment when the cool exterior of the actor faltered.

'Where did you find that?' asked Teddy, in a tone that sounded surprised. His eyes darted between the paper, Hugh, Bertie and back again.

'Answer my question first,' stated Hugh. 'Have you seen it before?'

'No, actually,' replied Teddy in quick, short breaths. 'I haven't.' In an attempt to be casual, Teddy turned his head away – although it came across a little more petulant than he had probably intended.

'You're sure about that, are you?' asked Hugh, not entirely convinced by Teddy's performance.

'Very sure,' replied Teddy, his voice was now firmer. 'I can confidently say I've never seen that note before in my life. Where did you find it, by the way?' he added, taking another attempt at nonchalance.

Hugh paused a moment before deciding that there was no reason that he couldn't reveal the information. 'In Miss Hamilton's make-up box, as it happens.'

'Is that right?' commented Teddy, letting out a low whistle. His face brightened and he laughed loudly. 'Maybe Arthur was blackmailing her to be in the play as well.' His face tensed into a smile – more of a smirk.

'Let's talk about the night of the murder,' Hugh said. 'What were your movements after the rehearsal?'

'Well, I took Jenny out to some little café,' Teddy recalled, 'somewhere nearby. She was nervous, and I wanted to take her mind off it, give her a bit of a treat. This was her first ever opening night as a professional actress, after all.'

'She stayed behind to rehearse for a while by herself, didn't she?' asked Hugh.

'Yes, that's right. I came outside for a bit of fresh air, you know. We'd been cooped up in there all day. I waited outside.'

'Why outside?' prompted Hugh.

'Smoking is banned in the theatre,' replied Teddy, rolling his eyes. 'I suppose that's what you get for building a tinderbox theatre out at sea. The whole thing is made from wood, you know. Could go up in an instant; at least, that's what they want you to think. You must have seen the "no smoking" signs plastered all over the place.'

Hugh shrugged, indicating that he had. 'You were outside with Charlie, weren't you?'

'Yes, actually,' replied Teddy, looking over at Bertie. 'He came out for a bit at well, same reason I expect.

That's the problem with this job, you spend too much time in dark rooms. This time of year, you're lucky if you get to see any daylight!'

'So, Jenny would have been inside by herself?' said Hugh.

'Yes, I suppose she would have,' replied Teddy, before letting out a gasp of realisation. 'You think she stayed behind to swap out the bullets in the gun?'

Hugh responded with a kind of noncommittal shrug.

'Well, I don't know if I can get on board with that idea,' said Teddy, brushing it off. 'I still don't think that Jenny is the type – whatever the type is. Maybe I'm not the right person to judge that sort of thing, but she's just too sweet. Too sweet to know anything about guns and murder, if you ask me.' Teddy thought carefully for a few moments more. 'No, hold on. She wouldn't have been alone with the gun. At least I don't think so. You'd have to check with Charlie. He'd have been around while Jenny was doing her little rehearsal, wouldn't he? He came out after he'd finished setting up everything for the show and she'd finished by then, the gun would have been put away. We were only waiting around outside while she was changing out of her costume, that's all.'

'You said she'd been nervous all day?' said Hugh.

'Yes, of course.' Teddy rolled his eyes like he was stating the obvious. 'But that wasn't because she'd been planning a murder, for goodness' sake! It was because she was worried about the performance. She'd been worried and kept going over every line, every movement.'

'The blocking?' said Hugh.

'See, you really are getting the hang of all this theatre

jargon, aren't you? Very impressive,' he added, with a cheeky wink in Bertie's direction. 'Yes, she was getting herself in a state, worried that she might not get it all right.'

'Some murderers rehearse their killings, you know. Practice them. They go through the motions in their head or act them out, over and over. That way you can build up courage, build up the confidence to go through with it.' Hugh turned to Bertie. 'What did you say you saw Jenny rehearsing when you left the theatre?'

For a moment, Bertie sat there a little dumbfounded. Processing everything that Hugh was saying and what he was suggesting. He swallowed before he spoke. 'The shooting scene.'

'The shooting scene,' Hugh repeated to Teddy. The group stood there for a moment in silence. The idea just seemed to hang in the air between them.

'Let's go on,' Hugh said eventually, when he realised that Teddy had nothing to add. 'What was the actual performance like?'

'Well, as far as I was concerned, there was nothing particularly out of the ordinary,' Teddy said. 'I know there was a bit of a fuss before we started, Robert being off ill and all that. Turned out that it wasn't that much of a problem after all. I think we were worried that it was going to be a bit of a mess with Arthur filling in. But he knew the lines and the blocking' – he directed the word "blocking" towards Hugh with a smile – 'and it wasn't that bad after all. Quite passable, really. I've certainly seen far worse performances at the end of a pier.'

Bertie agreed that it was rather impressive for Arthur

to fill in at the last minute. There were plenty of directors that couldn't tell you half of the things that were happening in their own play, not without consulting a script with their copious notes scribbled across it.

'Was that surprising?' Bertie asked.

'Was what surprising?' Teddy repeated back to him.

'That Arthur went on and did the show as well as he did?'

'I suppose so,' said Teddy, thinking about it. 'He's one of those directors that's pretty specific about everything – directing by numbers, you know. Move here, stand here, cross here, do that. Unfortunately, it doesn't leave much room for personal interpretation, which can limit one's talent a little. But he knew what he wanted all right. I suppose that means he must have known the play and the lines pretty well.'

'And how was the play for you?' asked Hugh.

'Well, it was fine really, I do an awful lot of running around though, helping with the sound effects.'

'How did that come about? You helping out?' said Hugh.

'Well, we're a bit short-staffed on this show, aren't we? Poor old Charlie is doing the job of three or four different people. Handy for you, though, I suppose. Fewer suspects hanging around the place.'

'Why is that? Money again?' said Hugh, not sure whether to direct the question to Teddy or Bertie.

'Yes, I expect so,' Teddy answered. 'It's not the most complicated play in the world – technically speaking – so Charlie can just about manage. Other stage managers would struggle, I think. But he's young, full of energy and can run about the place without breaking into a sweat. I expect a lot of the staff here are brought on for the summer season and are let go at the end of it. There's not enough work to justify keeping them on all the time, is there?'

'These sound effects. What does that involve?'

'Oh, it's pretty fun actually,' replied Teddy, his face lit up with enthusiasm. 'Mind you, it took me a lot of practice to get the timing right – Arthur was really specific about that. It needed to be right on the cue line, "Oh no!"' Teddy acted out the line in mock-dramatic fashion. 'Like I said, that's his style. The thunder is done by this huge sheet of metal that hangs from the roof. When you shake it, it makes the noise of a thunderclap, or something that sounds pretty close to it.

'Then, after all that, Charlie has to run around to the other side to bring down the curtain. So, after I've done a few thunder crashes, I take over from Charlie on the wind machine. He whizzes back around and does his thing. It took a while for us to get everything slick and in the right order, but after a few rehearsals we got pretty good at it, even if I say so myself.'

'Can you tell me about the scene, the one with Jenny and the rest of you all on stage?' asked Hugh.

'The shooting bit, you mean?' said Teddy. He stopped and thought about it for a moment. 'Well, Jenny did it all right. She shot her.'

The blunt statement shocked Bertie and Hugh for a moment.

'You're sure she did?' asked Hugh.

'Of course she did. Right in front of us all. Celia is a

great actress, but even so, that would have one hell of a performance if it wasn't real. I didn't think much about it at the time, of course, but looking back… Well, she was shot, wasn't she? No wonder it was convincing.' Teddy gave an involuntary shudder at the thought.

'You're certain,' said Bertie, standing up from the bench.

'Well, yes,' said Teddy. 'Of course, whether she meant to or knew that she was going to, is quite another matter. Like I said before, Jenny is just too sweet to do something like commit a murder. But if what you're asking is, did Jenny fire the gun that killed Celia Hamilton? I'm sure. It had to be her.'

Chapter Thirteen

Bertie and Hugh arranged to meet Constance in the same tearoom that Jenny and Teddy had dined in on the evening of the murder. The name of the tearoom – which neither Jenny nor Teddy could remember – was Lilly's. A small sign with a soft pink background and crisp black lettering hung from a wrought-iron bracket. It swung gently in the breeze.

The shop was simple and unassuming from the front. Bertie could well understand why it had been so forgettable. As they entered through the front door – accompanied by the tinkling of a small bell – he noticed that the inside was very clean and neatly kept. Crisp white tablecloths covered each of the square tables, which were set at angles from the walls. Well-worn bentwood chairs, although still looking very stable and sturdy, were placed around them. They selected one of the tables and took a seat. A small posy was displayed in a vase in the centre of the table top. Bertie was surprised to find that the flowers were real.

A young waitress emerged from the back of the shop to welcome them both. She carried a confused look on her face, as if she wasn't expecting any customers today. That was understandable; They were the only two people in the place. Rather than the black-and-white uniform typical of the Nippies that you'd find in a Lyon's Corner House, and the uniform that tea rooms around the country would try to emulate, she wore a neatly pressed shirt with white and green stripes; it seems somehow more appropriate for the seaside. Like every other waitress in the country, she wore the same standard white apron with a matching coronet cap.

Their order was taken. The waitress had taken great care to write it down neatly – even though it was just tea for three – before tucking the notepad into her apron and disappearing through a door at the back of the shop. She returned almost instantly with their drinks, placing them down in front of them. Bertie noticed that she made sure that the handles were facing the same direction – a nice touch. The pair of them nodded their thanks before she turned away.

'One moment,' said Hugh, before she could leave. 'Were you working here last night?'

'Working?' she repeated. 'Yeah, I was working.'

'I'm Inspector Chapman from Scotland Yard,' Hugh said. 'This is Mr Carroll who's helping me with my enquiries. I was wondering if you might have a moment to speak to us. Perhaps you could take a seat.'

The waitress took a moment, looking at the empty tables to her left, then to the empty tables on her right. 'Well, I'm not exactly rushed off my feet, am I? I suppose

I could spare a few moments.' She pulled out a chair and sat, perched delicately on the edge of it.

'What is your name?' asked Hugh.

'Dorothy. Dorothy Baker, if you want the whole thing. You can call me Dot, though. Most people do.'

'Okay, Dot,' continued Hugh. 'We're looking into the death of someone who was killed last night.'

'Killed?' repeated Dot with alarm. 'I don't know no one that's been killed.'

'No, I don't expect you do,' said Hugh. 'This was an actress at the theatre on the pier. We believe she may have been murdered.'

'A murder in Brighton?' she replied in shock. Bertie noticed, as was usual with the locals, that Brighton was pronounced without the "t". 'I did see that the whole thing was closed off on my way in and I did wonder to myself, what could that all be about? I couldn't very well stop to find out. I have a lot to be getting on with. But at least now we've solved that mystery. I don't know what I can do to help you about it, though, really I don't.'

'There were two people that dined here before the performance yesterday, between six and seven.'

'Oh, you think they were the ones what done it, do you?'

'We're not certain yet,' replied Hugh.

'They were actors, weren't they?' She stated this as a fact, rather than phrasing it as a question.

'You could tell?' interjected Bertie.

'Of course!' she boasted, happily. 'We get all types in here and actors are easier to spot than most, aren't they? You only have to wait five minutes before they can't stop themselves from telling you. On they go, talking loudly, broadcasting their stories for everyone to hear. I'm sure they're not *all* the same, mind you, but they do like to be centre stage, don't they?'

Bertie chuckled with a shrug of agreement. She was right. Not all actors were the same, but a lot of them tended to be quite similar.

'Were they disturbing the other customers?' asked Hugh.

'Other customers?' she repeated, with a hint of indignation. 'There weren't no other customers. They were the only two. No, I tell a lie.' She instantly corrected herself. 'There was an elderly lady sat over in the corner, there. Although she didn't seem too bothered by it. Maybe she couldn't hear them too well.'

'But you could?' asked Bertie. 'Hear them?'

'Of course, not that I was listening in or anything,' she said, protesting her innocence. 'Well, it's just that you couldn't *not* hear them. They were both very giggly – very excitable, if you know what I mean. It was their opening night last night, wasn't it? Yes, I think that's what they were talking about,' she said, answering her own question. 'I think she was a lot more nervous than he was – cue more nervous giggles.' She rolled her eyes.

'Now, he was very cool about the whole thing,' she continued, 'but he seemed to be much more experienced than she was. Very handsome too, not that you're asking my opinion on that or anything. Kept talking about how great everything was in London. London this and London that. How great it would be if she could move to London with him. London, I ask you! She was local though, I think. She looked and sound like she was at least.'

'Yes, that's correct,' replied Bertie. 'You seem to have got the measure of them alright. Very impressive.'

She gave a shrug, brushing off the compliment. 'Not really. They really were talking quite loudly, you know.'

'Did they mention anything about Celia Hamilton?' prompted Hugh.

'Celia Hamilton, from the movies?' she asked, surprised. 'No, I don't think so, at least not by her name. They were talking about some nightmare of a woman—'

'Yes, that would be her,' Bertie interrupted, with a smile.

'Well, yes then. "The way she was looking at me, I could have just killed her," that's what one of them said.'

'Hold on a minute!' Hugh exclaimed.

'Oh, for goodness' sakes, Inspector. You think I can't tell the difference between two people planning an intricate murder and when they're using a figure of speech?'

'You don't think it was anything more than that?' Hugh asked.

'Of course not, otherwise I think I would have mentioned it when you came in here asking all about killings and murders, wouldn't I? No, I think it was just them letting out some of their frustrations.'

'Well, I think I'll write it down anyway,' said Hugh, who had been writing things in his notebook throughout their discussion, doing his best to keep up with the fast rate of her talking.

'Whatever you want to put in your notebook is no concern of mine,' she commented cheekily. 'They really weren't acting suspicious or doing anything that might make me think they were planning on murdering someone. And if they were, they certainly weren't saying it out loud like they did everything else.

'Now, if you've nothing else to ask, I really should get back to my work. It's not too bad in the summer. We take some more girls on who spend half their time gossiping and making eyes at the customers, but they do help out a little. This time of year, who's got to deal with everything? Me, that's who.'

'Of course,' replied Hugh. 'I don't think we have anything else.'

Hugh looked at Bertie who shrugged, unable to think of any further questions. His mind was elsewhere, wondering what work the waitress might have to do in a tearoom that was entirely empty except for the three of them.

'Thank you,' said Hugh as the waitress rose from her seat and disappeared through the doorway that led into the back of the shop.

'"I could have just killed her",' Hugh read back from his notebook, before closing it and placing it on the table. 'What do you think of that!' He gave a playful tap on the top of the notebook to punctuate his point.

'Honestly,' replied Bertie, 'It's just a bit of a coincidence, isn't it? People don't go around planning murders using loud voices in a public space, do they?'

Hugh shrugged.

'I don't think it's blown the case wide open,' Bertie continued, 'has it?'

'No,' replied Hugh, defeated. Before he could

continue, he was interrupted by the soft tinkling of a bell. A cool breeze that made them shiver blew in through the open door. Standing in the opening was Constance, her expression blank and hard to read, although when she saw Bertie and Hugh waiting for her, she allowed herself a small smile of recognition before joining them at the table.

'Thank you for meeting with us,' Hugh said kindly. 'We just want to establish your movements from yesterday.'

'Sure, that's fine,' Constance replied in a quiet voice. It wasn't that she was timid in any way – in fact, she spoke quite confidently – but her American accent was soft. Bertie couldn't quite place it. He noticed that there was a lengthening of the vowels, suggesting perhaps somewhere in the south, but not to the extent that it came across as a drawl.

'You've not been over here for long, have you?' said Hugh.

'No, say a month or two. Before that, I was working in New York as a dresser at The Imperial.'

'And how did this come about?' Hugh questioned. 'I mean, you getting a job over here?'

'Well, Arthur and I had become friendly…'

'Friendly?' said Hugh, looking for clarification on the term.

'We had become friends, that's all,' she replied. 'We'd met six months or so earlier, while he was working in New York. He was there co-producing one of his shows that he'd brought over from London.' Hugh nodded at Constance, encouraging her to continue. 'I was the dresser for the lead actress, Evelyn Lane. Arthur would often come backstage to give notes or to talk to the cast. We would often speak while he was waiting for Miss Lane to be ready.

'He was always very polite, very charming. He'd ask me about my family, where I grew up. Now and then, he might take me for dinner so we could talk properly.'

'Forgive me for asking,' said Hugh, 'but would you say this was a romantic relationship?'

Constance looked shocked, to the point of being horrified. 'No, no! Of course not! Nothing like that!' Her eyes darted between the two of them. 'Is that what you thought? Is that what other people thought?' she added hurriedly, in a hushed tone. 'No, it was completely innocent. It was more like having a good friend.

'At some point, I'd mentioned that I always wanted to visit England one day, so we kept in touch. We wrote letters to each other and eventually, this opportunity came up. I was delighted. It was his idea, really. He had some feeling that Celia, who had been living in America for so long, would be more settled, more comfortable, if she had an American dresser. It was what she'd be more used to after working in Hollywood all those years.

'I used the little money I had saved and put it towards the cost of a ticket over here. But Arthur was very kind. He helped to pay the majority of the fare on my behalf.'

'Indeed.' Hugh let a note of disbelief creep into his voice. 'That does seem generous.'

'He is a very generous man, at least he has been to me. As I said, we stayed in touch and I think he thought of me like a family member.' She looked between Bertie and Hugh again, then added, 'He never had any children of his own, of course.'

Constance stopped talking suddenly. She took a sip of the tea in front of her instead.

Bertie watched her closely. He waited for her to replace the cup on the table. 'How old are you, Miss O'Neil?'

'Nineteen. Nineteen and a half, if you wanted to be completely accurate.'

'It's a long way to come for someone your age, isn't it?' said Bertie.

'Yes, I suppose it is. But I've always been a traveller, Mr Carroll. I seem to move around a lot. I was born in California but grew up in Arizona. I was about twelve or thirteen when my family moved to New York. I've never really felt settled anywhere to be quite honest.'

'Do you feel any more settled here?'

'Perhaps. After some more time here, maybe. I was adopted by my parents at birth, you see. I love them very dearly and they love me, but I think, perhaps, that I'll never be able to feel settled anywhere. I have so much that's unknown in my past. There are too many questions that will always be unanswered.'

Bertie studied the youthful face. While still clearly a very young woman, she appeared much more mature and carried the wisdom of someone who was older. She didn't appear sad or even angry at her life's situation, merely resolved that this was the way things were. Perhaps her understated quality was mournfulness. Mournful at the loss of those in her life that she would never know. She quickly took another sip of the tea as an alternative to continuing to talk.

'Is O'Neil your adopted name?' asked Bertie.

'Yes, it is.'

'Do you know your birth name?' asked Bertie.

'I do not. My parents were never told. If they'd known, they would have told me, I'm quite sure of that. They are the most wonderful parents you could ever wish for. I always had everything I could ever need or want. It was an idyllic childhood, really.'

'Perhaps we could return to last night?' said Hugh.

'Of course. What did you want to know?'

'What were your movements after the rehearsal finished?' asked Hugh.

'Robert and I returned to our digs, where we ate. I made a plate of sandwiches for us to share – I suppose he's already told you that our landlady is away? Apparently, that seems to be a regular occurrence at this time of the year, so we've been left to fend for ourselves.'

'How are you finding that?' said Hugh.

'Oh, it's an adventure! I don't think Robert is particularly happy about it, but I don't think I could tell you one thing that Robert *is* ever particularly happy about. I suppose he's been treating me a little like his personal housekeeper, but I don't mind that. I'm a practical person; I enjoy cooking. It suits me just fine.'

'But you've moved out now?' said Bertie.

'I have. Arthur thought it was better, on reflection, that I move in with him. He thinks that I'll be safer there, I suppose. Whether he actually suspects Robert of being a murderer, I couldn't say,' she added hurriedly.

'But he's the type of man that doesn't like to take any risks – I suppose that's why he's managed to be such a successful producer. He's very protective of me, which he shouldn't be, really. I can fend for myself. But I suppose he feels some responsibility for me – he's the one that brought me here, after all.'

'That night,' Hugh continued his questions, 'did you eat or drink anything else?'

'I don't really remember,' she replied. 'Tea, I expect. I know I've drunk plenty of the stuff since I arrived. You Brits seem to love it! I'd never even seen a teapot before I came here.'

'I'm just trying to establish if there was anything you might have eaten or drunk that night that was the same as Robert.'

'Ah, because he was unwell?' she asked, with a smile of realisation.

'Exactly that,' said Hugh, waiting for an answer.

'Yes, I can say for certain that we shared the same plate of sandwiches so if it was the food that upset him, it's very likely that I would have picked up something, too.'

'Triangles or squares?' asked Bertie. When he saw the confused look on Hugh's face, he clarified, 'the sandwiches.'

'You know Mr Carroll, I have no idea. It could have been either. It could have been both.'

'And the tea?' Hugh asked.

'It was all poured from the same pot.'

'Thank you,' said Hugh. 'That's all very helpful.' Hugh jotted down notes in his small notebook. Bertie tried to see what he had written, but it was unintelligible to him.

'Can you tell me what happened when Mr Laughton became unwell?' asked Hugh.

'Well, yes,' replied Constance. 'He just had a bit of a funny turn. Poor Robert, he's not exactly the perfect picture of a healthy man, is he? I suppose I shouldn't say that. It's not polite. He's a nice enough man. I don't think he takes care of himself very well, that's all I mean.

'It was only about five or ten minutes after we'd eaten, although I can't swear to that, you understand. He came over all clammy and sweaty.' Constance hesitated for a moment, then added, 'Well, sweatier than usual.'

'I have to say, that matches up to what I saw in the rehearsal that day. He didn't look like a man that was in full form,' Bertie added.

Hugh nodded to him and then encouraged Constance to continue.

'No, you're right, he wasn't then either.' Constance agreed with enthusiasm. 'I think at the time, I put it down to nerves. Sometimes even these old actors like Robert, who have been around the block a few times, still get nervous as an opening night approaches. It was only during the technical rehearsals when he started to get hot and flustered, you see. When we were in the rehearsal room, he had seemed more or less all right.

'I suppose, once you get on the stage, there are so many additional things to worry about. There's also the heat of the lights, and layers of costume to deal with,' she explained.

'You think, whatever illness he picked up, he was

already suffering the effects of it earlier that day?' said Hugh.

'Well, if that's what Mr Carroll thinks, I'd say it certainly looks that way as well. As I said, I don't think it can be from what we ate. I ate and drank the same as he did, and I was perfectly fine.'

'Okay,' continued Hugh, 'what about the rest of the evening? Can you tell me what happened next?'

'Well, Robert was very insistent that he should come and do the show – I mean, can you imagine? I said absolutely not, he should stay in bed, but he wasn't happy about it, not happy about it at all. He's one of those people who thinks the show should come above everything else. To come above your own health, though? I told him he was being silly. He carried on insisting that the show must go on. He said couldn't bear it if it was cancelled on his account.

'I said that I was sure it wouldn't be a problem for Charlie or Arthur to go on and cover for him. That seemed to calm him down a little. I know it's a horrible thing to say, but we weren't exactly full. Did it really matter? The little audience we did have probably weren't there to see Robert, were they? Now, I didn't say that to his face, of course.

'No – I insisted. He should stay in bed. Eventually, I persuaded him, and I left for the theatre promising that I'd sort everything out, make sure that the show would still go ahead and explain to everyone what had happened.'

'Tell me this, Miss O'Neil. We know that Robert

came over to the theatre later in the evening, so he can't have been completely incapacitated?' said Hugh.

'He was certainly dizzy, nauseous… At that point in time, he wasn't in any condition to be going anywhere. I dare say, with Robert's stubbornness, he may have been able to force himself to stumble down to the theatre. At the time, I certainly wouldn't have thought he could have managed anything more taxing than lying down in a bed.'

'But after ten, maybe fifteen, minutes' rest?'

'I really couldn't say, Inspector. You sometimes see people who have a funny turn for five minutes and can be back to normal in no time at all. Perhaps Robert is one of those people?'

'You don't think he could have been faking it?' said Hugh.

Constance looked surprised at this suggestion. 'Faking it?' she repeated with curiosity. 'Well, that's an intriguing idea. I suppose it's possible. He is an actor, after all. I can't think of any earthly reason why he would pretend, unless he somehow really is the murderer?'

'Back at the theatre. How did everyone take the news?' asked Hugh.

'Oh, there was a bit of a panic,' she replied. 'You would expect that, of course. It took a bit of persuading, but eventually Arthur said he'd go on, he knew the script well enough; he was pretty sure he could cover it. I think Charlie was relieved that he wouldn't have to go on himself. I don't think he's one of those people who relishes the idea of being on the stage. Besides, there's so much for Charlie to do during the show to keep everything running. There really was no choice. It had to be Arthur.'

'Did you know that Arthur had any acting ability? He seemed to do a pretty good job,' said Hugh.

'Acting ability? I didn't really think about it. I suppose he must have, being a director…'

'You'd be surprised,' interjected Bertie with a chuckle.

'I mean, I'm not a particularly good actress myself,' admitted Constance. 'But then, a maid's role is pretty much the same on the stage as it is off. "Fetch me this", "Do that". I was certainly more than qualified to do that. I think Arthur did a great job, in the circumstances. He knew all the lines. He stood in the right place. What more could you ask for?'

'I'd like to ask you about guns, Miss O'Neil,' Hugh said, changing the topic.

'Guns?' she replied, looking a little confused.

'Do you know much about them?'

'You think I know all about them because I'm an American?' she asked. 'Just because I'm an American doesn't mean I grew up in the Wild West, Inspector.'

'Did your family own any guns?'

'Yes,' she replied simply.

'So, you'd know your way around one – how to load and fire one, for example?' Hugh said.

'I suppose I would … if the need arose,' she replied. 'What's this about?'

'Did you spend any time by yourself, near the props table during the show?' asked Hugh.

'You saw the show, didn't you, Inspector?' she replied. 'My entire part requires me to collect things, bring things, whisk them away and so on. All I do, for most of the show, is move to and from that props table.'

'I see.'

'No, Inspector, I don't think you do,' she quickly added in defence. 'At no point am I ever there alone. Charlie's job, as the stage manager, is to make sure I take the right things at the right time. Every time I'm at that props table, I'm very closely supervised by him. So, if you're suggesting that somehow I could have tampered with that pistol without him noticing, you're very much mistaken.'

Hugh closed his notebook and returned it to his jacket pocket.

'Thank you, Miss O'Neil,' he said with a smile. 'You have been incredibly helpful. Of course, there was no reason you would have wanted to kill Celia Hamilton, is there?'

'I think it's pretty clear I have not, Inspector.'

'It's just all this running around after her,' Hugh continued. 'We know she wasn't exactly the easiest person to work for?'

Constance simply smiled in response to Hugh's question. 'You think I could do a job like this without a thick skin?' She seemed as if she was trying to hold in a laugh. 'Not a chance! If people like me couldn't look past some of the histrionics that happen behind the scenes, there'd be murders every night on Broadway!'

Chapter Fourteen

Hugh and Bertie walked down the hill as they left the tearoom and towards the parade, heading back in the direction of the pier. Despite the crisp, chilled air that swirled gently around them, the bright steely sunlight felt warm against Bertie's skin. The light cast a cool tone over everything it touched. It had the strange effect of bleaching the vivid colours of the seaside town around them; everything appeared in shades of blue-grey.

Looking down from their high vantage point, Bertie watched a carriage of the Volk's Electric Railway slowly trundle along, skirting the edge of the beach. It looked like it contained only one solitary customer. To his eyes it looked rather claustrophobic in the special "winter" car, with the passenger sealed in, protected from the elements behind the glass and wood. But then, he had never been particularly fond of very small, enclosed spaces.

Hugh spoke as they walked. 'You never considered – what's the term? – "treading the boards" yourself, Bertie?'

'Ha!' he exclaimed with a smile. 'Not even a bit.'

'Not even a little bit?' Hugh repeated.

'It's just not my thing. Standing up there on the stage, taking all the acclaim, the attention. I know there are some people who live entirely for those moments. Me? I'm happy where I am. I can work in my neat, tidy office. Just me and a typewriter, all by myself. No one looking at me.'

'Do you not get lonely?' Hugh said. The question came tinged with genuine concern.

'I have my secretary. She's always there. I'm not entirely sure what I'd do without her, quite honestly.' Bertie's hands remained in his pockets, but he still gestured freely as he talked, his coat flapping like the wings of a bird. 'Somehow, she takes my sloppily written pages – complete with their spelling mistakes, smudged ink and handwritten corrections scrawled in the margins – and turns them into beautiful pages of perfectly typed text. I find it's quite unnerving, her ability to do that much typing without making a single error or a mistake.'

Together, they continued walking towards the Palace Pier, which they could see stretching out into the ocean ahead of them. Today the sea was calmer, the surface of the water shimmering in the sunlight. Wheeling seagulls passed overhead, scouring the beach below for signs of leftover food from holiday makers. They were rather optimistic. The holidaying crowds had long since departed. At this time of year, the only people venturing onto the beach were fishermen or locals walking their dogs.

Hugh sighed. 'I'm not convinced we've been able to see the full picture of what went on last night.'

'Do you think that someone's been lying to us?' asked Bertie. 'Trying to throw us off the scent?'

'Quite the opposite. I think – at least, for the most part – people have been telling us the truth.'

Bertie smiled, and turned to Hugh as he walked, responding in an astonished tone, 'And that's a bad thing?'

'Perhaps... I think it might mean we've been approaching this from the wrong angle. The problem is, I haven't quite worked out what the new angle should be,' and then he added, with a sparkle in his eyes, 'yet.'

The Marine Parade started to curve a little and began descending towards the entrance to the pier. Hugh stopped for a moment, using the Aquarium building as shelter from the wind to light a cigarette. He took a long draw on it, thought for a moment, and then exhaled. He turned to face Bertie while he leant against the brick wall.

'If we take everything at face value, Robert has to be out of the picture as he was at home. And because the props table was under the watchful eye of Charlie, we can discount anyone who left directly after the rehearsal and didn't return until the performance. That's Arthur, Teddy and Constance.

'The only two people who could have been alone with the gun are Charlie and Jenny. Neither of those two seemed to have had any reason to kill Celia. Neither of them has ever met her before.'

Bertie mulled things over in his own head, trying to make a pattern of the jumble of puzzle pieces that were floating about in it. 'You said that we've been told the truth, for the most part,' he pondered. 'Who are the ones that have been keeping things from us?'

'I've got my theories,' replied Hugh, 'but you tell me… You've been in the interviews with me. What do you think?'

'I think that Teddy was lying,' Bertie said confidently, after a few moments of thought.

'Interesting…'

'That blackmail note. I think he was lying when he said he'd never seen it before. Something about his reaction.'

'Yes,' said Hugh, 'that's exactly what I thought as well.'

Bertie continued turning over the idea of Teddy as a blackmailer in his head.

'What would Teddy need money for?' Hugh asked Bertie.

'Nothing. Not really. Teddy is doing very well for himself, or so it would appear. Of course, there could be any number of hidden vices – he could easily be the type. Problems with gambling, perhaps? He could even be a drug addict. Although these are wild guesses, and he doesn't show any outward signs of that sort of thing.'

'That's the problem with addicts and gamblers. If they're smart enough, they learn how to hide their secrets. To the rest of the world, they can look like they're functioning perfectly well in life,' replied Hugh wisely. 'A friend of mine, on the force, told me that the Secret Service often recruits alcoholics, drug addicts or homosexuals. And that's because they're experts in being able to hide their secrets from the real world. I suppose it makes sense when you think about it.'

'So, you've never been approached by the Secret Service then?' joked Bertie.

'Now, you tell me. I'd be interested in seeing which one of those things you think I am,' said Hugh, in mock offence.

'Look, if Teddy was blackmailing Celia for money, she's no use to him dead,' said Bertie, quickly steering the conversation back towards the case in hand.

Hugh considered Bertie's thought for a moment. 'People can do extraordinary things in the heat of the moment. If they're put under pressure or if they lose their temper… If, perhaps, Celia decided she would no longer continue paying whatever it was that Teddy wanted. Perhaps he panicked? In that kind of situation, someone could easily decide to kill, on impulse. At that point, any sense of good judgement leaves you. You're not acting with thought. You're acting on instinct.'

'But this wasn't a murder carried out in the heat of the moment,' said Bertie. 'It had to be pre-planned. Someone swapped that bullet out, purposefully, in advance of the performance. They had to have done.'

Hugh sighed and then turned to continue his journey down towards the pier. Bertie joined, walking alongside him.

'I'm still not going to rule him out,' said Hugh, turning to Bertie as they walked. 'There's just something about him that I don't quite trust. He's a little too cocky for his own good.'

Bertie smiled, chuckling at Hugh's assessment of

Teddy's character. He wasn't wrong. 'You're right. He is cocky, but does that make him a murderer?'

'You'd be surprised,' said Hugh. 'Murderers are often very cocky people. Murder is easy if you can follow three very simple rules. Only do it once, don't leave any evidence and don't tell anyone.'

'Those rules seem simple enough,' said Bertie.

'You'd be surprised how many times they fall down on the last one. What's the point of getting away with the perfect murder if you can't boast about it? Murderers have egos too – big ones.'

Bertie and Hugh arrived at the entrance to the pier. They were waved through by the constable on duty and continued towards the theatre. After a minute of walking along the sun-bleached boards, Hugh turned to Bertie.

'This play of yours?'

'What about it?'

'How much of the action – where people stand and how they move – did you write? It's all detailed in the script, isn't it?'

'Not always,' replied Bertie.

'But I've seen the odd playscript in my time, just the amateur versions, of course, and they seem to be quite detailed.'

'Amateur dramatics?' said Bertie, in a surprised tone. 'I didn't count you as someone who would be into that sort of thing.'

Hugh smiled at him, amused at his reaction. 'No, unfortunately not. I once had to attend to a murder at a second-hand bookshop. They had a few playscripts on their shelves. I thought why not just thumb through a few pages, out of curiosity.'

'Well, every playwright is different. Some do like to write in a lot of stage direction, some don't. I put it in when it's absolutely necessary. If it's not vital to the working of the plot, I'm more than happy to let the directors and actors come up with most of it. They'll experiment through the course of the rehearsals until they settle on something that feels and looks right. Charlie would have made a note of all the blocking in his prompt-copy.'

'That's the copy of the script he has on his desk?'

'That's exactly it. When they publish the amateur version of the playscript, the "acting edition", very often it will contain those additional stage directions from the original production – and that all gets taken from stage manager's prompt-copy.'

Hugh took a few more steps before speaking again. 'So, this play. Where everyone was standing, it would have been the same from night to night, but not necessarily the same as the original production?'

'That's right. In fact, it would probably be quite different. The same goes for sound effects and lighting. Every director, every actor, wants to put their own spin on a play or a role. All that thunder and lightning at the end of Act One, to make it more dramatic, we didn't have any of that in the original. The staging of the shooting scene too, with everyone on stage, that was quite different too. There could be something in it?'

'How about some amateur dramatics right now, Bertie?' said Hugh with a note of excitement.

'Me and you?'

'Yes, I want to go through any differences between what people should have been doing during the play and what they were actually doing on the night. And you can be my scene partner!'

The theatre, still guarded and undisturbed, was empty. There was always a kind of magic, Bertie thought, to an empty theatre. Perhaps it came from his own, over-romantic, view of the theatre, but there was always seemed to be the lingering memory of past performances locked within the walls of a building. The enthusiastic response of the audiences and the emotions of the performers somehow persisted, encoded in the plaster and lath. Bertie didn't believe in ghosts but being alone in an empty theatre was the one thing that might almost convince him. Sometimes he felt as if he could still hear the reverberation from a roar of laughter or the percussive tapping of the applause from a long-departed audience.

Flipping some switches on a large and slightly scary-looking switchboard, the pair of them managed to turn on some of the lighting battens above the stage. Unable to decipher any of the other equipment – and through fear of electrocution – they decided that, as unflattering as the light cast solely from overhead was, it was at least sufficient to move around the stage without the risk of them falling off the front of it.

An unusual combination of colours splashed across the stage; these had been more carefully balanced in the performance to create a more natural looking light. Dots of red and blue light were splashed haphazardly around the walls of the set. They created weird patterns and textures. The lighting in the centre of the stage was more forgiving, although it still hit their faces at rather an unfavourable angle.

'There's something about the shooting scene that's bothering me. You be Celia this time and I'll be Jenny,' said Hugh.

Hugh and Bertie took up their positions on the stage, Bertie stood just behind the sofa, where Celia had been, and Hugh placed himself between the sofa and the wall.

'Downstage of the French windows. That's what Jenny said, didn't she?' confirmed Hugh. 'The change they made when they got to the theatre – Robert's suggestion. So that would place her about here.' He positioned himself downstage of the window and angled towards Bertie.

'There was something you said yesterday and it's been on my mind. It was about the gun. When did you last fire a gun? Not for a while, right?'

'A gun?' responded Bertie, with slight confusion. 'I don't think I've ever fired a gun.'

'How accurate do you think you'd be?'

'From this distance? I don't know, probably not very. How hard is it? I could probably point it in the right direction, I might even hit something if I was lucky…' He thought about it for a moment, then added, 'If it was a big target.'

'And Jenny. When was the last time that she might have fired a gun, do you think?'

'Well, I expect that she's just like me. I don't see why she would have ever fired a gun before, not before doing this show, anyway.'

'So, let's say that she'd be about as accurate as you. Maybe she'd be able to hit a large target, but with no real accuracy.' Hugh stood still, deep in thought for a moment, until his attention returned to Bertie and he began talking again. 'Would it surprise you to know that you can be hit by a bullet, and it not be fatal?'

Bertie admitted that, yes, that did come as a surprise.

'In fact,' Hugh continued, 'you can be hit by any number of bullets and still not be killed. It can be perfectly survivable.'

'It might be perfectly survivable, but it sounds like you would have to be incredibly fortunate.'

Hugh stopped and was still for a few moments before saying, 'Yes, she was incredibly lucky.'

'Celia?' questioned Bertie. 'But she's dead?'

Hugh rolled his eyes theatrically at his response. 'No. It wasn't Celia Hamilton who was lucky; it was Jenny.'

Now Bertie started to see what Hugh had been suggesting. 'You mean, for someone like Jenny, inexperienced and from that distance. For her to fire a shot that would be fatal...'

'Right through the heart. It's a pretty tough shot to make if you're not practised in the art. Not to add guns, like that little thing she had, aren't exactly the most accurate at the best of times.'

Bertie thought back over the events of yesterday. 'But she was practising,' he said. 'The day of the performance, she stayed behind to rehearse that scene. What do you think? Target practice?'

'Could be,' Hugh replied. He deliberated over the idea for a moment, before eventually speaking. 'Well, it's a thought, at least. But I think we'll leave it as a thought only. I'm not letting it become an idea.' He smiled at Bertie. 'Not yet.'

'But you still consider it unlikely that someone who seems to appear inexperienced with a gun would be able to fire a lethal shot from that distance?'

'I do.'

'And someone, if they swapped the bullet without Jenny's knowledge; they'd be relying on a lot of luck too.'

'Exactly.' Hugh stopped for a moment; his body frozen in thought. Suddenly, his eyes widened, and he sprang to life again. 'Wait here,' he announced before leaving the set through the door.

After only a few seconds or so, Hugh returned. In his hand, he held the red folder that had been sitting on the stage manager's desk. It contained Charlie's prompt-copy for the production.

'Bertie. You said that everything is recorded in here, everything about the performance? Where people stand and what they do?'

'Yes, that's right.'

'So, let's look at it a moment. I want to go through the performance and see what – if anything – was different.'

'You think there's a clue here?' asked Bertie.

'A clue?' Hugh looked at Bertie, his eyes glinting with

excitement. 'Yes. That's exactly what I think we're going to find.'

Hugh lay the book open on the small table that was set in front of the sofa and opened it. Charlie had removed the binding from the printed script and had separated out the individual pages, mounting each one neatly on a sheet of paper. The sheet of paper had a rectangular cut-out in the middle so that both sides of the script were visible.

On other pieces of plain paper, interleaved with the script, there was a handwritten list of any cues that were needed. A ruled line split the page into two columns, in the second of which were all the movements of the actors, recorded neatly in pencil. Sometimes, small diagrams accompanied the notes, with the initials of character names written next to arrows that had been drawn over a sketched plan of the set and the layout of the furniture.

Examining the blocking recorded in the script, Hugh turned the pages slowly. 'Any differences?'

Bertie shook his head, trying his best to use his memory of the performance last night and compare what he had seen with the neat notes in the script. 'Not yet. Not as far as I can see, anyway.'

'Hmm' agreed Hugh, as he returned his gaze to the page. After a few minutes more study, they arrived at the shooting scene. Bertie and Hugh sat a little more upright, invigorated with the expectation of discovery. On this page, would there be some discrepancy or some difference between the script and the performance?

Comparing the notes with their recollection of what

had happened on the night, they found themselves disappointed. From what they could remember, the performance had been completely faithful to the movements recorded in the script.

'Did we miss something?' said Hugh. 'This is exactly the same as the play we saw.'

'Yes, that's what I think too,' replied Bertie sadly. He wasn't quite sure what he had expected. Some glaring differences from the night before, perhaps. But no, there was no clue awaiting them on the page, like fingerprints on a windowsill or a shred of fabric caught on an errant thorn of a rosebush.

Hugh settled back onto the sofa with resignation. 'Well, that's that.' He put his hands behind his head and lay further back, his eyes closed in thought.

Bertie continued flipping through the prompt-copy idly. 'Back to the drawing board, then?' he commented, turning another page.

With his eyes still closed, Hugh replied, 'Not completely, I suppose. But there're still plenty of possible solutions floating around. I can't seem to start narrowing them down, though.'

Bertie, finishing his inspection of the script to the end of the first act, sat back on the sofa joining Hugh. 'Exactly as the script says. It went a little off the rails at the end of the act, but other than that, it was perfect.'

Hugh's eyes snapped open. 'What do you mean "a little off the rails"?'

'Oh, nothing really. Just the timings were a bit off, when people moved and said their lines in relation to the sound effects, little things like that. It's not surprising really, especially with Arthur doing it "off-book". Little things were bound to go wrong at some point, weren't they? He wouldn't be able to get it all perfect.'

Hugh sat upright and turned to Bertie. 'Show me.'

'It really is nothing,' Bertie protested. He sat back up, pointing to the last page of the act. 'In the prompt-copy the sequence of events went like this, Arthur, as the butler, goes to the sofa and says, "Oh no, she's dead," which is then followed by the thunder crash and the windows flying open. All that palaver at the end.'

'Right,' replied Hugh, 'and what actually happened?'

'The way I remember is that Arthur said, "Oh no" then there was the thunder crash and so on, and then he said, "She's dead".'

'And you call that going off the rails? I'm glad I'm not a performer in one of your plays. You seem like a very precise and demanding playwright,' Hugh chuckled.

'I said a little off the rails, if we're being fair. But, as far as I can see, it's the only thing that was different on the night. Perhaps it doesn't mean much at all, but…' Bertie trailed off.

'You think there is another possibility?'

'No,' replied Bertie. But then he reconsidered after a moment. 'It's fantastical, but maybe… Perhaps, if I were writing a play, a work of fiction, there might have been a way … a way I could have written it.'

Chapter Fifteen

Bertie and Hugh were now a familiar sight to the constable keeping guard at the entrance to the pier. He gave a nod of recognition as they exited through the barrier and on to the road. A few of the reporters, who were still waiting for any scrap of information, called Hugh's name, trying to get his attention. Bertie was also surprised to hear his own name called out by one of them, a reporter, perhaps, from the London entertainment scene. Unfortunately, the reflex triggered by hearing your name is a hard one to break. Automatically, he turned but immediately wished he hadn't. Now all the reporters that were gathered around him knew his name and also joined in, cawing like seagulls.

'Mr Carroll, are you assisting with the investigation?' a voice called from somewhere. All Bertie could offer was half a shrug as Hugh grabbed him by the waist, firmly guiding him through the small crowd and across the road. Sensing defeat, they didn't follow.

'Oh well,' said Hugh, 'I suppose you couldn't stay my little secret forever…'

After a few steps, Hugh stopped and turned back to face the pier entrance.

'Strange, isn't it?' said Hugh. 'There are no posters at this end of the pier.'

Bertie turned around to join Hugh. 'That's true,' he agreed. 'There's room for one,' he said, noticing two empty hooks from which a sign would usually be hung. 'Perhaps the cost of hiring a sign writer was an expense too far for Arthur. A bit of a shame really, it might have helped fill a few more of the seats.'

'It makes me wonder, though. As we've been walking around the town, have you noticed *any* adverts?' Hugh questioned. 'Posters in shop windows, that sort of thing? This is Celia Hamilton, after all. Where were the legions of crazed fans, the autograph hunters?'

Bertie racked his brain for a moment, trying to recall if he had seen any publicity for the play. 'No,' he answered, eventually. 'You're right. Perhaps it might be worth looking in a local paper? They might have placed some adverts there or at least posted an entry in the listings. No wonder they didn't have much of an audience. I'm surprised anyone knew that the show was even on!'

Hugh turned back, continuing away from the pier. He gestured to Bertie, inviting him to walk next to him as they ambled along the pavement. 'Is that how a try-out like this would normally be done? On the quiet?' he asked.

'I suppose it could be,' replied Bertie, 'if they wanted to keep it discreet for Celia's sake? I can understand that they might want to make sure that it was kept out of the national press, the London papers. They might not have wanted anyone getting hold of the story – that way you can still announce the West End run as a bit of a surprise. Launch it with a bang. You'd still need to advertise locally if you wanted to get a half-decent audience in. You would want enough people coming to see it so you could get a good read on their reactions and get any valuable feedback from them, otherwise what's the point of a doing a try-out in the first place?'

Hugh headed away from the seafront, crossing the road.

'Where are we off to now?' quizzed Bertie, following obediently after.

'I think we should look in at the Town Hall,' Hugh said.

'And what will we find there?' Bertie wondered aloud.

'Policemen, I hope,' said Hugh. 'That's where the station is. Thought it would be a good idea to pop in and see the local bobbies. Let them know how we're getting on.'

'Do we have anything to report?' said Bertie.

'Not unless anything has come of the idea you had at the theatre just now?'

'No. I seem to have lost all confidence in it,' Bertie admitted. It was one thing, sharing your theories with an old school friend; sharing them with the local police force was something else altogether. 'I'm still working on it though.'

After walking for a few more minutes, the Town Hall

came into view, along with the familiar sight of the traditional blue lamp with "Police" written on all four sides.

'I think we've found the right place.' Hugh nodded his head towards the lamp. 'It also has the distinction of being the only place in the country where a chief constable was murdered in his own station,' he added cheerily, before opening the double doors and walking in.

'Recently?' Bertie added, concerned, as he tentatively followed behind. He was left waiting for an answer that never came.

Hugh strode confidently in, speaking briefly and professionally with the sergeant on the desk. He gave a nod in reply and led them both down a short corridor where he rapped sharply on a door.

Half opening the door, the constable stepped inside and muttered some words of introduction that Bertie couldn't decipher.

'You can go right in,' the constable announced, standing aside to let the two of them enter. Behind them, Bertie heard the door click shut.

'It's about time,' said a polite voice. 'I've been wondering when you'd show up. Please take a seat.'

They did so, each taking one of the two wooden chairs placed in front of a highly polished desk. It had been darkened so much by the layers of varnish that had been added to it over the years, it was almost impossible to see what type of wood it had originally been made from. It was plain, neat and functional – seemingly very much like the man who was seated behind it.

'A pleasure to meet you, Chief Constable Bailey,' said Hugh. Bertie wondered if Hugh already knew the name of the officer or if he had simply read it from the triangular nameplate sitting on the desk.

'Edwin Bailey.' The officer introduced himself and shook Hugh by the hand. 'Your reputation precedes you, Inspector,' he said, straightening the papers on his desk.

Bertie noticed that everything was laid out on the table top at perfect right angles from each other. Everything about this man seemed precise, from the spotless uniform to the neatly trimmed, thin, white moustache that he sported on his upper lip. Even the way he spoke was clipped, as if each word had been measured with a ruler and cut to an exact length before allowing it to be expressed aloud.

'It's a pleasure to have one of Scotland Yard's finest detectives here in Brighton,' he finished, allowing himself a thin smile. Edwin Bailey appeared to be one of those people who kept his emotions neatly compartmentalised and seemed to dispatch them with the same efficiency in which he ran his office. 'Even so, if I'd been on duty last night, I'm not sure I would have handed over the reins to this investigation so freely.'

'Of course,' Hugh responded, 'it only came about because I was present at the time of the murder. I daresay you could have handled the matter just as well without me.'

'Oh, yes?' replied the chief constable, who seemed to suddenly relax a little more in Hugh's presence now that he had made this graceful concession.

'Yes,' Hugh asserted. 'I have complete confidence in the Brighton Police Force. It was only that I was there on the night, a first-hand account of what happened—'

'Well, that's very kind of you to say, Inspector,' said the chief constable, gently cutting Hugh off. 'We are also glad to have your expertise available to us and because of it, I expect that this matter will be put to rest swiftly. We do consider ourselves right on the cutting edge of technology here in Brighton. Over the last year or so, our experiments with using the wireless to communicate to our policemen have been met with great success. In fact, this summer we were able to issue a radio set to each of our constables on patrol for the first time.

'It has been a very efficient way of getting information out quickly to the men on the ground. I expect that many police forces will adopt the system in the coming years, but we're proud to say that Brighton was the first.'

Hugh seemed to be listening intently to what the chief constable had to say, although Bertie had to admit he wasn't paying as close attention. He was taking in the surroundings of the room, tracing the square meander border around the frosted windows of the office. The word "POLICE" was written in the centre, although from Bertie's point of view – inside the building – the text appeared backwards. Hearing his name said aloud brought his attention, sharply, back into the conversation.

'This is Bertie Carroll,' said Hugh, introducing him. 'He's been assisting me with the case.'

The chief constable gave him a piercing look, weighing him up. 'Now, I wouldn't normally advocate the involvement of an amateur detective,' he stated, in his matter-of-fact style, 'although I'm sure you have your reasons. In the past, we've found them to be quite a nuisance, something of a hindrance rather than a help. Not to say that's the case here.' The curt consolation was directed at Bertie.

'Certainly not, Sir,' said Hugh proudly. 'Mr Carroll has one of the finest minds in the respect of murder. And some quite good reviews too.' He couldn't resist adding the final comment.

'Ah,' the chief constable replied, with realisation. '*That* Bertie Carroll, are we? Well, if the inspector considers you a valuable associate, who am I to disagree with him?'

'A pleasure to meet you,' said Bertie, who couldn't think of anything else to say in response. He noticed that the policeman didn't offer him a handshake like he had previously done with Hugh.

'Well,' said the chief constable, unlocking a desk drawer and retrieving a small stack of files. 'Why don't you take a look at some of the background we've managed to dig out for you.'

The stack of folders was secured together with a thick rubber band. On the front, tucked under the band, there was a sheet of paper covered with handwritten notes. Bertie couldn't interpret any of the words upside down, but the writing looked impeccably neat; he assumed it was the chief constable's own.

'Now, Arthur Cochran,' he started, reading from his list. 'Not much there. He's a familiar name, of course. I believe we've had several of his shows tour through here. London based, so that would be in your back yard, so to speak, Inspector. Same with Teddy and the young American girl, both unknown to us.'

Hugh nodded, encouraging the chief constable to continue.

'Jenny and Charlie are both locals. Now, there's nothing to say as far as the boy is concerned...'

'But Jenny?' probed Hugh.

'Well, there's an interesting thing. There was a sad case, some eleven years ago now. It was one of the productions at The Grand Theatre, North Road. I'm afraid to say a young girl died unexpectedly during the run.'

'Murder?' interjected Bertie.

'Now let's not get too carried away, Mr Carroll,' he stated firmly. Edwin Bailey's tone hadn't changed, but Bertie got the distinct impression that he had just received a telling off.

'No, the whole thing was put down to an accidental overdose,' the chief constable clarified. 'For whatever reason, she and some of the other girls had started dabbling in some kind of dope.

'Of course, there was a thorough investigation at the time, but as far as we could see, there was nothing suspicious about the death. A tragic accident is what was concluded.'

'But what does this have to do with Jenny, Sir?' asked Hugh. 'She wouldn't have been old enough, surely?'

'No,' the constable agreed. 'Not Jenny. It was her father. Seems that he was the one pushing the stuff on those poor girls. Apparently, that sort of thing had been going on for years, under our noses. He was a regular on the crew at The Grand and this was his way of making a little money on the side. Every few weeks, with a new show coming through, there would be a fresh batch of clients for him to try and sell to. Like I said, a sad case. It reflected very badly on Brighton and on the local theatre community. A very sad time.

'Now, it all came out later on. He was up to his ears in gambling debts – not that it excuses things, of course. A father, trying his best to earn back enough money to raise his daughter. One wonders if he thought he would win big on the horses and give her everything she'd ever dreamed of.'

'And the mother,' interjected Hugh. 'What about her?'

'There never was a mother, I'm afraid,' the chief constable said, consulting his notes. 'According to what I have here, it looks like she died in childbirth. The father raised the child by himself. There was an aunt in Saltdean, it seems. She was always there to help and when the father was sent away to prison, she looked after Jenny. Presumably she still does to this day.'

'He didn't return to Brighton after his prison sentence?' questioned Hugh.

'Not as far as we know. Seems to have vanished off the face of the earth.'

'I wonder if Jenny knows about all this?' said Bertie.

'You'd have to ask her that, I suppose,' replied the chief constable. 'I expect she must know some of it, at least. Stories like that cast long shadows. People talk about them for years after. Very long memories people have, don't they? Still, it does make things more interesting for you.'

'I suppose so,' said Hugh. 'Although, does that make Jenny more likely to be a murderer?'

'Well, you never know,' commented the chief constable. 'Criminal tendencies can run in families, depending on their upbringing. If you come from a bad lot, I find that it often gets passed down the line. It's a sad cycle. Although, I'm not saying that's the case here, but we do see it. Now, that's not the only interesting thing.'

'It's not?' Bertie sounded surprised.

'In the records from the investigation, we found a witness statement,' he revealed. 'The show, when the girl died, had an actor performing in it by the name of Robert Laughton.'

'You're joking!' exclaimed Bertie.

The chief constable seemed entirely unmoved by Bertie's reaction.

'Was there any indication that he might have had something to do with the girl's death?' added Hugh.

'As I said, there was nothing suspicious about the death,' replied the chief constable. 'It was just an unfortunate accident. But still – I suppose funny isn't the right word – all these years later…'

Hugh and the chief constable continued to talk over some of the finer details of the case while Bertie tried to quietly contemplate how these new revelations affected their investigation.

Unfortunately, there was nothing more the chief inspector could give them. Jenny and Charlie were the only two Brighton locals. As far as the police records went, there was nothing else to add regarding the other members of the company.

The trio said their goodbyes with Constable Bailey's typical crisp efficiency and, only moments later, Bertie and Hugh found themselves standing outside in the daylight.

'Well, that was informative,' said Bertie.

'Yes,' replied Hugh, 'it was. It gives us plenty of things to think about.'

'Do you think all that stuff in the past, with Robert and Jenny's father, could be related to Celia's murder?'

Hugh sighed. 'I don't know yet. I don't see how that would lead to Celia being involved, but you never know what we might uncover. Of course, it could be one great big coincidence.'

'I thought there was no such thing as coincidences.'

'Only sometimes,' said Hugh. The hint of a smile flashed across his features.

'What he said about criminal tendencies running in the family? Do you think there's any truth in that?'

'I don't know if that makes her any more likely to be a murderer,' replied Hugh. 'There might be something in it. She was young, and he was an absent father. Could she still be somehow connected to the drug world?'

'And if we think Robert was drugged?' Bertie interjected.

'Could be... But it seems a bit thin. Besides, you wouldn't need access to hard drugs to make someone ill for a few hours.'

'God!' Bertie suddenly exclaimed. 'She made us all tea!'

'Jenny?' asked Hugh.

'Yes. During the break in the rehearsal, she offered to make us all tea.'

'You think she could have slipped something into Robert's cup?'

'There's no reason why not,' said Bertie, trying to recall the details of yesterday's events. 'We were all chatting away, distracted. She could have done anything without us noticing.'

'Well, that's very interesting,' said Hugh. 'What's also interesting is why Robert never mentioned any of this to us.'

'You think he's hiding something?' said Bertie.

'He might be. Something like that – the death of a young girl, on a show you're working on – it wouldn't be something you'd be likely to forget in a hurry, is it?'

The two of them stood in quiet contemplation for a while until Hugh noticed that Bertie was looking intently at him.

'Sorry,' said Bertie, his focus broken. 'I just realised something very important.'

'What's that?' asked Hugh eagerly.

'I have no idea what you look like in a police uniform.'

Hugh laughed. 'I'm afraid it's been a while. Only special occasions nowadays. Also,' he added, 'you would have been very disappointed. In my years as a constable in uniform, I'm ashamed to say I never looked as well turned out as our friend Edwin Bailey, back there.'

Chapter Sixteen

Bertie looked out through the gently curved bay window, across Regency Square. Even on a dull day like today, the crisp expanse of grass in the centre of the square was a deep verdant green.

Near the King's Road end of the square sat a war memorial with a bronze trumpeter perched atop it. From his high-up position, the soldier could look outwards, casting his gaze over the West Pier that stretched out in front of him and the vast expanse of ocean beyond.

Arthur was at the door to the room, his back to the large windows, thanking the proprietor for bringing up refreshments for them. A Royal Doulton tea set, with its Art Deco influences, had been placed on a low table that sat in the centre of the room. The octagonal-shaped cups were a bright shade of yellow with alternate panels overlaid in gold gilt. Each one sat on a matching saucer; Bertie noticed that the patterns had been carefully lined up between the two.

After closing the door, Arthur set about the elaborate business of making tea while he spoke.

'How's the investigation going?' he asked as he spooned sugar into his cup. He gestured, using the teaspoon in the direction of Bertie, then Hugh, by way of asking if they would like sugar in their tea. They both declined with a wave of their hands.

'Well, it's ongoing,' replied Bertie, as Arthur lay a cup of tea down on the table. Bertie walked over to the chair nearby and sat in front of it. 'There are plenty of possibilities, but the trick – as I'm learning, being a good student – is we have to work methodically eliminating them one by one. Then, eventually, we will arrive at the solution.'

'So, you're making yourself useful then!' Arthur emitted a small laugh. 'Yes, I thought you would be. Theatre can often be its own little world, with its own little language. At the very least, I thought you might be able to act as an interpreter to the inspector!'

Arthur placed the second cup of tea in front of Hugh, who sat next in the chair to Bertie. Arthur, however, did not take one of the remaining seats, but elected to stay standing. He balanced his cup on the mantelpiece. The teacups were pretty enough that it didn't look out of place, nestled there between a carriage clock and a vase of spills.

'Well then, ask away. I'll do my best to answer any questions you have,' he said eagerly.

'Tell me about Celia,' Hugh asked. 'Can you fill me in on your background together?'

'There's not really much to tell.' Arthur saw Bertie raise a disbelieving eyebrow in his direction. 'Well, okay.

There are plenty of stories I *could* tell, but in the main, there really isn't that much to say. It was a successful, happy marriage, for a time.'

'But only for a time,' stated Hugh.

'For most of the time.' Arthur sighed before continuing, recollecting. 'Celia was young and beautiful. She still is … was beautiful,' he added with a tinge of sadness. 'And we were very much in love, right until the end. We both were, I do believe that. I think, perhaps, that those looking in from the outside saw an ambitious young actress going after an older producer who was beginning to make a name for himself. From that, they drew the wrong conclusions.'

'They thought you were being played?' Bertie asked. 'That she was using you to further her own career?'

'Yes. Unfortunately, there were some that did think that. There were many people who said it behind our backs. Plenty more said it to our faces. But I don't believe she was ever using me. Now of course she would benefit from her association with me; that was natural. There were occasions when I would take a risk by using her in a role instead of a more established actress, but that's only because I knew she could do it. I believed in her. She was an incredible performer, you know. No one else could match her in that regard. Her acting style was always so natural.

'There were also plenty of times when she didn't get the job. She would still fight me for those jobs, lobby me, if you will, but she still respected my judgement as a producer. Once the decision was made, she might be angry but that was to be expected. She would always be disappointed when she missed out on a role, but she never held a grudge over the choices I had to make. Not once.

'You've seen her be controlling, manipulative, overbearing – and perhaps she was all those things. It was not an easy life, living with her. But, still, it was built on a foundation of love between us. I can promise you that.'

Hugh glanced at Bertie. He had not expected Arthur to declare – so openly – his love for Celia. From the expression on Bertie's face, it was clear that he hadn't been expecting it either.

'But it didn't last? You did eventually split from each other?' asked Hugh.

'We did.' A hint of regret flashed briefly across Arthur's face. 'The simple truth was that we wanted very different things. She was an ambitious actress and she'd always set her sights on Hollywood. I was becoming a very successful producer in London, but I had no intention of leaving that behind and starting over again in America. She wouldn't have that. When it came to her love for me and her ambition for herself, it was the ambition that was always going to win. She would let nothing stand in her way.

'Maybe I should have gone,' he added sadly. 'But these are the decisions that you carry with you for life. Perhaps the ambitions I had for the work I wanted to do in London, that was my equivalent. I let that win.'

'You said you wouldn't be able to produce your shows in America?' said Hugh. 'But you have gone on to produce shows since – in New York, for example.'

'Ah,' replied Arthur, 'hindsight is a wonderful thing.

It's very easy to look back now, when we've both managed to turn our careers into the successes they are today, but it wasn't like that back then. Yes, we were doing well, but we weren't well established yet. One false move, just one bad show, and it could have easily been curtains for either one of us. It still could. That worry never leaves you. You're only as good as your last show and investors will only tolerate so many flops before they lose confidence in you.'

'It would have been sensible for her to try to line up work before she left for America, wouldn't it?' asked Hugh.

'Of course,' agreed Arthur.

'But she wasn't able to do that, in the end?' pushed Bertie.

Arthur thought a moment before he began to speak. 'Before she went, she used to tell me about all the opportunities she'd been offered. She said she had a year's worth of work ready and waiting for her when she arrived.

'I don't know whether it was false confidence or whether she was trying to convince me, to convince herself. What actually transpired, when she got there, was it took a much longer time for her to land her first job. I don't know how long it was in the end, probably more than a year before she got her first big role and then, well… After that, the rest is history of course.'

'You never got a divorce? You're still married now, then?' questioned Hugh.

'Well, yes,' replied Arthur, who seemed to surprise himself at the answer. 'I suppose we are. We've been separated – living apart – for so long, I never really think of us as married. But strictly, in a legal sense, yes we still are.

'There was never any question of a divorce, of course. Celia wouldn't have wanted the scandal – not that she'd be the first Hollywood actress to get remarried. She never took my name, not professionally. She was always Celia Hamilton. Some people would have known, in industry circles, that we were married for all this time, but publicly … I don't think I even made it as a footnote in any one of the hundreds of articles that have been written about her. Our life in London was well in the past by the time she started getting her big roles.'

Bertie shuffled forward in his seat; it proved harder than he expected it to be given the cushion was remarkably soft. 'But that would mean that you would be in line to receive her inheritance? Isn't that how it works, Hugh?'

Hugh nodded in response and Arthur chuckled.

'Bertie!' Arthur declared. 'You always were able to sniff out the best motives!'

Hugh seemed less inclined to find the humorous side to the situation. 'Of course, it depends on the will. But it's a motive, isn't it?' he pushed.

Arthur's smile faded with a slight "Hmph" and his expression turned to one of thought. 'You know, I have absolutely no idea. I don't know if she even had a will, let alone what the contents of it were. I rather expect that I've been disinherited, quite frankly.'

'So it wasn't exactly an amicable separation?' suggested Hugh.

Arthur took a few steps forwards, towards Hugh. 'Now look here,' he said, somewhat angrily. 'I don't like what you're suggesting here. I have no need for money. I've done very well for myself. I'm certainly not the wealthiest producer there is in this industry, not by a long stretch, but I do all right for myself. She knew that. It's not a question of amicability. I'm sure she'd have rather left it to one of the charities she supports than to me.'

Arthur sighed loudly before settling down in one of the empty chairs. 'There really is no reason why I would want to see her dead. I put her in my play, after all. I was hoping that it would be a great success and go on to make me a decent amount of money. Without her in it, no one will come to see this play.' After a brief pause, Arthur caught sight of Bertie, forgetting that he was the playwright and added apologetically: 'No offence.'

'None taken,' replied Bertie, who held his hand up with polite submission. 'But I'm intrigued to know, why this play? Why this time and place?'

Arthur remained silent for a few moments before answering. 'She took an awful lot of convincing, you know. Celia, I mean. She wasn't keen on the idea, not at the start. I think she thought that returning to the UK, doing a theatre show … somehow it was an admission that her career was starting to take a turn. I said to her, it's not like that at all. I knew it would be hard to get her to come round to the idea, but I persisted.'

'And she did come round to the idea in the end?' said Bertie.

'Oh, yes.'

'You didn't have to pressure her in any way? Use

something from your past together to push her, to convince her?'

'What exactly are you suggesting?' asked Arthur, with a confused expression on his face.

'Blackmail, Mr Cochran,' said Hugh. 'We know that she'd received at least one blackmail note that she kept.'

'That's a ridiculous notion,' replied Arthur, offended. 'The fact that anyone would try to blackmail Celia at all, let alone that I would have done it.'

'But it's what happened,' said Bertie. 'We found the note. Someone must have been sending them.'

'Did she have enemies?' added Hugh.

'Of course not,' replied Arthur. 'Professional rivalries at the most, but nothing serious. Jealous actors who were hungry for success, perhaps. But she didn't have enemies. She might have been slightly abrasive from time to time, but underneath it all she wasn't all that bad. I promise you that.'

'So you convinced her by other means?' asked Hugh.

'Money! Those were the "other means". I convinced her all right, but it didn't come cheap! I had to make quite a considerable offer in the end. Nothing like the kind of figure she'd command for being in one of her films, but it was still quite a significant amount for a producer in the theatre, like me.'

'What about Brighton,' Bertie continued, 'the out-of-town try-out? Whose idea was that?'

'Hers,' Arthur answered quickly, then changed his mind. 'Mine. I think both of us thought it was a good idea to do a test run away from the limelight. Despite their outward appearance, the talent and confidence of actors is tragically fragile. On a stage or a movie set, they have their characters and their personas to hide behind – a mask, if you will. But behind the scenes, they can be incredibly vulnerable.

'Celia would never have wanted to put herself in a position where she might risk embarrassment in some way. This was a way of ensuring that she could build her confidence before we took the show into town, really make a success of it. I knew I could get the theatre cheaply this time of year...'

Bertie interrupted as Arthur's words trailed away. 'The transfer, the moving of the show into London, were you counting on that?'

'Yes,' Arthur replied, simply.

'To make back the money you invested in the show?'

'Of course.'

'Even with all the cost-saving tricks you've used?' said Bertie. 'The second-hand set, calling in a favour from Teddy, using Jenny, a local girl, with very little experience or expectations for a salary. You've even gone down the route of using a significantly cut down stage crew, trying to run the whole thing with only one stage manager and the cast pitching in with sound effects.'

Arthur smiled at Bertie's astuteness. 'You should have been a producer, you know,' said Arthur, as he stood from his chair, placing his hands in his pockets. He gave a loud sigh. 'You must have a producer's eye if you were able to notice all that. Even then, despite my best efforts to save money, this will still end up costing me a fair amount. Celia's fee, as I mentioned, was quite considerable. I also had to pay the travel expenses of getting her here in the first place and as you would expect, Celia Hamilton only travels first-class.

'Then again, that's the risk of being a producer. Sometimes you gamble and you lose, sometimes you gamble and you win, and when you win in theatre, your winnings can be quite significant. But are these things worth the risk? Was it all worth it?' Arthur let the question hang in the air, before quietly answering it himself. 'Of course.'

'It wasn't just Celia Hamilton's expenses you covered for her travel over here. There was also the maid, Constance,' said Hugh.

'Yes, that was indeed a cost,' replied Arthur. 'Not quite as much as Celia, you understand.'

'But all the same, that's still a significant expense if you're trying to save money, isn't it?'

Arthur looked at Hugh in silence for a moment before answering his question. 'It was a sweetener. Part of the deal. An American dresser, for someone who was used to America, used to the American ways for the past two decades or so. I thought it would help settle Celia in here a little more. Anything to make her feel more comfortable. Anything to convince her to do the job.'

'And did it?' interjected Hugh.

'Evidently she was convinced; she did the job.'

Hugh leant forward a little in his chair. 'Your relationship with Miss O'Neil,' he asked, 'how would you classify it?'

'Classify it?' repeated Arthur with a chuckle. 'What's there to classify about it? Of course, I'm fond of the girl, but that's about as far as it goes. She had rather an unsettled upbringing, moving all over the place during her childhood. Unfortunately, there are plenty more with a tougher upbringing than hers.

'Young as she is,' Arthur continued, 'she seems very assured about what she wants from life. One of those things she was assured about was visiting Britain one day. There was no way that someone in her position, with her income … well, she'd never have been able to afford the ticket herself.

'Being the old sentimental fool I am, I thought I could help out. Kill two birds with one stone, if you will. I could pay for her ticket over here and get my American dresser.'

'It was a very generous gesture of yours,' commented Bertie.

'Yes,' he replied, 'I suppose it was.'

Arthur returned to his chair and, with a long breath out, he was seated again.

'She's moved in here now, hasn't she?' asked Hugh.

'That's right, well I didn't want her staying with a mur—' Arthur stopped himself short of completing the full sentence.

'That's who you think did it then?' said Bertie.

'Well, it looks that way to me. It all fits, don't you think? I don't see who else could have done it. It was either him or Jenny, wasn't it? There's no way it could be anyone else. Now, that illness could very easily be Robert putting on an act, couldn't it? You've said yourselves, he's the only person unaccounted for that night; everyone else was on stage.'

'You think he could have sneaked into the theatre at

some point and swapped out the bullets?' questioned Hugh.

'I don't know,' replied Arthur. 'Why not? Now, Jenny could have done it; she might have her reasons. Maybe there's some hidden background to her that I don't know about. Not like Robert…' Arthur trailed off.

'Wait, what do you mean, "Not like Robert"?' interjected Bertie in a rush. 'Did he have a reason why he might want Celia dead?'

Arthur shifted uncomfortably in his seat. 'It's just a small thing,' Arthur admitted, 'but now, when you put everything together, it starts to look a bit different, doesn't it?'

'Go on,' said Hugh.

Arthur took a deep breath before beginning his story.

'Celia and Robert were in a show together – not one of mine, by the way – but it was a big show. It was a huge deal, a big break – not only for Celia, but for Robert as well. It was a good role, one that could have made his career.

'The play had terrible reviews. It didn't do well. It went against all the expectations it had going in. Everyone thought it would turn into the hit of the season but, alas, that wasn't the case. Robert was particularly singled out by the critics as being… How can I put it delicately? Not that great. In my opinion, he wasn't all that bad, but the hopes were so high for that show and for the people in it. It was always going to fall short.

'Celia, on the other hand … well, she always knew how to play the system. She had built a relationship with the critics. She'd have dinner with them or take them out for drinks. Nothing improper, you understand, but she'd be able to sweet-talk them. For the most part, she'd always be able to secure herself favourable notices. She played the game well and she almost always won.

'Robert didn't see it like that. I think he felt that Celia had cheated him out of those good reviews, that he was somehow cheated out of a career and that he'd have to resign himself to playing vicars and butlers – something which he does very well, by the way. Nothing to turn your nose up at, if you ask me. I think he's always blamed Celia for that in some way, that she hurt his chances. Always held it against her. That's why it was strange…'

'What was strange?' asked Hugh.

'Well, he *wanted* to be in the play. He asked me. I didn't think anything of it at the time – I needed a butler and here was one ready made. I said I couldn't pay very much, but he said that didn't matter. He just needed a job to tide him over for a few weeks.'

'But for him to murder her?' said Bertie. 'You really think that's something he's capable of?'

'Someone did though,' replied Arthur, 'didn't they?'

'It just seems like a long time to bear a grudge, that's all,' said Bertie. 'I'll admit he's not become the huge success that he might have dreamed of, but at least he's been in very steady employment all these years. Most actors can't say that, can they?'

'Do you think he really may have been responsible?' asked Hugh.

'I don't know. I'm saying it's a possibility,' said Arthur. 'Even so, it seemed likely enough to me that I thought I should move Constance into a room here. Just in case, you understand.'

'I think that's all we need from you for now. We may want to talk to you again at some point,' said Hugh, rising from his chair. Bertie followed his lead and did the same.

'I wouldn't worry about that. I don't think any of us are planning on leaving anytime soon,' said Arthur. He ushered the two of them to the door. 'Anything I can do to help, let me know. I want to get to the bottom of this as much as you do.'

Arthur opened the door, letting Hugh out into the corridor.

Bertie stopped on the way out. 'Don't worry Arthur, what is it the butler says in Act Two? "We will find our murderer before the day is out!" That's right, isn't it?'

'Yes,' mumbled Arthur, sounding a little disheartened. 'Something like that...'

As Hugh and Bertie exited into the corridor, the door closed softly behind them.

Chapter Seventeen

The round face that appeared in the doorway looked startled. Her eyes blinked twice. The first was to adjust to the light, the second time was in confusion.

'Mrs Saunders?' said Hugh.

'I am she.'

'I'm Inspector Chapman from Scotland Yard. This is my associate, Mr Carroll,' he added, with a nod at Bertie. 'Can we come in for a moment?'

'If you're after Charlie, he's not here,' she said bluntly. 'Although you're welcome to come in if you want, I expect he'll be along soon.'

'That would be great.'

On hearing Hugh's response, her face transformed into a wide smile and seemed positively enthused to have two such distinguished guests all to herself. She turned, beckoning the pair of them to follow her in. 'Of course, I know all about you, Mr Carroll,' she called over her shoulder as they walked down the small hallway into a bright kitchen.

'You do?' Bertie replied.

'Oh yes,' she said cheerily. 'You could say I'm quite a fan. We all love a good murder, don't we!' Suddenly her smile vanished, and her mood changed as she realised the seriousness of the situation. 'Goodness me, I am sorry! I mean a good murder mystery, not real murders, because of course…' Flustered, her words trailed off.

'That's quite all right, Mrs Saunders, I understand completely,' said Bertie giving reassurance, as he realised that the end of her sentence would never come.

A tentative smile crept back onto her face, but her cheeks were now slowly reddening. 'Oh good,' she said, although she tried to temper her enthusiasm from then on. 'I saw one of yours on tour at the Theatre Royal, end of last year I think it was. And I've seen one or two of them in London as well. *Death Comes at the Close* would it have been? Charlie sorted out the tickets for me. He's done quite a few shows up in London now.'

'That's quite a commute,' commented Bertie.

'Well, when he's up there he stays with friends or other people he knows, most of the time. Can't be going up and down on the train all the time. He'd have nothing left to show for it after the fare. Of course, he comes back on weekends when he can; he's a good boy like that.'

'Is he?' mused Bertie automatically. She seemed to take this as a signal to elaborate more and the words began to tumble out of her again.

'Oh yes, a very good boy. We're very proud of him, you know. We're a very theatrical family, after all.'

'You are?' questioned Bertie, who was now genuinely interested in the family's theatrical roots. As Charlie's mother began talking again, he caught a look from Hugh. It seemed clear he thought that they should really start getting to the point.

'Yes. Well, my father used to be the Master Carpenter at the Royal years ago. And Charlie's dad, he's a Dayman at the Hippodrome. That's where he is now and that's where we met. You wouldn't know it, because I'm not much to look at now, but I used to be a dancer there. Not much of a mover now, am I,' she joked, 'but of course, that was a long time ago. It was a lot of fun, even though I'm not sure I was ever very good at it.'

'Oh, I'm sure that's not true!' exclaimed Bertie lightly. Now the slightly over-the-top mannerisms and sheer exuberance of the woman in front of them made sense. There was something about performers, even those who had long retired from the art, they still always loved to perform.

Before she could start talking again, Hugh began. 'Well, Mrs Saunders—'

'Mrs Saunders?' she responded cheerfully. 'No, you can call me Jill.'

'Well, okay then, Jill,' Hugh began again. 'We'd like to confirm Charlie's movements on the day of the murder.'

'Of course, of course,' she brushed it off. 'Now then, can I get you a cup of tea? Sit down, sit down,' she gestured with both hands at the kitchen table. It was small, rectangular, with a red and white tablecloth that had been neatly pressed. Before they could decline, cups and saucers were being rattled out of a nearby cupboard.

'We're fine, Mrs Saunders. Jill.' Hugh tried to interject over the noise. 'Honestly.'

'Oh, that is a shame,' she said, closing the cupboard. She picked up her own half-drunk mug from next to the sink and brought it over to the table where she sat. 'Well, anything I can help you with.'

'Last night, your son came back here?' asked Hugh.

'Yes, that's right. Sausages it was, if you have to know. It's not right doing an opening night on an empty stomach now, is it?'

'Did anyone else eat with you?'

'No, just us. Harry – that's his dad – he wouldn't be back until later. That's the problem with the theatre, isn't it? Throws your mealtimes right off. You either end up eating far too early or halfway into the night. How are us housewives supposed to cope?' she asked. It sounded like she really wanted an explanation from one of them. 'In, sit down, eat, out again. That's how it was. There's no time on opening nights. Lots of things to be done. I'm sure he doesn't eat properly when he's up in London. How can he? Well, luckily, he's got his mum down here for this one.'

'And how was this one?' asked Bertie. 'Did you talk about the show yesterday evening?'

'Oh, they work him too hard. They've got him doing the job of about four people down there. He was telling me about the technical rehearsals. Seems like a nightmare! Very slow progress, but they got there – my Charlie always makes sure of that. Of course, these shows are so very technical now, aren't they? All these sound effects and lighting. Seems like that Arthur is very demanding, knows exactly what he wants. Well, that's all very well, but unless you've got a good stage manager to hold it all together, you could be in a world of trouble.'

'Did you notice if he had a key with him?' asked Hugh, when the torrent of words had finally come to a stop.

'Key?' she repeated with a blank expression. She blinked twice. Clearly, there were no more words left to come.

'Yes, Mrs Saunders. We believe he had a key that unlocked a safe in his possession,' Hugh suggested.

'A key?' she repeated again, in the same dumbfounded tone as last time. 'A key to a safe?' She looked confused. 'I don't know how it works in your household, Inspector, but I don't make people turn out their pockets on my doorstep. How on earth should I know what he's got in his pockets? I ask you!' she exclaimed with a roll of her eyes.

'No, I see your point,' Hugh conceded. 'It would have helped us out a great deal, so it was worth a try.'

'I suppose there's no harm in asking,' she seemed to agree. 'Lost it, did he?'

'No,' Hugh said with a sigh. 'Why do you say that? *Does* he lose things?'

'No. He's very particular my Charlie is. Everything neat, everything in its place. That's why he's so very good at what he does,' she said, beaming. 'I tell you, that producer was very lucky to get someone as good as my Charlie.'

'Why is that?' questioned Bertie.

'For what they're paying him? It's hardly very much

for all the work he has to do. Of course, it's that Miss Hamilton, God rest her soul.'

'Celia?' asked Bertie. Both his and Hugh's ears had pricked up at the mention of her name. 'What's she got to do with it?'

'Well, of course!' she exclaimed. 'Charlie is obsessed with her!'

Hugh and Bertie looked at each other, surprised.

'Obsessed, Mrs Saunders?' Hugh questioned, unconvinced.

'He's probably seen every single one of her films – some more than once. He collects all those magazines, doesn't he? I don't know what he wants with all that. He's always been a fan of cinema – can't keep him out of the bleeding place sometimes. The others he likes, they come and go, but Celia? Well, she was always his favourite. I took him to see one, when he was just little, and when she came on the screen his face just lit up. From that moment, he's just loved everything she's done.'

'I had no idea,' admitted Bertie.

'There's probably not a single thing about her life that my Charlie doesn't know. He'll have read every interview, read every book. Knows everything, he does. I don't know. I suppose they say it's not healthy, being obsessed like that. He doesn't mean any harm by it, of course. He's not one of those crazed fans you read about, those ones that follow them around or anything. No, those people aren't right in the brain, are they? Something probably happened in their youth, didn't it? Wouldn't happen if they had a proper mother figure around, would it? Not my Charlie. No, he's a proper fan.'

'How did he feel about working with her?' asked Hugh.

'He thought it was wonderful. Well, that was the thing... That's how Arthur got him to do it for next to no money.'

'Work on the show, you mean?' clarified Bertie.

'Well, yes. A bit rum, if you ask me. Taking advantage of a young boy like that. I'm sure he's doing it for a fraction of what he'd usually get paid. But Arthur knew he was a fan and he used that when he negotiated his fee. I suppose it works out all right, Arthur gets him on the cheap and my Charlie gets to meet his heroine.'

'And what was it like, meeting her?' Bertie pressed.

'Well, that was the thing, weren't it? He's absolutely in love with the Celia Hamilton you see up on the screen, but that's not the Celia Hamilton you get in real life, is it? She's very different. I think he was a little disappointed in the end. In the movies, she's beautiful, elegant, charming. In real life, well ... I wouldn't say she was the complete opposite, but not very far off it. Never meet your heroes, that's what I say. They'll only let you down.'

'Was he upset by it all?' asked Hugh.

'Upset?' she exclaimed, dramatically. 'He was distraught, poor thing. Now, that was just the shock, I suppose. The first day, the first rehearsal, he went in so excited. He was crestfallen about it all. Mind you, he just knuckled down like he always does. Eventually, he started enjoying the rehearsals again, came to terms with it I suppose: the reality.'

'So, he got used to it then?' Bertie questioned.

'Yes. He'd never let get personal feelings get in the way. He's a professional and always acts as one,' she proudly replied.

At that moment, the scraping of a key could be heard in the lock. The trio around the table spun their heads to look down the corridor that stretched all the way to the front door. The door clicked open and in stepped Charlie, closing it behind him. As he looked up, he was startled to see three expectant faces looking back at him down the hallway.

'Oh,' he said. 'Hello everyone.'

Charlie trudged down the corridor and stopped, hovering just outside the doorway to the kitchen. 'Come to ask more questions, have you?'

'We did,' confessed Hugh, 'but your mother has been most enlightening.'

'She has, has she?' said Charlie, his eyes narrowing suspiciously. 'What exactly have you been saying?' He cast a look of accusation in her direction before returning his attention to Bertie and Hugh. 'Well, now I'm back I can speak for myself.'

'Actually,' said Hugh, accompanied by the noise of the chair scraping backwards on the floor as he stood up, 'I think we've got everything we need.'

Bertie joined Hugh by standing. Mrs Saunders looked rather saddened that her guests were leaving so soon.

'Oh,' murmured Charlie, as he stepped aside to let them both pass.

'Thanks for all your help, Mrs Saunders,' announced Hugh. 'We'll see ourselves out.'

Bertie and Hugh headed towards the door. Charlie's eyes followed them every step. Just as they reached the door, Hugh stopped.

'Oh, there was one thing,' he said as he turned to face Charlie. 'The gun in the play?'

'Yes, what about it?' Charlie asked.

'Jenny said that after the shooting scene, she put the purse with the gun in it back on the props table.'

'That's right,' confirmed Charlie. 'I was there with her. I saw her do it, if that's what you mean?'

'When we found the gun,' Hugh continued, 'it wasn't in the purse. It was sitting in its place on the props table. Did you remove it and put it back?'

A confused expression flitted across Charlie's face for a moment. 'No.' He thought carefully. 'No,' he said again, more confidently this time, 'that's not right. It stays in the purse.'

'You're sure of that?' said Bertie. 'Might you have taken it out, ready for a later point in the play?'

'No,' said Charlie again. 'It stays in the purse ready for when it goes back on for Act Two. There's no reason for me to take it out.'

'Curious,' said Hugh.

Charlie stood there, still deep in thought, before letting his eyes return to Hugh. He shrugged. 'Sorry.'

'Don't be sorry,' said Bertie. 'They're all clues, aren't they, Hugh?'

'That they are.' Hugh smiled. 'The tricky part is knowing how they all fit together.'

'No further questions?' said Charlie. It sounded like he was disappointed.

'No further questions,' replied Hugh. 'Come on, Bertie.'

With that, Hugh opened the front door and the two of them headed out, down a few steps to the pavement. Behind them, Charlie closed the door.

'What do you think, Bertie?' asked Hugh in a low voice.

'Well, we were wondering where Celia's fans were and it looks like we found one! Do you think it changes anything?' added Bertie.

'It could be a motive?'

'Why would he kill her?' Bertie asked himself aloud. 'He adored her.'

'Perhaps he turned? Sometimes, these sorts of fanatics aren't exactly the most mentally stable, you know.'

'But this is Charlie we're talking about,' said Bertie. 'He's a stage manager.'

'It wouldn't be the first time a famous actor or actress lost their life by way of a supposed fan,' Hugh explained. 'And this damn discrepancy with the gun. Come on.' He invited Bertie to walk alongside him.

Bertie glanced back for moment. The wavy glass in the lattice window of the front door blurred everything and it was hard to make out the details through the diamond shaped glass. Maybe it was a trick of the light, or a shadow of a nearby tree, but he could have sworn that there was a figure watching them closely as they set off down the street.

Chapter Eighteen

'No, I got it right here,' said a cheery female voice at the end of the telephone. 'You want me to read you a bit? It's pretty bad, you know!' She broke into a long, lyrical laugh. It was infectious and made Bertie smile.

Bertie's secretary, Gertrude Williams, had been taking a look through her small archive of newspapers and yearbooks, of which she kept a meticulous record. At one time he had tried to decipher the hundreds of index cards that she would use to cross-reference and track down information, but he soon gave up. It made no sense to him. It was much more efficient to let her do her thing and, almost always, she'd be able to come up with some useful insight or other.

Even though she'd lived in London for at least a decade, her West Indian accent remained as strong as it was the day she'd arrived. She had come to work as his secretary almost by chance. Bertie had always sent his scripts off to a typing agency; while he could just about wrangle a typewriter into doing what he wanted, it would rarely be perfect. He would correct the mistakes by hand on his own typescript first and then send them off to the agency to be copy typed. When it arrived back, it would be neat and error-free with the typing agency's stamp on the front, accompanied by the typist's initials.

Unfortunately – or perhaps, fortunately, in this case – he was so short of time when he was rushing to produce the script for his second West End play, he asked the agency to send someone over so that it could be copy typed as he wrote. Originally the agency had wanted to send someone from their secretarial pool, but Bertie, not requiring someone to answer phones or deal with his correspondence, said he just needed the fastest typist they had. Picking up a previous script of his, he noticed the initials "GW" on the front cover and asked if, perhaps, they could send her over.

She had arrived at his front door completely unfazed after wrangling a large and heavy typewriter up the stairs. Bertie recalled her first words to him, 'Well it's nice to be out of the office for once, although I sure am glad you don't live on the top floor!'

The typewriter had been set up and within minutes she was already churning out pages of perfectly typed text. From that moment, they'd got on like a house on fire. Unfortunately, she had to return at the end of the week, although Bertie swore the moment he could afford to, he would engage her full-time.

Incredibly, the second play had been a huge success and it meant that Bertie could keep good on his promise. He always wondered why she'd been relegated to the agency's typing pool for years; she turned out to be a first-class secretary. An ardent fan of the theatre, Bertie would always ask her along to the opening nights and the parties that he was regularly obliged to attend. Bertie had always been very shy at parties. He would much prefer to sit quietly in the corner and wait for the whole thing to be over. Together they made quite the team and Miss Williams was generally able to provide enough theatricality for both of them.

Bertie had telephoned back to his London flat, wondering if she'd be able to track down a review for the doomed show that Robert had been involved in. Of course, Gertie (which is how she was affectionately known by him) was able to surface the relevant article in only a few minutes. While she was searching, he updated her on the goings-on in Brighton and why he hadn't returned yet.

'Here it is. "Playing opposite Miss Hamilton was Robert Laughton. Indescribably cumbersome, his face had little variation during the course of the evening, except for the ability to swap between two fixed expressions: sternness and festivity. He was sadly unable to exhibit the experiences and sensations of his character while his voice remained far too monotonous to portray the emotions that occurred during the play",' she quoted down the telephone line.

'So, not exactly a glowing review?' chuckled Bertie.

'I daresay that you've never had one as bad as that. Not yet, anyway,' she added cheekily.

'And Celia, what does it have to say about her?'

'Nothing, as far as I can tell,' she said. 'Nothing over

and above all the basics really, who she is, who she plays. That's all.'

'Well, the dinner and the drinks must have worked then.'

'Oh, is that how she does it?' Gertie exclaimed into the receiver. 'She really was a crafty sort wasn't she?'

'Very crafty indeed. She wouldn't let anything stand in the way of upholding her good image.'

'Maybe you could learn a thing or two from her, you know.'

'Miss Williams, I'm not sure what you're suggesting,' responded Bertie in a jovial fashion. 'My image is excellent. Well, I thought it was anyway,' he added in a low murmur.

'Well, of course, you write very good plays, but that doesn't stop people from trying to make them worse. Speaking of which…'

'Oh dear,' replied Bertie, 'tell me the bad news.'

'Mr Littler has requested some cuts in your latest draft. I spoke to him on the phone this morning.'

'Oh,' said Bertie, sounding surprised. 'At least it was nice of him to call. Normally, he just does what he wants when it comes to that sort of thing.'

'Yes, I did think it was unusual. There are enough changes that it's worth doing before we send it out to be Roneoed. Better to do it now, rather than having to correct all the duplicates by hand later. Reading between the lines, I suspect it's more likely that his leading lady – Miss Mathews – is the one who has requested the cuts.'

Bertie sighed. 'Did they sound like very important lines?' he asked.

'Quite important,' Gertie chuckled, 'but they also contain some very long and hard to pronounce chemical names.'

'Ah, I think you might have stumbled across the real issue there,' Bertie replied, thankful for his secretary's astuteness. 'I tell you what, I'll try to take a look at them tonight to see if I can find something easier to pronounce.'

Bertie fell silent for a moment.

'Are you still there, Mr Carroll?' Gertie enquired.

'My original script for *Murder by Association*. Can you dig it out for me? There's something I want to look up. A line.'

Rather than hearing an affirmative response from the usually efficient secretary, a noise that sounded like a loud tutting was transmitted down the phone line. If he hadn't known her better, he would have thought it was a fault on the line.

'Mr Carroll, I don't know what you carry that bag around with you for, if you never look in it!'

'My bag?' Bertie repeated. The bag she was referring to – a very fashionable leather briefcase – was sitting in his hotel room, unopened since he had arrived.

'Yes, I put your copy in there before you left. I thought you might find it useful. I did mention it before you left, you know.'

'Sorry, I'm sure you did,' he apologised. 'Well, in that case, I'll look it up when I get back to my room. Thanks, Gertie, you're a real gem. I don't know what I'd do without you.'

'No I don't know what you'd do without me either.'

Even down the phone line, Bertie could tell that she was smiling.

Chuckling to himself, he replaced the receiver and exited onto the street. In the phone box next door, Hugh was still talking animatedly into the handset. His voice was muffled and Bertie was unable to make out the details of his discussion.

Hugh's eyes flitted up for a moment, meeting Bertie's. He gave a wave of acknowledgement before returning to the task of scribbling things down in his notepad. He was deep in conversation with Scotland Yard, seeing if his colleagues back in London had managed to surface any more useful information.

While he waited, Bertie watched a man across the road walking a small dog with a long body. The man was clutching a bag of fish and chips. The dog trotted alongside him, looking hungrily up, while seagulls circled greedily overhead.

After a few more minutes, Hugh hung up the receiver and emerged from the telephone box. 'Sorry, didn't mean to keep you waiting.'

'Not at all,' Bertie replied. 'Any new information?'

'Some,' said Hugh, reading from his notebook. 'Our counterparts in America report that they were able to locate the orphanage where Miss O'Neil was adopted from, but there were no records available.'

'Because they don't exist?' asked Bertie.

'No,' said Hugh, thoughtfully. 'Because they appear to be missing. They had a record in the index cards, but when they went to retrieve the file, it simply wasn't there.'

'Lost?' Bertie thought aloud.

'Quite likely. Files get moved around, things get misplaced from time to time.'

'That's not unusual?'

'Unfortunately, it's not,' Hugh confirmed.

'So, we'll never know who Constance's parents were?'

'Unlikely, but you never know. There's always information around. There was a woman who still worked at the orphanage and remembered that Constance's mother had wanted her to be adopted under complete anonymity.'

'Is that strange?' said Bertie.

'Not necessarily, but uncommon enough that it stuck in the woman's mind.'

'Anything else?' asked Bertie.

'Just confirming everything else that people have told us, departure and arrival dates from America… It all seems to line up.'

Hugh flipped back through a few pages of his notebook, reviewing his notes. There was a brief flash of annoyance before, with a flick on his wrist, he neatly tore out a page. He flipped the book closed before pocketing it and then folded the torn page in half.

'Wait,' said Bertie quickly. 'What's that?'

'Nothing,' replied Hugh, 'it's blank.'

'But why did you do that?'

'Tear it out?' asked Hugh. 'It's a silly thing really, but I missed out a page before I started writing just now. I don't like the idea of having a blank page in there, and I don't want to go back and fill it in, because I prefer to have everything written down in the order I found it out.'

Bertie chuckled to himself. 'That's adorably fastidious, but that's not quite what I mean. Why did you fold it in half?'

'I don't know. I guess that's just what I do. Habit, I suppose. I was going to throw it away. Should I have screwed it up in a ball? I could have made you a paper plane if that's what you'd prefer?'

Bertie stopped Hugh from talking by putting his hand on his shoulder, as if to prevent him from going anywhere, while he ran over some of the things they'd learnt in his mind.

'I've just had a thought,' Bertie said. 'The blackmail note…'

'What about it?'

'Was there anything that you found odd about it? Something that was off?'

'Off?' repeated Hugh. 'No, I don't think so.'

'It was a plain piece of paper, wasn't it? Crisp, clean…' Bertie left a pause, for effect. 'And unfolded. There was no crease in the paper.'

'I don't see what that has to do with anything?' replied Hugh.

'The first thing you do, after you've written a note, is fold it in half.'

Hugh looked down at the scrap of paper in his hand. 'Yes,' he said, with more enthusiasm, 'I see what you mean.'

'You fold it to put in an envelope, don't you? And even if you don't put it in an envelope, you're likely to fold it in half and write the name of the recipient on the outside.'

'So, you're saying it's the opposite of what we originally thought? Celia Hamilton wasn't receiving blackmail notes…'

'No, she was sending them!' said Bertie, finishing Hugh's sentence for him. 'That note we found in her make-up box wasn't meant for her. She was the one who had written it, but she hadn't got around to sending it.'

Hugh nodded in agreement. 'But in that case, who was she blackmailing? Why was she blackmailing them? That doesn't make sense at all, does it? Celia Hamilton was a rich woman.'

'When we showed that note to Teddy, he said that he hadn't seen it before, right?'

'Yes, that's right.'

'Now, I don't think he was lying. I don't think he *had* seen it, but there was a glimmer of recognition in his eyes. I think he was telling the truth. But perhaps he'd seen other notes that were just like it!'

'But I still don't see why Celia would need to blackmail Teddy?'

'You're right, it can't have been for money,' confirmed Bertie.

'And I don't see what Celia would have on Teddy that she could blackmail him with.'

'Oh no?' said Bertie, concerned. 'I'm afraid I have a pretty good idea.'

Chapter Nineteen

Teddy shrugged his shoulders in a noncommittal way. The unfolded blackmail note sat on the low coffee table in front of him. He was lounging in a large, squishy, chintz armchair in the living room of his digs and was doing his very best not to pay any attention to the note that lay incriminatingly on the table.

Teddy was staying with the legendary Basil Grainger, the landlord of these digs who was well known to travelling actors across the country. He had once been an accountant, although one could hardly imagine such a loud, brash personality doing such dull, routine work. He would often keep his lodgers up quite late into the evening, recounting stories that had been told to him by his previous visitors in the years gone by. He had a distinctive flair for storytelling. Tales that would be dull and uninteresting in the hands of others would be told in a way that would captivate and delight his unsuspecting audience. On other nights, he would accompany himself on the well-played piano and encourage others to join in the singing with varying degrees of success. The composer of choice tended to be Ivor Novello, someone of whom Basil was an ardent fan; a signed photograph sat atop the piano and was, like everything else in the room, kept spotlessly clean.

It was rarely a boring visit when you were staying in the Grainger household, although even Teddy – who was always enthusiastic and upbeat, and one of the few who could match Basil in that regard – had to admit that another round of *Keep the Home Fires Burning* might be enough to put him off Ivor Novello for life.

'You've not seen this note or any other like it?' repeated Hugh for the second time.

'There was a glimmer of recognition when we showed it to you last time,' Bertie pushed the note across the table a little further, while Teddy redoubled his effort to pretend he couldn't see it. 'I think you've seen a note, perhaps even more than one, very similar to this before.'

Teddy folded his arms, defensively. 'And what if I have? Does that make me the murderer?'

'Not necessarily,' replied Hugh, 'but any information we get will help us complete the picture and get us closer to finding out who really did do it. It might even prove your innocence.'

Teddy shifted uncomfortably in his seat. 'And how close are you?' he asked. 'To finding out who it was, I mean.'

'There are many lines of enquiry we're looking at right now and we're entertaining all of them,' said Hugh, in a matter-of-fact manner.

'How about you Bertie?' Teddy said, his mood lightening a bit as he turned to the playwright. 'Perhaps you'll be the one to solve it?'

'I have my theories...' he replied.

'I knew it!' said Teddy with enthusiasm. 'I bet you'll solve it, Bertie. You're very good at all this.'

'I don't know,' Bertie admitted. 'There seems to be a pretty big difference between writing this kind of thing and solving this kind of thing. Well,' he stumbled for the words, 'they're two very different things.' He inwardly cringed at his lack of vocabulary in the moment.

'And the note,' Teddy said. 'What are your theories about the note?'

Bertie looked over at Hugh, who gave him a kind of half nod, half-shrug as an indication he should proceed. 'We noticed—'

'You noticed,' corrected Hugh.

'I noticed,' continued Bertie, 'that this note hadn't been folded. To me, that would seem to be a clear suggestion that it had never been sent. That means whoever was in possession of this note wasn't the recipient. They were the sender.'

'Oh, very good, Bertie.' Teddy's response trod a fine line between genuine enthusiasm and sarcasm. 'See, you *are* good at this.'

Teddy shifted in his seat again before continuing. 'So, who was the sender?' he asked, trying to sound as innocent as possible.

'I don't think I need to tell you, Teddy. I think you already know.'

Teddy shifted one more time, knowing that the game

was up. He combed the hair away from his face with his fingers.

'Celia,' he admitted with a sigh. 'It was Celia, for God's sake. She was the one sending them to me. You already mentioned that you found it in her dressing room. It doesn't take a genius to put it together, does it? You're right, by the way, I've never seen this particular note before, but I've seen plenty of other ones like it. Perhaps this one was meant for me, perhaps it was meant for someone else. I really couldn't say, but I recognise the style – quite unique, wouldn't you say? It's her all right.'

Hugh sat quietly, processing this admission. 'But why would Celia need to blackmail you?' he asked. 'Blackmail anyone? Surely it wasn't for money?'

Teddy gave a wry chuckle and then smiled in Hugh's direction. 'Celia never desired money, Inspector. Even if she had all the money in the world, it wouldn't buy her what she really wanted.'

'And what was that?'

'Power,' replied Teddy. 'Simply power. She was a master manipulator. In any situation that she found herself in, she'd always be able to architect it to suit her, for her benefit. She would always make sure to put herself at the top of the pyramid. A manipulator of people, yes. But why, I hear you ask?' Teddy allowed the words to hang there for a moment, for dramatic effect.

'I think she did it to get what she wanted, to get her way. Of course she did. But most of all, I think she did it for fun. I think it amused her. The idea that she was able to cast her spell of misery over anyone she chose. Why did she do it to me? I have no idea. We have no prior relationship. I met her for the first time just four weeks ago. But I was new. Fresh meat. And I suppose I wanted something…'

'And that was?' said Hugh.

'I wanted an in. I had this wild idea that I might want to get involved in the film industry. I'm doing well in plays and all that in London, but Hollywood? Well, that would be a completely different experience, wouldn't it? I wanted to see if I could make my way into movies. She'd been working out there, and working very successfully, for years. I was hoping she could give me advice, give me some introductions out there. Give a pal a leg up, you know.

'Well, that's what set us off on the wrong foot. That cemented the relationship we were going to have from then on. I wanted something from her and she knew that she'd be able to hold it over me. My carrot. Something she could use to control me. She could make me do whatever she wanted. Of course, I already knew about her reputation. People had warned me. Robert warned me. He had past dealings with her. He knew her game.

'But I wouldn't play. Teddy Howard will not be manipulated. So, I did the worst thing imaginable – in her eyes at least. I ignored her. Ignored her comments. Ignored her snide looks. "I can make or break you", that's what she'd say. Well, she might be able to make me in America, but I wouldn't let her break me here. She's got no power over here. Not anymore, not really. Of course, that wasn't going to stop her trying, was it?

'Rehearsals were a nightmare, criticising Jenny, Robert, Constance – the poor darlings – but she couldn't work her magic on me! I carried on being my cheery self the whole time, didn't I! Well, she didn't like that, did she? Not one bit.

'That's when the notes started. It was her last attempt to try to exert some power over me, I suppose. What she thought she was trying to blackmail me with, I don't know.'

'Oh no?' interjected Bertie.

'I really don't, Bertie,' said Teddy, using a tone of mock innocence. His voice had suddenly gone quite high.

Bertie took a long pause and his eyes met with Teddy's. A long, interrogating glance. It was a somewhat futile attempt to break down the wall Teddy had built between himself and his interviewers. However, Bertie continued; he had already got Teddy to admit to being the blackmail subject in the letters.

'Everyone in this industry has secrets,' said Bertie. 'We all do. Some are known by very few, some are shared openly inside our community. For the most part, those secrets seem to stay out of the eyes and ears of the public. Could it be that one of those secrets, a secret of yours, was what Celia was threatening to reveal, perhaps to one of her journalist contacts? We know what a powerful relationship she has built up over the years with entertainment critics on both sides of the Atlantic. Was there something that really could end your career?'

Teddy gave his biggest sigh yet – it was almost to the point of theatricality.

'Fine. Actors, dancers, directors, most of the other people in this industry,' Teddy started. 'Everyone's usually too caught up with themselves. They don't notice people, not really.

'Writers like you, however, that's a different matter. They're always studying people; they know how to interpret them – their codes, their characters, their habits. It's all material to go into the next play, the next book, isn't it? You never know when all those observations will come in handy.'

Teddy paused for a moment, lighting a cigarette. His tone changed, becoming much more serious. 'It's why I don't doubt for a moment that you'll be good at this detecting lark. You notice everything. You notice, of course, my character – what I'm like. You notice how I act. Now, I have to admit, I am a thoroughly interesting person. Perhaps you should put a character like me in one of your plays one day? I think your audience might find that rather stimulating.

'But of course, actors like me ... good actors. We know how to observe people, too. I observe people's voices, their mannerisms. I observe the way they walk, the way they act. Everybody has secrets and if you know what to watch for, you can see them plain as day. You have your secrets too, don't you, Bertie? I wonder what your inspector friend would think of that.'

Teddy blew a cloud of smoke accusatorially towards Bertie. Bertie could feel Hugh's gaze burning on the side of his face but didn't dare return it.

'Now,' Teddy continued, 'would one prefer to be a member of the majority instead? I don't know, that seems a silly notion to me. After all, the majority of people aren't actors like me; fewer still are playwrights like you.'

'Like me?' Bertie repeated. He had attempted to respond with a tone of innocence, but fell far short.

'Who says that being in a minority, like we are, is a bad thing? I think it's rather wonderful. Who wants to be just plain normal?'

'And you're saying that's what she was blackmailing you with?' said Bertie, continuing the questioning.

'Yes, that's my secret, if you can even call it that. Perhaps I should have held it closer to my chest than I did. My personality is too loud to deny myself those feelings. I'm far too busy celebrating them. Would I have been the first actor on the stage to admit that I'm far happier in the company of other men? No. Would I have been the first actor in Hollywood? Certainly not!

'However, would it have been the end of my career if she'd have spoken to one of her journalist friends? I suspect it would have been. Who's going to cast me, a pansy, as their big romantic lead? I can't quite see it, can you? Where does that leave me? Another confirmed bachelor all my life? God, I might end up like poor old Basil here, although I rather think I would have better levels of taste in my soft furnishings.

'Theatre has always been a safe place for those of our kind,' he spoke directly to Bertie. 'Now, that might not be the end of me. But as I'm sure you know as well as me, darling, it is completely illegal. The inevitable conclusion of our kind of love is that it ends in jail. It would take next to nothing to have me locked up. My career wouldn't survive that – I know I certainly wouldn't.'

Hugh cleared his throat. 'Well, Mr Howard, you've given us our most persuasive motive so far.'

Teddy leapt to his feet. 'Absolutely not!' he objected at full volume. 'Tell him, Bertie. You've worked it out, haven't you? I know you have! You know who really did it, don't you? Tell him.'

Teddy's arms gesticulated wildly as he protested, his voice pleading. The ash from the end of his cigarette was sent flying across the room. 'Murder, for goodness' sakes! It wasn't me, I tell you. It wasn't me! Bertie, make him see sense!'

'Please, Mr Howard,' said Hugh, who had also risen from his chair in an attempt to calm him. 'Please, sit down.'

Teddy threw himself back down in the chair before adding, 'This is ridiculous!'

Hugh remained standing and paced slowly around the room in thought. 'You do see how this looks though, don't you?'

'Of course I do,' replied Teddy. 'Obviously, that's why I didn't say anything when you showed me that note the first time.'

'Well, lying about it certainly doesn't help your case,' said Hugh bluntly.

'Now look here,' Teddy protested, switching his gaze between them. 'I didn't lie. Technically, I didn't lie. You asked me if I'd seen that note before and I said I hadn't. That was absolutely, completely, true, thank you very much.' He finished the end of his sentence like a petulant child.

'You do see why it's a compelling reason, don't you?' Bertie added in a gentler tone.

'Well, it would be quite a compelling reason if you ignore the fact I didn't actually do it,' complained Teddy. 'If I'm faced with a choice between going to prison for murder or, well, for the other thing, I don't see that either one is more favourable than the other.

'Besides, I told you, I was laughing it off. I wasn't giving her the upper hand; I wasn't letting it get to me. I had no reason to try to get her to stop.'

'But it did escalate, didn't it?' said Bertie. 'When the notes started arriving, that was when it started getting worse?'

'Yes, but murder! Me! Murder?' His histrionics were starting to sound a little more desperate now. 'I didn't go near that gun before, during, or after the show. And here I was, thinking you were on my side, Bertie.'

'Before, during, or after,' Bertie repeated. He was distracted for a moment, deep in thought.

'Exactly,' Teddy said, triumphantly. 'I don't know how you expect me to have, somehow, shot her, without being able to get anywhere near that damn gun. I never even touched the bloody thing.'

'Well, if that's the case, Mr Howard,' Hugh said, 'we have to return to the very real possibility that Jenny intended to shoot Miss Hamilton. But you're convinced that idea is impossible.'

'Why would Jenny want to murder Celia? It makes no sense. None at all,' Teddy stated. 'There's absolutely no reason whatsoever for Jenny to do it. No connection, no previous dealings, no anything. Of course, Jenny got given a bit of a hard time by Celia during rehearsals, but so did everyone. That's hardly enough to drive someone to murder, is it?'

'I don't know, Mr Howard,' said Hugh. 'Isn't it?'

The question hung in the air. Teddy leant forward – stubbing out the cigarette in a decorative ashtray filled with other cigarette butts – before he allowed himself to have the quiet, final word. 'No'.

Chapter Twenty

The long walk to Robert's digs was largely spent in silence; the only exception was when Hugh had asked Bertie to confirm or provide directions. The grand houses of Regency Square, and those closer to the seafront, were slowly being replaced by ones that were smaller and less well kept.

Rows of squat, plain terraced houses stretched out in front of them, the smooth rendered finish leaving them featureless and uninteresting. Some of the homes, in a valiant attempt to fight back against their plain appearance, had been painted in pastel colours that made them stand out from the boring, whitewashed majority.

The pair of them arrived outside number forty-two, the address that they had for Robert's digs. The outside of the building had been painted a pale shade of blue. Two long, thin cracks stretched from the base of the wall, where it met the pavement, up to the first floor and disappeared under the windowsill.

Arthur had now moved Constance into his hotel, for

additional protection, but Bertie was surprised that he had been happy to let a young girl stay somewhere like this in the first place. Although, beggars can't be choosers. There wasn't enough money in the production for everyone to afford the same first-class level of accommodation as its star performer.

As Bertie reached out his hand to knock on the front door, Hugh leant out to stop him by gently holding his wrist. 'What Teddy was hinting at. About you…'

'What about me?'

'All that language, dancing around the subject, being a member of the minority. Was he suggesting what I think he was?' Hugh's voice sounded concerned.

'Now who's dancing around the subject?' Bertie paused a moment before continuing. 'What do you think he was suggesting?'

'You know I'm a police officer,' said Hugh, his expression hard to read.

'You're also the oldest friend I've got.'

'We go back a long way,' said Hugh. 'That's a lot of time that's past.'

'This thing with Teddy?' asked Bertie. 'We don't have to pursue that any further, do we?'

'That depends.'

'On what?'

'Whether it's something that matters or not. If it becomes relevant, we might not have a choice.'

'But if we do have a choice?' asked Bertie.

'Then we'll make the right decision,' said Hugh. He moved his hand to Bertie's shoulder, guiding him to look directly at him. His voice became serious. 'You know if you're ever in trouble...'

'I should always call you.' Bertie tried to brush it off as a joke, completing the sentence in a light-hearted tone.

'I'm being serious.'

'I know you are,' replied Bertie. This time he was completely serious too.

A moment passed, with their eyes locked together, where nothing was said.

'Shall I knock?' asked Bertie, finally breaking the tension.

Hugh nodded.

After a few moments, Robert appeared at the door. He seemed a little disgruntled, as always, but on the whole he seemed surprised.

'Oh, it's you two, is it?' he said, holding a hand up to shield the daylight from his eyes. 'I suppose I should invite you in.'

Robert ushered them into a small, dimly lit sitting-room. Sunlight valiantly tried to penetrate the dusty net curtains that hung in the window, but ultimately failed to do so.

'We wanted to talk to you about a play you were in,' said Hugh. 'One where you were playing opposite Miss Hamilton in London. The reviews it got...'

Robert made a noncommittal sound. 'Oh, you found out about that, did you?' He sat in an armchair that had seen better days and indicated a sofa opposite for Hugh and Bertie to sit down.

'That play was decades ago,' he continued. 'I didn't

think it mattered! I don't see how it could have any relevance to what happened here, surely?'

'You don't think it's relevant?' Hugh repeated. 'You don't expect us to believe that, do you?'

'I expect you'll believe exactly what you want to believe.'

'So, you don't blame Celia?' asked Bertie. 'For the way your career turned out?'

'The way my career turned out?' exclaimed Robert, confused. 'For heaven's sake, what does my career have to do with anything?'

'It's fair to say, isn't it,' started Bertie, in an attempt to be delicate, 'that your career never really took off. And the play you did with Celia didn't exactly help with that. The relationship she had with some of the critics, she would encourage them to give her favourable reviews, which might mean the rest of you would be left out in the cold.'

Robert sighed and his usual brash demeanour faded a little. He started to explain, speaking earnestly and softly. 'Perhaps, at the time – and this was a long time ago mind you – there was some resentment over it. I was young and ambitious, and I thought that I would be able to make something of myself.

'I'm sure you know, Bertie, as well as I do, when it comes to show business, you can't predict these things. There are the haves and the have-nots. There are those who will be able to break through and those that won't. I was always the latter. However much I tried – and believe me I did try – that kind of star quality would always end up eluding me.

'Back then, I was young and very stupid. Just like every other young actor, I thought I could be famous one day. In many ways, I was just like young Teddy is today. Of course, he has that quality that I never did. Does that mean he'll succeed? Perhaps not, but at least it means that he's got a fighting chance – a better chance than most.

'I can look back now, with age and with hindsight, and I know I never really had that chance. It was never going to happen for me, but I made the best of it, didn't I?'

Robert gave a small chuckle and started talking in his trademark bolder voice again.

'Vicars and butlers!' he announced with a theatrical slap on his thigh. 'It's a damn good trade, you know. Of course, I complain about it from time to time; it's not exactly high art, is it? But it pays the bills. Being an actor isn't the most reliable way to make a living; if I wanted that I should have become a bank manager, like my father was. However, you must remember that I've been one of the lucky ones. I've been able to work steadily and consistently for – well – as long as I can remember. Now, that's nothing to be sniffed at. There are plenty of actors who are much worse off than me.'

Robert paused a moment, reflecting on his surroundings. 'Well, perhaps not that much worse off!' He emitted a single shotgun laugh. 'I'm not saying this thing, this resentment with Celia, never existed. It did. I didn't much like her and I don't think that she ever liked me. And if there was any situation – like that damned play of ours – that might reflect badly on her, she'd do whatever it took to make sure she came out smelling of roses. Whatever it took,' he repeated, 'even if it came at the cost of throwing everyone else under the bus. Quite frankly, it was terrifying. I think she'd sacrifice a child if it meant protecting her career. She could be quite an appalling woman sometimes.

'But now, that's all behind me. History. It's all in the past. And not just in the past by a little bit either, a long, long way in the past.'

'But didn't all that come flooding back when you had to work with her again? Even after all these years? Bringing back up all that resentment and pain?' said Hugh.

Robert looked between the two of them before answering. 'Yes, it did. But it was different. Everything is much more distant now. I can remember the feelings I had at the time, but they're faded. Everything is dim, dulled. If you've got some fanciful idea that those feelings were, somehow, rekindled the day we walked into the rehearsal room, they weren't. I can promise you that.'

'But rehearsals with Celia were a nightmare, weren't they? She wasn't very nice to you,' Bertie said.

'She wasn't very nice to anyone. She wasn't back in the day. She wasn't this time round. Even after all those years, a successful career and a large ocean between us, she hadn't changed at all. So yes, I must admit, rather than have any old feelings rekindled, we all got some lovely new ones that the cast could share between us!' he said, trying to lighten the mood again.

'Feelings against Miss Hamilton?' said Hugh.

'Yes. But enough to kill her?' Robert scoffed. 'That's

ridiculous. I'm an old man now. I've lived my life. I'm not going to commit murder – if that's what you're suggesting – as some kind of revenge. I've come to terms with it all – my time, my career.'

'And your career now?' asked Bertie. 'How's that going?'

'It's going fine. Why?'

'Arthur tells us you were the one that contacted him about being in the play.'

'Along with a dozen other producers,' Robert replied with a roll of his eyes. 'At my age, roles can be hard to come across. I'm not too proud to seek out work myself, even if it doesn't pay that well.'

'You're also the only person that remains unaccounted for on the night,' Hugh said.

'Well, we've been over that, haven't we? There was no one else here to vouch for me, so I don't know what you think I can do to prove it. Quite frankly, I can't wait to leave this dreary place,' Robert said, looking around. 'It wasn't my choice of accommodation, I can tell you that. I don't know what else there is to say about it.'

'There's also a second play that you've neglected to tell us about,' said Hugh.

'There is?' asked Robert, looking genuinely dumbfounded.

'I'm afraid we don't know the name,' added Bertie, 'but it was here in Brighton.'

'I've done several plays in Brighton over the years. Any other clues that might help me remember which one it was?' said Robert.

'Yes. A young girl died,' said Hugh, bluntly. 'An overdose.'

'Good Lord. Yes, that does ring a bell. That was in Brighton, was it?' He closed his eyes, trying to recall something. 'No, I can't tell you the name of the play, but I remember the circumstances now. Poor young girl. A very silly thing for someone like her to go in for drugs. Of course, there were rumours of murder or suicide at the time, but I think that was just people's imagination running away with them; that's what happens when you're in a building full of "artistic" types. It was just a tragic accident, I seem to remember. Very sad business.'

'That's not the only link,' added Hugh. 'There's Jenny.'

'Jenny?' A confused Robert repeated. 'She wouldn't have been old enough, surely? It was years ago.'

'No, not Jenny herself,' said Bertie. 'It was her father. It seemed like he was the one who was pushing the drugs.'

'Well, would you believe that?' Robert sounded impressed. 'How on earth did you find that out? I don't see what this has to do with Celia's murder, though? She almost certainly would have been in America by then.'

'Seems like a coincidence though, doesn't it?' said Hugh. 'Two deaths in Brighton, both of them on plays that you worked on?'

Robert's face puffed up before he exploded. 'Well, it is a blasted coincidence, isn't it! Neither one has anything to do with me. Our theatre world is positively minuscule. I'm sure you'd be able to find half a dozen people who worked on that show with some connection back to me,

Arthur or Celia. Charlie too,' he added. 'He's from a theatrical family that goes back years. It doesn't mean anything. A coincidence is exactly what it is.' He sat back in his chair and folded his arms.

The three of them sat in silence for a moment. There really wasn't much else to say.

Bertie cocked his head, as something occurred to him. 'You don't have your script here, do you, Robert?'

'I can get it if you want. It's upstairs somewhere.'

'If you don't mind,' replied Bertie. 'I would look at mine, but it's back in my hotel room.'

'Checking we were getting all the lines right, were you?' Robert joked as he extracted himself from the chair with some difficulty.

'My very efficient secretary packed it for me. I don't know what she thought I was going to do with it, but it turns out it might come in handy after all!'

Robert disappeared for a few moments. Bertie and Hugh could hear his heavy footsteps ascend and then descend the creaking staircase.

'What's this about?' asked Hugh, with a quizzical expression on his face.

'Not sure, actually,' replied Bertie, who seemed a little absentminded. 'It's just something that occurred to me earlier, but I want to double-check.'

Robert returned and threw the script in Bertie's direction. He put his hands out to catch it but missed; it sailed through them and landed on his lap. It was a dog-eared, well-thumbed book – the published version of the script which had been professionally printed and bound. Robert had scruffily marked each of his lines with a large pencil tick. Some indecipherable text was scrawled in the margins, which must have made some sort of sense to the actor, even if he was unable to interpret meaning from any of them.

Bertie flipped through to the back half of the script, searching for something. He snapped the book closed and tossed it lightly back onto the coffee table in the centre of the room.

'Find what you were looking for?' asked Hugh.

'No, interestingly, I couldn't find it at all... Tell me, Robert, how long does it take you to learn lines?'

'Learn them?' Robert repeated, while he thought about it. 'I suppose it would depend on the show, really.'

'But generally, if you had to say?'

'Generally? A few days, maybe a week or two. It's easier when the lines are written well,' he said, in Bertie's direction. 'But roughly about that. When you've done it as often as I have, you get pretty good at it. It's like a muscle you exercise; the more you do it, the easier you find it.

'You have to become good at it, especially if you're in rep, learning the lines of the next show while you're performing in the current one. Things can come unstuck pretty quickly if you can't stay on top of it all. You don't want to come in and do your Bertie Carroll lines halfway through William Shakespeare! Ha!' Robert laughed at his own joke. 'The trick of rep – although I'm sure a playwright would be horrified to hear this – is that as long as you get the gist of the line right, all the other actors will help you muddle through it. A bit of light improvisation never hurt anyone! These days, I'm coming up against my age, so it takes a little longer. Luckily, it seems that as the roles start getting older, the fewer lines you get in the play.'

'Thank you, Robert. That was helpful,' replied Bertie, still deep in thought.

'You look, to me, like a man who is on to something,' said Robert, affectedly.

'Yes.' Hugh was looking at Bertie, impressed. 'I was going to say the same thing.'

Bertie gave a shy smile. 'Well, I'm not convinced I'm on to something – not yet. But I've suddenly had a thought and it's starting to make things a lot clearer.'

'Let me know if you ever want to share anything with me,' said Hugh.

'I'll think about it,' said Bertie with a smile. 'I'll definitely think about it.'

Chapter Twenty-One

Hugh was sitting on a stool at a tall table, tucked away in one of the corners of The King and Queen public house. The pub had recently undergone a rebuilding in mock Tudor style. It somehow made the place both new and old at the same time. The daylight outside had almost faded completely and the stained-glass windows were lit only by a dim glow. The gloom of the bar, accentuated by its dark wood floors and large black timber beams, seemed to reflect his current state of mind.

On their way to the pub, Bertie had disappeared back to his hotel room to retrieve his bag. He had just returned and Hugh could see him across the room with his foot resting on the wrought-iron rail, waiting to be served at the bar. He hoped that the bag Bertie had brought with him would contain some good news.

Hugh returned to his own thoughts. To him, the case seemed impossible. He reflected on the advice that he had given Bertie previously: be patient, gather as much information as possible and, given time, the solution will eventually present itself. Now he had to admit that his own patience was wearing thin. Could it be that his own crime-solving methodology was going to fail him for the first time? Up until now, it had been foolproof.

Ordinarily, there would have been something that emerged from the information they'd gathered. A feeling or an idea that stood out as being different, something that didn't quite fit or sit right among everything else. Sitting here today, each one of his thoughts seemed as incomprehensible as the last. Each theory he tested was as impossible as the one that preceded it. In any normal case, he would be concerned, but now he felt a tinge of embarrassment. This time, he had an accomplice working alongside him, although that shouldn't have made any difference. Not only did Hugh need to figure out the case for his superiors and make sure that justice was done, but there was also something else. He found himself with an overwhelming desire to impress Bertie.

Two dimpled glasses were set down on the table with a dark beer contained within – not too dissimilar in colour to the dark brown varnish of the table. They were followed shortly by a sheaf of papers, which landed with a loud thunk on the table, snapping Hugh out of his muddled thoughts.

'Two pints of their best mild,' said Bertie with enthusiasm. 'If I'm going to think like a policeman, I may as well drink like one.'

'I'm not sure thinking like a policeman will help all that much. This policeman is still getting nowhere with the case.' Hugh's expression remained fixed somewhere between concern and despair. He forced a smile to his face. 'Cheers,' Hugh added, as he held up his beer glass. Bertie returned the gesture, before taking a small sip from the glass.

'That…' said Bertie, with a cocked head and surprised expression on his face, 'is not as bad as I was expecting, quite frankly!'

Hugh laughed and nodded towards the pile of papers on the table. 'What's that then?' he asked. 'More clues?'

'Well, I can't be sure, but there just well may be,' Bertie replied.

He flipped the inch-thick document over, revealing the front cover. It was bound with – what had once been – two shiny brass fasteners. They had dulled and tarnished with age. In the top right-hand corner, written in a hand that Hugh recognised, were the words "Rehearsal Draft". Further down the page, in typewritten text, it read:

ASSOCIATION WITH DEATH
By Bertie Carroll

'Your handwriting hasn't changed much since school, has it?' said Hugh.

'Unreadable, you mean?' Bertie joked back. 'No, not really.'

'So, what's this, then?' asked Hugh. 'Your version of the script?'

'Yes, the final rehearsal draft. This is my copy, with all my notes.'

'And what does that mean?'

‘It means that this script is the last version I ever wrote,’ Bertie explained. ‘Now, there are always changes in rehearsals, things that get cut or tweaked. All of those bits are what has been written in the margins or lines that have been crossed out.’

Hugh flipped through a few pages of the script. There, just as Bertie had described, was text with lines drawn through them or additions added in pencil.

‘Any major re-workings of a scene get sent off for re-typing, but I like to keep the original as it is for my own records,’ Bertie continued. ‘If there any big re-writes or new scenes that get added, I put them at the back.’ Bertie thumbed through the last few pages of the script. ‘Although in the case of this show, it looks like there were just a couple…’

‘I’m sure even Shakespeare didn’t get it right on the first try,’ commented Hugh with a smile. ‘So how does this help us?’

‘Well, this isn’t the script that the current cast is working from. They’re using the published script, which is different. That version of the script is as it was first performed, the one produced from the prompt-copy. If there were any changes or cuts that had been made, they wouldn’t have been included in the published version.’

‘So…’

‘So,’ Bertie continued, ‘I’m afraid I got something wrong earlier.’

‘You did?’ said Hugh, sounding a little surprised. In his opinion, Bertie hadn’t put a foot wrong in the entire investigation.

'Yes, and it's been bothering me ever since,' Bertie admitted. 'It's when we were talking to Arthur. One of the lines from the show.'

'You got it wrong?'

'Not quite,' Bertie explained. 'I'm pretty sure I quoted a line that was never in the show at all!' He flipped open the script and flicked through the pages towards the back. 'There is it,' said Bertie, pointing out the line in the script.

~~*PARKER: We will find our murderer before the night is out!*~~

'Parker? Not the most imaginative name for a butler, is it? You came up with that all by yourself, with no help from anyone?' Hugh joked. He looked back at the page again, scanning the lines, and then turned to Bertie with a quizzical look. 'But it's crossed out?' he said.

He was right. A neat pencil line stretched through the middle of every letter in the sentence.

'That's right,' confirmed Bertie. 'It was cut. It was never in the show. Thank God, quite frankly. It would have been a bit over the top. Still, I was young and foolish back then, but perhaps that's why it stuck in my mind; that's why it came back to me when we were talking to Arthur.'

'So, what's this all about?' asked Hugh, who was trying to follow Bertie's thought process.

'Well, if it was never in the show, it was never in the published script. That's what I was checking when we were at Robert's digs. I wanted to look at his script to see if that line had made it in,' Bertie explained. 'It hadn't. It wasn't there. If it was never in the script, that means that no one involved in this show should have ever heard it before. Including…'

'Including Arthur,' agreed Hugh. 'He would have never heard it.' Hugh thought for a moment more, then added excitedly, 'He would never have committed it to memory!'

'Exactly,' Bertie continued. 'Remember, we're talking about someone who knows the script well enough to pick up the part of the butler and do it off-book with next to no notice. When I quoted that line from Act Two, why didn't he correct me?'

Hugh nodded in thought. 'Perhaps he was just being polite?' he said. 'I mean, you are the writer, after all. Isn't it rude to correct the author?'

'I suppose it's possible,' mused Bertie, 'but that isn't the impression I got. He just categorically agreed with me. You'd think if it was a line you didn't recognise, you might look confused for a moment, at the very least?'

'Perhaps he didn't know the second act as well at the first act?' Hugh continued, thinking out loud. 'The second half of the performance never took place, so we don't know what would have happened. Perhaps his performance in the second act wouldn't have been so impressive? Maybe he would have had to take the book on with him?'

'That's right,' said Bertie, with a glimmer of recognition. 'The second half never took place,' Bertie repeated under his breath. He sat for a while with his own thoughts before Hugh interrupted them.

'Well, that seemed to set the machinery whirring,' commented Hugh. 'Have you had an idea?'

'I have,' said Bertie. 'Only an idea... But if I pull on that thread, it opens up a whole new set of possibilities. What was it Teddy said earlier? About the gun? He didn't go near it before, during or after the show. Before, during or after,' Bertie repeated to himself.

'What do we know about the gun?' he continued. 'It only had two sets of fingerprints on it. Jenny and Charlie's. For a while, we thought there might have been more than one gun – maybe a gun with a silencer. But what if we discount that idea? What if there really was only one gun? Where else could it have been? Who else would have had access to it?'

'We know the gun was under Charlie's watchful eye for pretty much the whole performance, don't we?' said Hugh, working through the idea.

'What if I look at this as a writer? When I look at the whole thing as if I was writing one of my plays, it doesn't work, dramatically speaking. Jenny is far too obvious a suspect, so who else could I pin it on?'

'I thought in plays and movies, it was always the least likely person?' commented Hugh, joking.

'That's not always true, Hugh,' chuckled Bertie. 'And that's something I try hard to avoid. But if Jenny is too obvious, that's because someone wanted to try to pin it on her. And if someone went out of their way to make it look that way, it means that the actual murderer *must* have been someone else. It's the only thing that makes sense.

'Before, during or after,' Bertie repeated. 'I think

we've been distracted all this time. We've been focussing on the wrong things. We've been focussing on the moment of the murder, the shooting in the play. What happens when we look either side of that moment? Where was everybody? What were they doing? Where was the gun?'

'We know that the gun was locked away until the performance started,' Hugh commented. 'And Charlie had it in sight the whole time. He saw it when it went on stage for the murder scene and when it came back off again.'

'But then what happened after that?' said Bertie. 'What happened after Celia Hamilton was shot? When you think about that, more possibilities open themselves.'

'They do?' asked Hugh, who was confused by Bertie's reasoning.

'Yes. Things start to make more sense. They start to fall into place.'

'So who did it?' questioned Hugh eagerly.

'I'm not sure,' admitted Bertie. 'I don't know, at least I don't know for certain. Not yet. There are a few more questions that need to be answered.' His face lit up with a moment of realisation. 'And the most important of those questions is, why does Constance have a photo of herself in her dressing room?'

'It is?'

'Absolutely!' exclaimed Bertie. 'On the night of the murder, you were an excellent policeman. You are very good, aren't you?'

'If you say so,' Hugh replied, his modesty getting the better of him.

'I mean, you didn't let anyone leave the stage without being searched. The stage, the set, the crime scene. It's been completely undisturbed. Nothing could have left the theatre or been removed from it.'

'That's right, we searched everyone before we left the set. No one had anything of importance, did they?'

'No, they didn't,' Bertie agreed. 'And the stage has been guarded this whole time?'

'Yes, there has been a constable stationed there, making sure no one can interfere with anything on the stage or in the theatre.'

'We never found a bullet,' said Bertie. 'But I think that maybe we were looking in the wrong place. We never found a second gun, and that's because there never was one. But we never found a silencer either?'

'Suppressor,' corrected Hugh, out of habit.

'Right,' said Bertie. 'We never found a suppressor, yet there must have been one!'

'Must there?' quizzed Hugh, struggling to follow Bertie's train of thought. 'I thought we just ruled out a second gun?'

'I have an idea, just an idea, mind, but I need your permission. Tomorrow morning, I think we should open up the crime scene again, say we're done with it. Allow everyone in the company to come back to the theatre and collect their belongings, then send them home.'

'And you think that will help us?' asked Hugh, a little sceptically.

'Help us?' repeated Bertie. 'I think it's going to tell us exactly who the murderer is.'

'Take me through it. Step by step,' said Hugh.

‘I will,’ replied Bertie, glancing down at his wrist-watch. ‘But first I need to make a call to a newspaper. And Hugh?’

‘Yes, Bertie?’

‘I think we’re going to need more than just one beer!’

Chapter Twenty-Two

It was raining again. One by one each member of the company filed in through the stage door and set off in the direction of their dressing rooms. They did so sombrely and silently, ready to pack up their belongings. Charlie headed in the direction of the stage and Bertie followed closely behind.

'Give us a hand with this, would you?' asked Charlie, indicating a large rectangular wicker basket at the corner of the stage.

Bertie nodded, picking up one side of the basket by its rope handle, leaving Charlie to lift the other end. Between them, they carried it over and set it down in front of the props table. Charlie flipped open the top of the basket to reveal a pile of blankets and old newspapers inside. He watched closely as Charlie retrieved a stack of the newspapers and set about wrapping the props up carefully, placing them neatly in the basket to be protected by the blankets during travel.

'What's going to happen to all of this?' asked Bertie, indicating towards the props on the table.

'Put into storage, probably. I imagine that it will sit around gathering dust somewhere.'

'And the set?'

'We've got a crew coming in tomorrow to take it down. It's looking a bit tired now, but with a bit of fresh paint, I wouldn't be surprised to see it out on tour again.

'Apparently, the crew here haven't had to do a get out on a wet day in five years, if you can believe that.' Charlie smiled. 'I think their luck is about to change,' he said, his eyes flicking up to the roof where the gentle sound of rain drumming on the outside could still be heard.

Bertie was distracted by the sound of footsteps descending the stairs from the dressing rooms. He turned to see Arthur coming back down onto the stage. He gave a nod of recognition towards Bertie and Charlie but didn't say anything. Instead, he wandered through the doorway and onto the set with a sober expression on his face.

'How about you?' Bertie said, who seemed to be looking off into the distance, rather than returning his attention to Charlie. 'What will you do next?'

'Not another murder mystery, that's for sure! No offence,' he added at the end.

'None taken.' Bertie turned, allowing himself a smile in Charlie's direction.

'I think I've had my fair share of murders for a while – real or staged.'

'Me too. Although, I'll keep writing them as long as they're in demand. It's what pays the bills after all! Look, let me leave you to all this,' said Bertie, gesturing to the remaining props on the table. 'I'm just going to pop onto the stage and say my goodbyes to Arthur – to all of you, in fact. Maybe you should let the others know, we'll all meet up there when they're done?'

Charlie nodded. Bertie left him to continue with his work and followed Arthur onto the set. When he entered, Arthur had his back towards him and was adjusting the flowers in one of the vases, getting them ready to be packed up.

'Arthur,' said Bertie, announcing his arrival. Arthur, slightly startled, turned to face him.

'Oh, Bertie!' said Arthur with relief. 'It's you.'

'Nice flowers,' commented Bertie.

'They are, aren't they? I was going to bunch them up, give them to the two girls, Jenny and Constance. I thought it would be a nice touch, or something, after everything that's happened. Seems such a shame to let them go to waste, wilting here in the dark.' Arthur gave the flowers in the vase a little wiggle. 'Of course, it turns out they're fake! Oh well, it was a nice idea, I suppose. I expect they'll get packed up with the rest of the props,' Arthur said with a gloomy expression.

'I hope you didn't lose too much, putting on the show?'

'Well, yes. I did,' Arthur admitted. 'I'll be all right, I suppose. There's always the next show and then the one after that... One of them might do well enough to cover the losses on this one – unfortunately it's like that sometimes. You won't hear many producers telling you this, but producing shows is a terrible way to make money.

You have to spend so much money to mount a production in the first place and then earn enough to cover the running costs while it's open. I'm sure if I'd just left my money in a bank account, I'd be a richer man than I am today.'

'I thought the first rule of producing is that you never put your own money into a production,' Bertie commented.

'This one was more of a passion project, I suppose. It was all on me,' said Arthur. He looked around the set wistfully.

'I see,' said Bertie. 'That's why you were trying to do it as cheaply as possible.'

'Oh yes. Although nothing ever really comes cheap. It always ends up costing you something,' he added thoughtfully.

At that moment, Teddy walked onto the set. 'Bad luck, old chap,' he said in Arthur's direction. Arthur nodded in response.

Charlie followed in, closely behind Teddy. 'Maybe I'll see you on another one, in the future,' he commented optimistically. 'We all thought we'd meet up on the stage – Bertie's idea. You know, give us all a chance to say our goodbyes before we disappear off into the sunset. We're all free to go now, investigation-wise, aren't we?'

'Oh yes, that's right,' said Bertie.

One by one, the remaining cast members filed in. Jenny first, then Constance, with Robert trailing closely behind. Jenny and Constance both carried a small suitcase each. As he was more well-travelled, Robert's suitcase was larger and considerably more worn and battered.

'I suppose I should say something,' said Arthur, noticing the assembled cast, with expectant looks on their faces. 'It's rarely good news when a producer and his cast gather on the stage in any circumstance, let alone this one. I'm sorry we're closing before we even got started. And Celia... Well, we didn't just lose our leading lady. I lost an old friend and the world lost a star. But thank you, all of you.'

'Well, that's that!' added Teddy cheerfully, breaking the silence.

'Not quite,' came a quiet but firm voice from behind them. Everyone swivelled round to see where the voice had come from. Hugh had appeared in the doorway of the set, blocking the way out. 'Perhaps you should all take a seat.'

'Golly,' exclaimed Teddy. 'Does that mean you're going to tell us who did it?'

Hugh gave a wry smile. 'I hope so. Although I have nothing to say on the matter,' he admitted. 'But Bertie, I think you might like to say something?'

All heads turned back to face Bertie. Each of them seemed to study him closely. Their faces showed a mixture of expressions, from interest to concern, and perhaps – from some – a little disbelief.

'Perhaps you *should* all take a seat,' said Bertie.

The members of the company did so. Constance and Jenny sat on the sofa, with Teddy perching himself next to Jenny on the armrest. Robert reclined into a comfortable armchair, but Arthur elected to remain standing instead of taking a seat in the remaining occasional chair.

Hugh loomed reassuringly in the dark – the lights

above the stage didn't quite penetrate into the doorway where he waited. The shadowy figure looked a little threatening perhaps, but it was a reminder to everyone of the police's involvement in the matter. Hugh's presence also seemed to calm Bertie, who suddenly had found himself a little nervous. He was grateful for the support.

'I'm afraid this is a little different from what I'm used to,' he admitted to the group. 'Despite my profession, I'm not a great public speaker. I prefer to write and re-write my words until I know exactly what I want to say. Unfortunately, in real life, that's not an opportunity that one ever gets afforded.'

'Don't worry, Bertie,' said Teddy with encouragement. 'We're all behind you.' He looked around at the others for support. Only Jenny joined him by nodding her agreement.

Bertie took a breath and a look around at the gathered faces, some looking more eager than others. Robert looked decidedly grumpy, although he suspected this was quite usual.

'This murder, on the face of it, is simple. During the play, Jenny took a gun that had, at some point, been loaded with real bullets and used it to shoot Celia.' Bertie directed his gaze at Jenny. 'At any time, between picking up the gun – shortly before your scene – and the actual shooting on stage, you could have slipped a real bullet into the gun, couldn't you?'

'Could I?' Jenny protested. 'I don't even know how to get the bottom of that thing slid out, let alone load it. Let alone know where to get hold of a bullet in the first place.'

'No, that's quite true,' agreed Bertie. 'And then we come to motive…'

'Yes, motive,' started Jenny. 'I don't have that either. I don't have a single reason why I would kill her.'

'But it's safe to say you didn't particularly like her?'

'Like her? Well, no, I didn't particularly take to her, if that's what you mean?' said Jenny, with a bemused expression on her face. 'I don't know what happens up in London, Mr Carroll, but down here we certainly don't go around shooting people just because we aren't particularly fond of them.'

'No, you're right,' Bertie agreed. 'We try not to do that in London either, and certainly not on an opening night.'

'But I am a murderer, aren't I? If shooting someone makes you a murderer, then I did do that. Despite my protestations of innocence, I'm not, am I?' She looked up at Bertie with a solemn expression.

'I think we have a little way to go before I can answer that question. However, one thing I'm almost certain of is that you never came here with the intention of murder.'

Teddy, next to Jenny, took her hand in his and gave it a gentle squeeze for comfort.

'So, if we assume that Jenny didn't swap the bullet in the gun,' continued Bertie, 'who did?' He looked around the room at the remaining suspects. 'As far as I can tell, there's only one other person who had access to that gun.'

'Me,' came a quiet voice from the corner of the set. 'It's me, isn't it? I'm the only other person who could have done it.' Stepping forward and out of the shadows from the side of the stage was Charlie. The stage manager, usually preferring the dim light backstage, was now placing himself centre stage, into the spotlight.

'Yes, I'm afraid so,' confirmed Bertie. 'The gun was locked away in a cabinet, to which only you had the key.'

'And no one else goes near that gun during the show, except for me,' added Charlie, apparently incriminating himself further.

'And Constance,' corrected Bertie as he turned to look at her. 'You said yourself that the majority of your part is bringing things to and from that props table.'

'I have no reason for killing her,' said Constance. 'We've already been over that. Charlie supervises me every time I'm at that props table, I couldn't have slipped anything past him. Why would I want her dead?'

'You were the one who worked closely alongside Celia, the one who would get the full force of her displeasure.'

'That's simply something that comes with the job,' she responded. 'It's certainly not a reason for murder.'

'But,' continued Bertie, 'if either of you did go near that gun, if one of you tampered with it, we only have the other's word to say that you didn't. You could be covering for one another. There is, however, a problem. Charlie – as far as we can tell – also has no reason for wanting to see Celia dead.'

'Well, good,' commented Charlie. 'I was going to say—'

'Except,' Bertie interrupted, 'we've now learnt that you were a huge fan of Celia's. There wasn't a thing about her that you didn't know or a film of hers that you hadn't seen.'

'Well,' he started in defence, 'I don't see how—'

'To the point of obsession?' Bertie asked, interrupting again.

'No, not like that!' Charlie protested. 'Sure, I was a big fan. That's why I wanted to do this show. But why would I want to harm her? That doesn't make any sense.'

'It wouldn't be the first time a death has occurred at the hands of a crazed fan, would it?'

'I object to the phrase "crazed fan",' complained Charlie. 'I wasn't obsessive. I was just a normal fan – someone who enjoyed the work she did, the films she was in. There's no law against that, is there?'

'There isn't,' agreed Bertie. 'But it's safe to say that perhaps out of everyone here, you would have been the most disappointed when they finally met the real Celia.'

'Look, it's true. It's always dangerous, meeting your idols. Imagine finally meeting someone you've looked up to for years, only to find they didn't match up to your expectations. It was a let down, sure. But murder? I may not have been the biggest fan of Celia, the person, but I was still a huge fan of Celia, the film star. Her work still stands apart from the rest. She was the greatest actress of her generation, in my opinion. I still loved her for that. The idea that I would want to harm her is absurd,' he finished.

'If we take things on the face of it, only you, Jenny, or Constance could have interfered with that gun, either while the others were out of sight or if you were working together. But while you all had the means, only Jenny had the opportunity. But what about motive? Well, that for me is the most important one and Jenny didn't have it. The one person who was most able to commit the murder, seems to be the one person who was the least likely to do it. However, you did have a motive. Perhaps...?' Bertie trailed off, leaving his words floating there as a question.

'Exactly,' Charlie said, folding his arms. 'Only perhaps.'

Robert shifted impatiently in his seat. 'Well, who did do it then?' he interjected grumpily.

'We've been working under the assumption that the gun that killed Celia was the one that Jenny was holding, that someone switched the blanks for real bullets. But there is another possibility.'

'You mean I might not have been the one that shot her?' asked a relieved Jenny.

'No, you might not have done,' said Bertie. 'What if the blanks were never swapped? What if no one else touched that gun between the rehearsal and the performance? In that case, Jenny couldn't have been the one who shot Celia, because there were never real bullets in the gun while she was holding it. There was another possibility came to us, perhaps someone else could have fired a gun, at the same time?'

Charlie shifted his weight to the other foot. 'But there would have been two gunshots? We would have heard,' he said.

'That's what I thought too,' Bertie agreed. 'But then I thought about silencers or, as I was corrected by the inspector, suppressors. The sound of a gunshot cannot be silenced completely, but it can be reduced – reduced to such a point that it could be disguised behind the sound of a gunshot from Jenny's gun, if it happened at the same time. Timing would have been vital, of course, but this is a place full of people who are experts in dramatic timing.'

'But who could have done that?' asked Arthur.

'Me again, isn't it?' said Charlie, guiltily? 'You've said it before. Everyone else is onstage at the moment of the shooting, except for me.'

'That's true, but if we take you at your word – that you didn't want to see any harm come to Celia – there must have been someone else,' argued Bertie. 'But there was someone else. Someone who had the opportunity and, more importantly, a motive.'

Bertie turned to face the irritable figure, sunken into his chair. 'I'm talking about you, Robert.'

'Me! Come off it, Bertie, old boy.'

'You blamed her,' said Bertie, 'for ruining your chances of becoming a real star. Even after– '

'I told you, that's all water under the bridge. This is ridiculous,' he interrupted.

'Even after all these years,' said Bertie, finishing the sentence he had started.

'That's not the case,' protested Robert.

'You were unaccounted for.'

'I was ill.'

'Or pretending to be,' responded Bertie. 'What an easy thing it must be for an actor to feign an illness. You had the motive and the opportunity.'

'And the means?' asked Robert. 'Where on earth would I get a gun from?'

'Hugh,' said Bertie in the direction of the inspector, who was still standing nearby in the doorway of the set. 'Tell me about the gun again, the one in the show.'

'What do you want to know?' he replied. 'It's a small semi-automatic, not very powerful. Mostly used for personal protection, things like that.'

'You mentioned that a gun like this could often be found being used by the staff of institutions like banks, isn't that right?'

'Yes,' Hugh agreed, 'they would have been a common purchaser of that type of gun.'

'Robert,' said Bertie, returning his attention to the actor. 'Your father was a bank manager, was he not?'

'Well, yes,' he confirmed, 'but I don't see what that has to do with—'

'There were three letters etched on the side of this gun,' Bertie interrupted. 'BBL. Which is quite likely to stand for Barclays Bank Limited. Robert, can you tell me what bank your father worked for?'

'Well, it wasn't bloody Barclays Bank!' Robert exploded. 'I can tell you that!'

'Okay,' said Bertie, a little thrown. 'I admit that was a bit of a shot in the dark. Even so, it might be easier for you, more than anybody else here, to get your hands on a second gun of the same type. Perhaps seeing the gun in rehearsals, seeing those bank markings on the side … is that what gave you the idea?'

'No,' he protested.

'Perhaps, if you were able to source a second gun, you would also be able to get hold of a suppressor for that gun, feign an illness, and return to the theatre on the night of the performance. The show is impeccably rehearsed, down to the last detail. Everyone knows the timings exactly. Firing a second gun, precisely at the same time as Jenny, would have almost been too easy for an actor of your experience.'

'It just isn't true!' Robert rose from his seat. 'And if you know who really did it, I suggest you get on with it!' He dumped himself back in the armchair with a loud huff.

'Drama, Robert! Drama!' said Teddy, clearly enjoying the proceedings. 'I think this is all rather good, isn't it?'

'Unfortunately, Robert, until we can prove it was someone else, you remain a strong suspect,' said Bertie.

'I don't know why you're keeping us all hanging on like this,' Robert protested. 'It's enough to give a man a heart attack.'

'I suppose it's my turn next,' said Teddy.

'Yes, I suppose it is,' said Bertie.

'On account of me being blackmailed and all,' Teddy announced with a smile, boasting to the rest of the group.

At the mention of the word blackmail, the room exploded into disorder, although Teddy tried to settle everyone down quickly. 'I really didn't mind though,' he commented in an innocent sounding voice.

'No, I don't want to talk about the blackmail – although that did give you a very good motive. It was something else. There was something you said earlier. It sparked a thought.'

'Well,' said Teddy in a low voice. 'I'm glad I helped.'

'When we were talking, you told me that you'd never been near the gun before, during or after.'

'I did?' said Teddy, sounding surprised at his own words.

'You did,' repeated Bertie. 'And that got me thinking. We've covered before and during the moment of the shooting. What about after? Perhaps there never was a second gun. Perhaps there was a second opportunity.'

'Oh, come off it, Bertie,' said Teddy. 'We all saw Celia being shot, didn't we?'

'This whole time, we have been overlooking something. While Celia wasn't the most pleasant person to work with, she was something else…' said Bertie, looking around the group. 'An incredible actress. You've all said as much, haven't you? You, Charlie, you said it just now, she was one of the best actresses of her generation. Arthur, you told me how you always admired her acting style, so natural.

'What if what we were watching on stage wasn't Celia Hamilton being shot? What if we were just watching a talented actress give a very skilled and convincing performance?'

'But it was so real,' came Jenny's timid voice. Teddy gently squeezed her hand for comfort.

Bertie watched Teddy mull over the idea before speaking. 'You mean she was never actually shot during the show. She was killed at some other point?'

'That's exactly what I mean,' said Bertie. 'For the last fifteen minutes of the first act, after Celia was supposedly shot, we've all been under the assumption that she was already dead. But instead, what if she was perfectly well and alive, waiting just out of sight behind that sofa, exactly as she was supposed to? Exactly as it was rehearsed?'

'Come off it, Bertie,' came the firm voice of Arthur, from the other side of the stage. 'This is getting rather fanciful, isn't it?'

'Perhaps it is,' admitted Bertie. 'Perhaps it is. But if we move the timing of her death, the circumstances change. The fact that any of you could have murdered Celia Hamilton becomes a very real possibility.'

'But we would have heard, wouldn't we?' asked Charlie. 'You said yourself, just earlier; even with a silencer on the gun, we'd have still heard something.'

Bertie nodded in agreement. 'That's right. We would have still heard something. So now we need to look for the opportunity, a moment in the play. Who had the opportunity, at the right time, where the sound may be disguised or hidden?

'Perhaps Teddy or Charlie, positioned behind the French windows at the end of the act? The perfect angle to be able to shoot from outside the set. We know that you, Teddy, were left alone at the end of the act while Charlie ran back round to the other side to bring in the curtain.'

'Now look here,' said Teddy. 'I was stuck behind that backcloth doing the sound effects. I couldn't see onto the stage from there, let alone shoot someone. Besides, I'm just an actor – probably a terrible shot!'

'I can quite believe that,' replied Bertie. 'And that's another point that struck me… I can't imagine any of you are expert marksmen. Hugh – the Inspector, I mean

– tells me that a gun that small wouldn't be very accurate anyway. It would have taken a lot of luck from that distance. A gun that small isn't that powerful either, yet we know the bullet passed directly through Celia. Right in here,' Bertie indicated to a spot directly over his own heart, 'and right out the back again. Whoever shot her must have been standing right in front of her.'

Jenny made an uncomfortable noise.

'A gun that small, from that kind of distance, wouldn't have been capable of performing such a feat. So, we have to conclude that whoever shot Celia is more likely to have done it from close range. And with that, only one solution presents itself.

'This murder relied on meticulous timing. It relied on perfect choreography. It relied on the fact that everyone would be in the right place at the exact time. It was callous, cunning and could have only been possible by you all working together.

'This murder was planned and rehearsed until it was perfect – and that surely makes you all accomplices to murder.'

The room erupted in protest. Bertie held up his hand to calm them and the hubbub quickly subsided.

'What I mean is, you are all accomplices to murder, even though you were never aware of the roles you were playing. You were all directed to be a part of it, and that means only one person in this room could have staged this murder. Arthur.'

Chapter Twenty-Three

A hush fell over the entire room. Even the noises of the sea seemed to fade into silence.

'Preposterous,' Arthur scoffed. 'Absolutely preposterous.'

'No,' said Bertie plainly. 'I don't think it is. This murder was planned, rehearsed and performed almost as if it were a play. That means that it can only have come from the hand of a director. Why else was this obscure play of mine even chosen? I admit, myself, that it's far from my best work, yet here it is being staged for the first time in years! But it had the right characters and the right setting, didn't it? You knew you would be able to tweak and change it to make your murder work.

'Why else put it on during the off-season, in this theatre, when it's the emptiest? Because it was cheap. Why reuse an old set from one of your old productions? Not only because you knew you could make the blocking for the murder work, but it was cheap. You got Teddy for a knockdown price in return for a role in London.

Charlie came cheap because he was a fan of Celia's. Jenny didn't cost much because she was inexperienced and local, and Robert needed a job. You always planned to lose money on this production, but that was because you thought it was a price worth paying. However, a producer is still a producer, and a producer is never going to lose more money than they have to. This production was never meant to make money, it was never meant to transfer into London. It was made only for one purpose. To kill Celia Hamilton!

'You ensured, with your blocking, that everyone was on the stage during the shooting scene. You knew that suspicion would be thrown upon Jenny; she was holding the gun, she was the only person who could have done it. The idea that anyone else could have been the murderer was completely impossible. But precisely because it was impossible, that meant that someone else *had* to have done it. That was your mistake. Jenny had no reason to kill Celia Hamilton.

'So, we looked for the changes. The changes between the original production and this one. Almost nothing had been changed. The odd line tweak here and there, the odd change in where people stood. But, all in all, it was pretty faithful to the original. It was only the shooting scene that you changed to your advantage, in an attempt to frame Jenny. However, there was another difference later in the play, after we'd already seen Celia shot.'

Suddenly Charlie exclaimed, 'The sound effects!'

Bertie smiled. 'The sound effects. Why add the thunder and lightning sound effects, turning the end of the act into something that was right out of a Victorian melodrama? Now, it would have never been enough to mask the sound of a gunshot, but it would have been enough to mask the sound of a gun with a suppressor attached. You were the one who picked the gun for the show, you were the one who could choose a model that you were able to fit a suppressor to.

'And here's where the choice of play becomes important. In *Murder by Association*, the body is found – behind the sofa – by the butler. Yes, here things didn't diverge from the script – as written. But here was where things diverged from what I'd seen during the rehearsal earlier that day. Luckily for me, I saw that rehearsal. Perhaps if I hadn't, I would never have known there was anything different about the evening performance and you might have got away with it.

'Robert. Can you remember your blocking for the moment you find Celia?'

'Of course,' he replied. 'I bend down behind the sofa for a moment, stand up and announce – rather grandly – "Oh no, she's dead" and then all the business with the thunder and the doors happens.'

'Exactly. But that's not what happened when Arthur did it that night, was it? He said, "Oh no" and remained bent down behind the sofa for a moment longer while the thunder and lightning were happening. It was only after that he stood up and announced, "She's dead". A tiny difference. But enough of a difference. It was at that moment, I believe, you shot Celia Hamilton.'

'Bertie,' stammered Arthur in protest, 'this is ridiculous. Just because I got a bit of the staging wrong? Do you think that's proof of me killing Celia? It's an incredible story, but it's simply ridiculous. Of course, I didn't do everything perfectly. I only went on at the last minute. You can't expect—'

'But you did,' said Bertie. 'That was your final mistake. You did do everything else perfectly. You knew the lines; you knew the staging.'

'Yes, I'm the director.'

'And no director I know of, including yourself, could have jumped on the stage and been word perfect at a moment's notice. But yet, by some miraculous feat, here you were. You had to have planned it. With Robert as the butler, you had cast someone who was a similar size and shape to you; you would be able to slip into his costume at the last minute. But you needed to learn the lines. You had to be word perfect, because without both hands free it would have been next to impossible to subtly pull a gun out behind that sofa in full view of an audience.

'The rest of the company was taken care of. You already knew that the set was designed in such a way that no one would be able to see what you were up to behind the sofa. You staged the scene so that Jenny was downstage, far enough that she wouldn't be able to see you, and you placed Teddy and Charlie out of the way, behind the backcloth, to do the sound effects. Still, it was a hell of a risk.'

'It's quite simply not true,' said Arthur. 'You can't tell me that I'm a murderer, just because I'm able to remember some lines, for goodness' sake.'

'But you didn't,' said Bertie calmly. 'You didn't know all the lines. I incorrectly quoted a line from the show to you, a line from Act Two. Except now I know that line was never in the show, it was never in the published script. That's the script you all had, the one you were working from. But you had no idea that I'd got it wrong. If, as you say, you knew every line in the show – even if it had just been the butler's lines – you would have known that I was mistaken. You would have known that line didn't exist.

'You only ever learnt the lines for the first act – only the lines you *needed* to learn. You never committed Act Two to memory and the only reason that explains it is that you knew Act Two would never take place.'

'This is absolute fantasy,' exclaimed Arthur.

'No,' replied Bertie, 'I don't think it is. You were able to retrieve the gun before your final entrance of the act. It was left in the purse on the props table, the only time in the show when it's unattended. Charlie had to go over to the other side of the stage; he's with Teddy doing the sound effects, located where they are because of the design of the set. We never thought about it being unsupervised, because we never looked at the movements of the gun *after* the supposed murder.

'And where was the bullet this whole time? That was something that never made sense. If the bullet had made it through Celia, while she was standing up, where was the bullet hole in the scenery? It should have punched a hole in the canvas or been embedded in the wood, but we looked and there was nothing. Just like everything else in this murder, we were looking in the wrong place. We didn't think to look beneath our feet. This floor cloth is old and tired. It's full of holes made by years of actors walking over it, burn marks from cigarette butts, drilled holes for scenery. One more hole, made by you firing a gun while Celia was lying on her back? It would simply go unnoticed among the others while the bullet disappeared through the stage and, quite likely, out to sea.

'After Celia had already been shot in the play, there was plenty of time for you to slip a live bullet into the gun and screw on the suppressor while the stage left wing was unattended. You could go on to the stage, commit murder and return the gun to the props table before anyone noticed. That's why you added that extra bit of staging at the end so that the butler would exit the stage. You needed to get the gun back onto the props table while Charlie's back was turned, bringing in the curtain. He'd be hurrying back over from the other side so quickly, he would be unlikely to notice that it was missing as he ran past. However, in the rush, you just forgot to do one thing: to put the gun back in the purse.'

'Well, why weren't my fingerprints on the gun?' said Arthur, protesting his innocence.

'Well, that's the simplest answer of all!' exclaimed Bertie. 'In the play, the butler wears gloves!'

'This is all getting rather convenient,' Arthur grumbled.

'Yes, it is, isn't it?' replied Bertie dryly.

'I suppose you've managed to come up with some fantastic reason why I wanted my wife dead, of course? A wife who I still loved dearly…'

'I believe that,' agreed Bertie. 'I believe that you did love Celia dearly. I think you still loved her all those years ago when she left for America, and she did you. Now, how shall I put it?' he pondered. 'Perhaps there was one last night of passion before she left?

'What was unknown to you, unknown to Celia even, was that when she left for America, she was pregnant. You confirmed as much yourself. Robert told me that she'd boasted of having work lined up for when she arrived, but that never happened. She didn't work for over half a year or more.'

'Because she was having a baby?' asked Teddy, mouth open.

'I think that's right,' said Bertie. 'That was my way into the whole case. Perhaps here was a motive for murder – finally. It was Robert who planted the idea in my head when he said that Celia would have sacrificed a child for her career. Tragically, I think that's exactly what happened. She gave birth in secret and, not wanting her career to be held back by the burden of motherhood, used the services of an orphanage.'

'She gave her own child away?' said Jenny.

'I'm afraid so,' agreed Bertie. 'And Arthur, you knew nothing about this. For all those years, you were completely unaware that you had a child on the other side of the Atlantic. Celia never told you. You would have had no idea. But you found out, somehow.

'I think it was all revealed to you on a visit to New York, on one of your shows, with a young dresser.'

'Constance!' exclaimed Teddy. 'Is that right?'

Constance sat stony-faced, expressionless.

'That's right,' confirmed Bertie. 'The orphanage, who had strict instructions that a child should be adopted under complete anonymity, to make sure that Celia's secret did not get out. But there wasn't just one child. There were two children. Two girls. A picture in Constance's dressing room put me on to it. I thought that it was strange for someone to have a picture of themselves. But I don't think it was a photograph of Constance.' He turned his attention directly to Constance, speaking consolingly. 'It was your twin sister, wasn't it?'

Slowly, hesitantly, Constance nodded.

'Can you imagine the betrayal?' Bertie said. 'Keeping two daughters a secret from their own father? From each other? The pain of separating a pair of twins who should have been brought up together? Imagine the horror you would have felt discovering that after all these years.

'But it couldn't be kept a secret completely. I think somehow you found out, didn't you, Constance? You had those photos from a newspaper pinned up in your dressing room and, judging by their stamp on the back, they were recent prints at that. I think it was you who visited the orphanage, under some other pretence, and removed those files.'

Tentatively, Constance spoke. 'I did.'

'But what triggered all this? It's because she died,' said Bertie, delicately. 'Last night I contacted the newspaper, the same newspaper you must have written to, Constance, to get a copy of those photos that were run alongside the story.'

'It's true,' Constance said. 'It was by chance, really, but these things often find a way, don't you find? One of the chorus girls had brought a local newspaper back with her to New York and there it was, a photograph of me. She was looking right back at me, identical in every way. A smudged, black-and-white photo of her and one of all the family. Dead in some kind of tragic fire.

'That was the only photograph I ever had of her. She had an awful childhood with those people, years of abuse and neglect, and for it to end like that… It was just awful. And all the while, I never needed to ask for anything. I had a wonderful childhood, everything I could possibly want. It just wasn't fair. It wasn't right.'

'And that's what hurt the most. Both of you, you could have had a wonderful life here, with your own father,' Bertie said. 'But he never knew – the truth was kept from him as well – and for that, Celia had to be punished. The death of your sister, Constance, and your child, Arthur. It was too much and you planned it together, your revenge.'

'No,' interrupted Arthur. 'Constance had nothing to do with it. It was my plan, my idea. She is completely innocent; she had nothing to do with it. It was me and me alone. No one else.'

'No,' said Bertie. 'She isn't innocent in this. There was one wrinkle that I couldn't iron out. If it was just you working alone, how did you ensure that you would be able to take the place of Robert?

'Constance is the only answer. You made sure that she was put up in digs with Robert in a house where you knew the owner would be away; you've toured Brighton enough times that you know the patterns of the landladies and you knew this one would be away visiting her sister. That way, you could make sure that Constance was in a position to make meals for her and Robert. And to poison him that evening.'

'Poison?' exploded Robert. 'Good God!'

'Not a lot, but just enough to make sure you'd be out of action for the evening. You ate the same food that evening, you drank tea from the same pot. But here's what I think it comes down to, triangles or squares. Your sandwiches. You said you don't have a preference, but before the performance I think you had the option of both. Perhaps the triangles were poisoned and the squares weren't? Either way, Constance could eat from the same plate as you and avoid getting ill herself. Although, in the end, she didn't get the dose quite right. Nothing could keep you out of action for long. Once an actor, always an actor. You'd do your damnedest to make it to the theatre, even if it was only at the interval. If anything, that worked in their favour. Another suspect and one whose movements couldn't be accounted for. During the investigation, when you saw that we weren't buying the idea that Jenny did it, you tried to shift the blame on to Robert. Someone who had a motive and the opportunity, but it didn't work.'

'Look here,' protested Arthur. 'You've got no proof of anything. This is all a lovely story, but there's not a shred of proof. We don't know for sure that Jenny or Charlie didn't slip in a real bullet at any point between the rehearsal and the show.'

'And we don't know where the suppressor ended up,' mused Bertie. 'Do we?'

'No,' he agreed. 'We don't. This could all be fiction. Another fantastic piece of fiction, from one of the foremost murder mystery writers in the country. This could be a complete invention, like something right out of one of your plays.'

'No. You're wrong. In one of my plays, I would never be so uninspired and boring to use the tired cliché of the butler doing it! And you're wrong about the suppressor, too.'

Arthur looked startled.

'And this,' Bertie said, 'is where we come across another wonderful piece of luck. On the night of the murder, we were fortunate enough to have a chief inspector in our midst. After you shot Celia, you returned the gun and your butler's gloves to the props table, as normal.

'But there, the plan went awry. You thought you were going to have plenty of time to get rid of the suppressor, drop it off the end of the pier, perhaps. However, Hugh – being an excellent policeman – made sure that everyone was searched before being allowed to leave the stage that evening. That presented a problem to you, how to get rid of your evidence.

'This set has been guarded and sealed since the night of the murder. Those flowers. Just now, I caught you fiddling with them. Of course, you tried to cover by saying that you were hoping to make a gift of the flowers to our two actresses here. That was a lie.

'You've been working in the theatre for your whole life, more than long enough to know that using real flowers in a play is considered bad luck. There was absolutely no reason for you to go near those flowers or that vase, but I remembered that you were standing near that vase on the night of the murder as well. So, unless I'm very much mistaken, that suppressor – with your fingerprints on it – is either still in that vase or in your pocket as we speak.'

Arthur took a stumbled step towards the door in the set. He quickly stopped himself, realising that the exit was still blocked by Hugh. He spun on the spot, now facing the French doors. At the same moment, a constable stepped into view, blocking his path. He turned once more, looking out towards the auditorium – the only escape route left.

Arthur tried to calculate whether he would be able to make the leap down from the stage and out of the doors before someone caught him.

Bertie took a step to his left, in an attempt to block the way. Arthur surged forward, grabbing him by the collar.

'You meddling little playwright!' he exploded. 'You have no idea what it's like! All these years, denied a family, denied two daughters. And to know, all the time that I was here, that I could have saved them from their pain. I knew Celia could be a nasty piece of work, awful sometimes. But to be cruel, Bertie. To be this cruel! You!' he puffed. 'Bertie. You ruined it all!'

With that, Arthur surged past him, pushing him to the floor. Arthur's eyes were firmly fixed on the back of the auditorium and the exit. He was going to make a run for it.

As Bertie fell, he reached out an arm in an attempt to soften his landing, but as he did so he caught the foot of Arthur who was dashing towards the edge of the stage.

Arthur tripped, fell over the front of the stage and disappeared from view with a loud bang.

Bertie stumbled back to his feet, flanked by Hugh and the police constable. Together, they gingerly peered over the front edge of the stage.

In a crumpled heap on the floor lay Arthur. With great effort, he rolled over onto his back, only to see the three of them looking down at him. The police constable was now brandishing a set of handcuffs.

'Mr Cochran,' said Hugh, 'I think you'll find you're under arrest.'

The constable hopped down from the stage, helping Arthur to his feet and leading him away. Hugh turned to Constance.

'You're a sensible young girl. I take it you'll come with me a little more easily.'

Constance nodded. 'I don't regret anything you know,' she spoke quietly, addressing the group. 'She tried to hide it – the truth – but she wouldn't let herself. The name she put on the birth certificate. It was Cochran. That confirmed it. She could lie about everything, but even she couldn't bring herself to lie about that. Even so, it's no consolation. She was evil. She deserved it. I'm absolutely sure of that. Arthur asked her, you know, on the day of the murder, whether there was anything she would have done differently in her life. She said there wasn't and she meant it. She never regretted a thing. I thought this would make things right again, make things equal – for us, for her. But now … it's the strangest feeling. I don't think it's changed anything at all.'

A silent tear rolled down Constance's cheek before, delicately, Hugh led her away.

'Gosh, Bertie!' came the excitable voice of Teddy, after a few moments of respectful silence. 'That was better than a real play!'

Robert seemed to signal his agreement by way of a jerky nod in his direction.

'What will happen to them?' asked Jenny quietly.

'You know,' replied Bertie, 'I have absolutely no idea. I've never accused anyone of murder before.'

'In that case,' announced Teddy, 'I think that all debut performances deserve a first night drink! How about it?'

'It's eleven o'clock in the morning,' Jenny reminded them all.

'You know what,' said Bertie – his heart rate still raised – 'I think that sounds like a great idea!'

Chapter Twenty-Four

In the bar at The Old Ship Hotel, the group had managed to track down a member of staff who was happy to supply them with their much-needed drinks. Bertie wasn't sure if it was due to the addition of alcohol, but he was almost certain that Robert was smiling.

'Well done, Bertie,' he boomed, as he shook Bertie's hand. 'I'm sure we'll be seeing this adventure, or one a lot like it, on the stage before too long!'

Bertie gave a noncommittal shrug, which made Robert emit a small chuckle. 'I think I might take a break from playing butlers for a while, but you never know. You might be able to add in a vicar's role for me! See you soon, Bertie! See you soon, everyone and all!' Robert's voice reverberated around the room of the hotel bar as he turned to leave.

'Is that right?' asked a still timid Jenny. 'Will you write a play about this?'

'You know what,' replied Bertie, honestly. 'I've not even thought about it. I really don't know.'

'Nonsense,' said Teddy. 'I think we've got the next Bertie Carroll hit lined up and ready to go! The only problem you're going to have is finding someone who is devilishly handsome and charming enough to play me!' He laughed.

'What will you do?' Bertie asked Jenny.

'Well, Teddy has said he'll put me up in London for a while. I think he's got an idea that I might be able to find some acting work.'

'Of course you will!' Teddy enthused. 'I'm sure we'll be able to fix you up with one of the Sunday Societies and then get you into a proper run of something. You are very good after all, isn't that right, Bertie?'

'That's quite true,' Bertie replied. 'And you, Teddy?'

'Well, after not a lot of thought, because I really didn't need to think that hard about it, I've decided to put my dreams of moving into the film industry on hold for a little longer. God knows I don't want to end up like Celia, do I? Stick to what you're good at, eh Bertie? I think that's the best plan for now!'

Bertie smiled at Teddy. 'Yes, I quite agree,' he said. 'I think I should like to return to writing crimes from behind my typewriter and not solving ones in real life!'

At that moment Hugh appeared in the doorway at the entrance to the bar, returning from the formalities that had been required at the police station. He hovered at a respectable distance, although Teddy was quick to notice his presence.

'I should think that your policeman friend should be quite grateful,' Teddy leant in and whispered to Bertie in a conspiratorial voice. 'Saved his bacon somewhat, didn't you?'

Bertie gave a small chuckle. 'I'm not sure I did, you know. I'm pretty sure Hugh would have solved it, with or without me.'

'Yes, I'm sure he would have,' Teddy said, before adding excitedly, 'but with not as much flair! That's what really counts!'

'He's right, Bertie,' added Jenny. 'You really were quite wonderful!'

Teddy leant back in, speaking in a hushed tone. 'He is – you know – rather quite handsome, isn't he?'

Bertie looked over at Hugh, catching his eye. Hugh flashed a wide smile back in his direction.

'He is,' agreed Bertie, 'if you're into that sort of thing.'

'I think we both know that you are,' whispered Teddy, before bursting into another hearty laugh.

With that, the trio said their goodbyes. Teddy and Jenny left, heading in the direction of the train station. Their chatting, giggling and gossiping slowly faded into the distance.

Hugh strode across the room greeted Bertie with a powerful hug. 'Congratulations, detective!' he joked, reaching out to shake Bertie's hand and flashing another wide smile that instinctively made Bertie grin in return.

'Not so much detective work as being incredibly lucky, I would have thought,' replied Bertie.

'Nonsense. Half the detectives in the police force couldn't do what you just did. That's probably the writer in you. All those things you notice, all those things you observe.'

'I don't know about that. What I do know is theatre,' said Bertie. 'I know that if a real flower gets anywhere near a stage, the director is always the first one to lose it!'

Bertie drained the last of his drink and together with Hugh, stepped outside. Finally the rain had stopped. The sunlight was dazzling as it shone down, bouncing off the wet road. The cool crispness of the air somehow made everything look pin sharp. There was barely a cloud in the sky and no breeze to speak of. Perhaps, tomorrow, the theatre would keep its record of never having a get out on a rainy day after all.

The two of them walked across the road to the railings of the parade.

'All of this. It was all chance, wasn't it?' Bertie admitted.

'You really think that?' asked Hugh. 'I think you're not giving yourself enough credit.'

'I never should have been at the theatre. I only popped in to see the dress rehearsal when my plans changed because of you. If I hadn't seen that rehearsal and noticed that the staging had changed, ever so slightly, perhaps they would have got away with it. Jenny would be going to prison for murder because, by all accounts, it really would have looked like she'd done it.'

'Thankfully, we'll never know,' reassured Hugh.

'It was only by chance that Constance even saw that newspaper and that was what triggered this whole sequence of events. It just shows, now and then, the things that you think are impossible – things that might have a once in a million chance – they do happen.'

'And for Arthur to have the nerve to take the chance on that night,' Hugh added. 'To take that risk? It just shows, if you really believe in doing something, even something like that, you have to take a gamble. Take that chance.'

The two of them stopped talking, avoiding each other's gaze, instead choosing to look out towards the sea. The sun, now almost overhead, meant that the two piers were glowing white on either side of them.

'Fancy a swim?' asked Hugh. 'Lovely day for it.'

'You can't be serious! It's absolutely freezing.'

'You'll get used to it. I promise.'

Together they walked down the ramp that led to the cobbled beach, Bertie a little reluctantly.

'I know you've got this mad idea that an early morning swim clears your mind and awakens your senses, or whatever nonsense you go on about,' joked Bertie. 'I'm sure the only reason your mind is clear is that it's absolutely frozen solid. It's complete madness.'

'Trust me,' replied Hugh, removing his coat and unbuttoning his shirt.

'You're completely ridiculous,' said Bertie.

Hugh proved quite persuasive. After a few more unsuccessful protests from Bertie, it was only a short time later that the pair found themselves standing at the water's edge, dressed only in their underwear. Bertie felt quite inadequate standing next to Hugh's muscular frame, not to mention how ridiculous he thought they must look to passers by.

'On three,' Hugh proclaimed. 'Two, three!'

Hugh grabbed Bertie by the hand and half led him, half dragged him into the freezing water at a run.

Bertie, who was rather fond of a warm bath, found the water ice cold and not at all to his liking. He swore, loudly.

'Brilliant!' shouted Hugh. 'Isn't it?'

'No!' Bertie shouted back as he struggled to catch his breath. 'It's not bloody brilliant!'

Even on a warm day, he would have found the water far too cold for him. Today, the temperature was far below any normal person's limit of acceptability. After flailing around and fighting his instincts for some time, he found Hugh had been right. Eventually, Bertie's body did begin to acclimatise to the water's temperature; either that or he was now so numb he couldn't feel anything anymore.

As the actions of staying afloat started to become automatic and thoughts of the coldness subsided, the chill of the water began to bring a kind of calmness over Bertie. It was just as Hugh had said.

Hugh swam past with strong, powerful strokes while Bertie bobbed about in the waves.

After a few more minutes, Bertie found that his mind had emptied and thoughts of the recent murder had completely disappeared. Right now, there was nothing else he could think about in the world.

It was only him, Hugh, the water and the endless sky.

About the Palace Pier Theatre

For the purposes of this book, I have attempted to resurrect the Palace Pier Theatre, although in some cases I have had to use a little bit of artistic license.

The Palace Pier was the third pier to be built in Brighton, after the West Pier and the Chain Pier, for which it was an intended replacement. It is the only one of the three piers still in operation today. The Chain Pier was destroyed in a storm in 1896 and the West Pier has fallen into disrepair since its closure to the public in 1975.

The seaward pavilion on the Palace Pier originally opened in 1901, two years after the pier's official opening, in the May of 1899. It contained a theatre with raked seating which was used for musical concerts although, only ten years later, plans were drawn up by architects Clayton & Black for extensive renovations.

The 1911 remodelling transformed building into a 1,300 seat theatre, comparable with many other regional theatres. The roof was raised so that a fly tower could be built and scenery could be hoisted up above the stage, and a studio was added to the front of the building.

During this refurbishment, an impressive stained glass dome and ceiling were added to the theatre auditorium. New comfortable, upholstered, tip-up seats were installed throughout the auditorium — which had now been split into a stalls and an upper circle. These original seats were eventually replaced by ones donated from the Theatre Royal, Drury Lane in the 1950s.

The tradition of Drury Lane donating its seats to other theatres has continued to this day. In 2019, when the seating was replaced, the old seats were donated to three venues around the country.

I believe that the seats and house curtain at the time of this novel would have been red, although it seems as if the proscenium's pelmet and curtains were removed around the time of the Second World War. At some point after this, all the drapery and upholstery became blue.

During the remodelling, additional dressing rooms were added backstage. There is an account I found that describes the star dressing room as having a window which looks down onto the stage, but this is something that unfortunately I couldn't corroborate with the plans I uncovered during my research. I'm sure that Celia Hamilton would have appreciated that feature so she could keep an eye on everyone below.

In 1940 the theatre and pier were closed because of the Second World War, with a central section of the pier being blown up as a defence measure. The pier reopened in 1946 and the theatre continued to run into the 1970s.

The Palace Pier and its theatre can be seen in many films including *Brighton Rock*, *Carry on at your Convenience*, *Quadrophenia* and *Oh What A Lovely War!* In the latter film, the West Pier is used for the exteriors but the Palace Pier was used for the theatre's interior. If you're sharp-eyed, there are a few brief shots of the backstage area and the steps up to the dressing rooms.

During some demolition work on the pier in 1973, a barge broke free from its moorings and caused significant damage. Part of the theatre was left hanging perilously over the sea. In 1986 the theatre was dismantled and stored, prior to a planned restoration. At the time it had been described as the finest remaining example of a theatre at the end of the pier.

Unfortunately that restoration never happened and the whereabouts of the theatre building are now unknown.

Acknowledgments

It's just the author's name that appears on the front of a book, but there are many more who made it possible through their help, advice and support.

First to Stuart, Huckleberry and my supportive family. Huckleberry, our miniature dachshund, gave me quiet comfort as he snoozed while I wrote nearby. Stuart, my husband, was the first person I shared an early draft with and he was able to put his detective skills, well honed over our many years of reading Agatha Christie novels and watching the adaptations on TV, to good use.

Many thanks to all the staff at The Keep in Brighton who were able to assist with my research into the Brighton area and the Palace Pier Theatre. They were also gracious enough to refund my parking when I accidentally arrived three days before my booked appointment!

A huge debt of gratitude goes to Matthew Lloyd's website arthurlloyd.co.uk which is an excellent jumping off point for anyone who's interested in "lost" theatres or the history of theatre buildings. It was there that I first encountered The Palace Pier Theatre in Brighton and the inspiration for setting of this book.

The work of the Theatres Trust is vital in making sure that more historic venues aren't lost, like the Palace Pier Theatre. Many thanks to Kate and Sofia at the Trust who were able to dig out a variety of plans and articles from their archives for me.

Thanks to Tess O'Hara at BPA who gave some useful advice and Iain Maloney who provided some excellent analysis and gave me additional insight into the book.

Thanks to Emma Mitchell for editing the text and getting it into a more presentable state.

Mary Torjussen really went above and beyond proof-reading this book. I'm grateful to all her extra comments and advice that have really elevated the final text.

Victoria Hyde at Insta Book Tours has been incredible, along with her merry band of bloggers. I've really enjoyed getting to know you all and it's been wonderful to have your support on my journey to publication.

A special thanks goes to the producers of Dear Evan Hansen – the production I was working on when the theatres were closed due to Covid-19. They were able to use the government's furlough scheme to continue support to their backstage workers throughout the pandemic. Without it, I never would have had the opportunity to start writing this book. It is especially appreciated when many in the industry did not receive that same level of support from their producers or theatre owners. You may have noticed that The New Theatre (these days called The Noël Coward) where the production currently runs gets a brief mention in Chapter Two. To everyone in the stage management, sound and automation office (no, we don't all fit at the same time), thanks for your encouragement.

If you leave aside the part about the murder, this book is a tribute to the many wonderful people I have had met during my varied career across many of London's theatres. Some of those shows have been great (and some less so!) but each of them was always a joy to work on because of the people that were involved in them, both onstage and off.

I have always loved the world of theatre and, for me, that started at The Braintree Dramatic Society. Thank you to Chris Buist who invited me along and thank you to the members who were willing to trust a 15 year old to operate the lighting desk for their productions. It was there that I was introduced to Agatha Christie – perhaps for the first time – through her play, *Spider's Web.*

Finally to Dad, from whom I inherited a passion for reading and, more recently, an appreciation for single malt whisky. He would have been beaming to see my words in print.